WHEN THE WORLD TURNS DARK: A POST APOCALYPSE EMP THRILLER

AFTER IT TURNS DARK BOOK ONE

JACK HUNT

DIRECT RESPONSE PUBLISHING

Copyright © 2022 by Jack Hunt

All rights reserved.

No part of this book may be reproduced in any form or by any electronic or mechanical means, including information storage and retrieval systems, without written permission from the author, except for the use of brief quotations in a book review.

This Book is licensed for your personal enjoyment only. This Book may not be resold. If you would like to share this book with another person, please purchase an additional copy for each person you share it with. If you're reading this book and did not purchase it, or it was not purchased for your use only, then you should return to an online retailer and purchase your own copy. Thank you for respecting the author's work. : A Post Apocalypse EMP Thriller

WHEN THE WORLD TURNS DARK: A POST APOCALYPSE EMP THRILLER (AFTER IT TURNS DARK Book One) is a work of fiction. All names, characters, places and incidents either are the product of the author's imagination or used fictitiously. Any resemblance to actual persons, living or dead, events or locales is entirely coincidental.

ISBN: 9798799188047

For my Family

ALSO BY JACK HUNT

If you haven't joined *Jack Hunt's Private Facebook Group* just do a search on facebook to find it. This gives readers a way to chat with Jack, see cover reveals, enter contests and receive giveaways, and stay updated on upcoming releases. There is also his main facebook page below if you want to browse.
facebook.com/jackhuntauthor

Go to the link below to receive special offers, bonus content, and news about new Jack Hunt's books. Sign up for the newsletter.
http://www.jackhuntbooks.com/signup

After it Turns Dark series

When the World Turns Dark : A Post Apocalypse EMP Thriller

When Humanity Ends : A Post Apocalypse EMP Thriller

When Hope is Lost : A Post Apocalypse EMP Thriller

When Blood Lies : A Post Apocalypse EMP Thriller

The Great Dying series

Extinct

Primal

Species

A Powerless World series

Escape the Breakdown

Survive the Lawless

Defend the Homestead

Outlive the Darkness

Evade the Ruthless

Outlaws of the Midwest series

Chaos Erupts

Panic Ensues

Havoc Endures

The Cyber Apocalypse series

As Our World Ends

As Our World Falls

As Our World Burns

The Agora Virus series

Phobia

Anxiety

Strain

The War Buds series

War Buds 1

War Buds 2

War Buds 3

Camp Zero series

State of Panic

State of Shock

State of Decay

Renegades series

The Renegades

The Renegades Book 2: Aftermath

The Renegades Book 3: Fortress

The Renegades Book 4: Colony

The Renegades Book 5: United

The Wild Ones Duology

The Wild Ones Book 1

The Wild Ones Book 2

The EMP Survival series

Days of Panic

Days of Chaos

Days of Danger

Days of Terror

Against All Odds Duology

As We Fall

As We Break

The Amygdala Syndrome Duology

Unstable

Unhinged

Survival Rules series

Rules of Survival

Rules of Conflict

Rules of Darkness

Rules of Engagement

Lone Survivor series

All That Remains

All That Survives

All That Escapes

All That Rises

Single Novels

Blackout

15 Floors

Defiant

Darkest Hour

Final Impact

The Year Without Summer

The Last Storm

The Last Magician

The Lookout

Class of 1989

Out of the Wild

The Aging

Mavericks: Hunters Moon

Killing Time

PROLOGUE

Friday August 5
Over the Atlantic Ocean
125 miles southeast of Miami

Ten thousand feet in the air the swirling storm lashed the steel bird without mercy.
Inside a rugged Orion turboprop aircraft — modified to withstand a violent beating — a team from the NOAA known as the Hurricane Hunters felt like they were riding a rollercoaster through a car wash.

They weren't alone.

The U.S. Air Force Reserve 53rd Weather Reconnaissance Squadron were also supporting the ten-hour mission in a WC-130J aircraft heading toward a secondary tropical storm nearby. They could tell where they were based on the glowing green radar in the flight deck control panel. It was a good thing because beyond their tiny windows, deep inside the eye wall, the crew couldn't see anything because of blinding rain. Even in daylight hours a storm like this could turn the cabin dark.

Multiple jarring jolts and large oscillations made regular turbulence seem like child's play as the plane banked left into the wind.

Strangely the flight through the hurricane was far less bumpy than the times when storms were forming or dissipating, as in those moments a storm wasn't stable. Still, it didn't stop the flight and weather crew from muttering a prayer under their breath. They weren't afraid of the storm as much as they felt a huge responsibility to do their job right. Lives depended on them. No matter how many times they'd done this, it was still dangerous and mother nature was known to throw curveballs.

And that's exactly what she had done that evening.

As the tropical storm moved across the Atlantic, the National Oceanic and Atmospheric Administration had deployed aircraft toward the southeast.

Twice a day — for the first few days — Noah Lockhart and his team had ventured out morning and night for close to nine hours to get readings before any onshore warnings occurred.

Six days before landfall, the National Hurricane Center had issued its first tropical storm advisory as storm winds strengthened. Then, in a freak of luck or what seemed like it, four days out from the storm making landfall, shear winds and an upper-level low weakened the swirling mass and the hurricane watch was downgraded to a tropical storm warning. Within another twenty-four hours all watches and warnings had stopped.

It truly was a classic case of the calm before the storm.

Had it remained that way, perhaps things would have been different, but it didn't.

In a flash of unpredictability, it strengthened and intensified, curving north and picking up speed as if mother nature had changed her mind.

By evening, less than two days before landfall, the National Hurricane Center began issuing warnings for the Bahamas and portions of Florida as the storm became a major force to be reckoned with. With sustained wind speeds of 157 mph, the threat was now almost upon them.

Noah radioed back to the Aircraft Operations Center in Lakeland, Florida.

"Hurricane 04 to hurricane control, we're approaching the eye."

The radio crackled. "Copy that, Hurricane 04."

A host of sophisticated recon tracking equipment would soon measure wind, pressure, temperature, and humidity, allowing them to grasp the severity of the building threat.

Noah clenched his jaw. He'd flown these missions countless times but this one unnerved him enough to call his wife and tell her. His wife thought he was having a meltdown but this felt different.

"Is it me, or does something feel very off about this one?" he asked.

Bella, his co-pilot beside him, replied, "Reminds me of Ida, the way that got big so fast. A rapidly intensifying storm, the NHC called it." She chuckled. "The NHC sure love their fancy names. A little too late for those that died."

Flying at 210 knots air speed, the plane thrashed in the grasp of the worsening storm. Noah felt another wave of terror course through him. He was familiar with the feeling but no pilot got used to it. They simply put their trust in their training, the equipment and history. They'd done this enough times and always returned home.

Noah slapped away the paranoia creeping into his mind. *It's fine. You'll be okay.* Reassuring words were backed by history. The last Hurricane Hunter to go down was in 1974. Technology was better now.

"It's how fast it's moving toward land. It should make landfall in the next twenty-four hours." He shook his head in disbelief. "The way it died down and then rose back up again. It's like it came up out of nowhere on purpose to not give us enough time."

Time. Time was what made the difference with hurricanes. With modern satellite technology, the National Hurricane Center usually had a heads-up almost a week out — the general public, often less than that.

Noah reminded himself that a good portion of hurricanes never even made landfall, they simply fizzled out, and the majority that did amounted to some localized flooding and nothing worse than a bad thunderstorm. That's why many seasoned Floridians waited until the landfall path and timing were set in stone before evacuating. For some that was a mistake.

A lot of it boiled down to unpredictability. While forecasters were confident they could track a hurricane's movement and predict where the storm might travel, and when and where it might land — loops, hairpin turns, and sharp curves combined with shifts in direction had proven fatal.

Hurricane Elena was proof of that. It had developed near Cuba, entered the Gulf of Mexico and then when it was about to hit the Gulf Coast, it unexpectedly veered toward the east, then stalled just west of Cedar Key before going northwest toward Mississippi.

Hurricane Andrew, well, that had taken a good ten days before breaching U.S. shores. Of course, there were always the anomalies like Hurricane Ida that formed on the 26th, became a hurricane on the 27th and made landfall two days later.

The fact was, no two storms were alike. But that was the thing about the weather and climate system: it could be chaotic and not behave the way they expected.

That's why they were here.

While the NOAA monitored forming storms through satellite imagery and provided that data to the National Hurricane Center, there was somewhat a void in collecting data over the ocean because satellites had trouble seeing through clouds — so, there they were about to release dropsondes into the storm's eye wall, which would improve data and forecast models. It would give them a real-time look at the storm that had quickly evolved from a tropical depression to a tropical storm and now shifted up through hurricane categories.

"Okay, get ready," Noah said.

The P-3 Orion continued its path, buffeted by howling winds and fear-inducing up and downdrafts before punching through the wall and entering the relatively calm eye. For a moment it felt like they were in another world, a place where dreams were good and nightmares were a distant memory. But it wouldn't be long before they entered the belly of the beast again. They would fly through and out the eye, then circle back and do it again until they had completed four passes. The plane would crisscross in a triangular pattern through the storm to measure the central pressure and surface winds around the perimeter of the eye.

"Release."

The first of thirty dropsondes the size of an 11-inch-long tube was released.

Not far behind him he could hear the weather crew spouting off readings. The plane itself was measuring wind speeds while the sensors on the dropsondes would transmit data back to the weather technicians through radio waves ready to be sent to the meteorological services in real-time.

The whole process from beginning to end was a well-oiled machine.

Once the data was uploaded to research teams at the Hurricane Center, predictions would be made by federal forecasters and formal reports would advise state agencies and the powers that be to prepare for the projected path of the storm, and if need be, evacuate.

"How fast is it moving?"

A tech in the rear threw out a few numbers.

Noah glanced at Bella. "At that rate it could make landfall by late evening tomorrow."

As they flew out of the eye for the third time and back into the wall, a sudden jolt of vertical wind made the plane bank hard to the left. Noah gripped the controls, white knuckling it as Bella monitored for hot spots of severe weather.

It wasn't the speed of the wind that could destroy the plane or cause loss of control, it was a shear, a sudden change in vertical or horizontal wind. It was the reason why they never flew through tornadoes. The plane like many airliners was specifically designed to fly in winds over 150 miles per hour. His mind recalled that as he struggled for control. But the hurricane wasn't acting like it normally did, it was building in pressure and wind speed at an unusually accelerated rate and shifting and changing in an irregular pattern almost like a tornado, as if controlled by some unseen force.

Again, the plane pulled from the left, this time from a horizontal wind, then from the right.

"Noah," Bella cried out.

"I've got it!" he bellowed.

And for a split moment, he did, and then a violent shear wind caused a loss of control that not even he with eighteen years of experience could recover from. The plane went into a spin, spiraling down, the last thought he had was of his wife, as they became Hurricane Fiona's first victims.

1

Saturday, August 6
The Black Hills, South Dakota

Scout Miller was a survivor long before the lights went out.

The sixteen-year-old had already stared into the eyes of darkness and knew what lurked inside. Fear. Suffering. An endless cycle of uncertainty. Now, what lay before her was hope and a life free from shackles — of course, if she didn't die on this mountain.

Where am I? she asked herself. *It doesn't matter. You're out. Keep running.*

As sunshine warmed up the endless grasslands and craggy mountainous terrain, Scout blocked out the pain of sharp rocks and sticks digging into her bare feet as she staggered onward, stopping every few feet to lean up against a tree and catch her breath.

The smell of the earth was intoxicating. New. Fresh. The light overwhelming. The sight of it all was magical. For a moment she almost forgot she was running for her life.

Scout breathed in deeply, letting fresh air fill her lungs and replace the pungent stench of that place.

Would it ever leave her nostrils?

Back there, she'd struggled to breathe. The filth. The debris. It was a hoarder's paradise. Scout lifted her eyes up through a canopy of lush leaves. Squinting. Seeing it for the first time at this angle. She wanted to stare at it forever, mesmerized and in awe, but she couldn't afford to.

Not now. Later. Once you're safe.

As she pressed on, twigs cracked with each footfall.

She darted left, then right, weaving her way around tree trunks, pitching sideways down a slope, pushing through bushes.

It all looked the same. Trees for miles, nothing but an ocean of evergreen.

Shooting pain coursed through her joints with each step. Months of being made to kneel had made her legs feeble and lacking the strength to escape. Her muscles were loose and bandy with hardly any form. Her eyes dark and sunken from a lack of food and water. The only taste held in her mouth was acidic, bile that she had thrown up a day earlier. Why had they kept her this way? They'd thought of everything. She never understood the importance until now.

It was to keep you weak. Dependent on them. Unable to think clearly.

There was still so much about the way they treated her that made no sense. Would she ever know the truth? Right now, she didn't care. All that mattered was putting as much distance as possible between her and home.

Home?

Could it be called that?

It wasn't a home but a prison.

Even though it was still dark out, it wasn't what she might encounter that scared her, but who. Them. Were they out looking for her? She strained her ears to hear but could only make out the sound of birds chirping their morning song. Shadows of trees stretched toward her, beckoning her on to freedom; thorns and brambles raked at her exposed skin like her ragged nails that had grown too long. A portion of her dirty white T-shirt and pink pajamas caught on a limb and shredded. She yelped like a dog.

A dog, she thought.

A gust of air hit her and she caught her own scent. The smell was atrocious, worse than any farm animal, and yet they'd treated their own animals better than her.

Scout weaved through the trees, her bare feet stomping the forest floor blanketed in leaves, dirt and twigs. She wished she knew what this place was but had only gotten glimpses through a dirty window nailed shut. She splashed through a creek and scrambled up a muddy embankment, her small hands clawing at the earth.

Each breath was ragged as her heart tried to keep up with her legs.

She wasn't sure what she would say or do if she saw someone. Tears streaked her cheek, wet and salty. She wiped them away with the back of her hands, smearing soil across an already muddied face.

"SCOUT!"

The gut-wrenching cry cut through the quietness, her name driving deep like a dagger. So many times, she'd heard it. Back then she had no place to hide. Here, she had the entire world. Scout spun around at the sound of that voice. Taking cover behind a thick tree, she peered out, scanning the crest of the hill on the opposite side of the creek, searching for her pursuer. Her heart pounded hard. Her mouth went dry. Would they catch her now?

How close were they?

If captured she would be punished severely, far worse than times before.

She'd almost died the last time she'd spoken out of turn. They'd choked her until she went unconscious. What would they do now? Kill her? Kill her like they had Elijah?

Elijah.

Tears welled up again. He was gone. Never coming back.

It was strange to think that she'd lasted this long. That any of them had. Pushing her aching back away from the tree, Scout burst into a sprint, not allowing her mind to think about losing her footing. All that mattered was outrunning her captors.

Terror caught in her throat.

Her mind was a playground of jumbled thoughts like someone turning inside an ocean wave, unable to catch a breath. She wanted to stop and rest but the only clear thought pushing through the madness was panic.

Go. Move it!

The rest was a blur.

She wasn't sure how far or how long she ran. An hour, two? How could she know? She never saw a clock in the house. Days were nights, nights were days. Just an endless cycle of humiliation and fear.

Then, out of the blue she saw an opening, a grassy meadow followed by a clearing that led up to a two-story log cabin with a red metal roof and a cedar wraparound porch. The lower foundation of the house was made of large cobblestones. It was more beautiful than anything she'd ever seen on Elijah's stolen cell phone.

She wanted to scream for help but would her pursuers hear?

Would the owners of the cabin take one look at her and send her away?

Bursting out of the dark forest into the bright morning sunshine, she couldn't see any movement beyond the windows. Was anyone home? Hurrying up to the door, she banged furiously and stepped back, waiting for an answer. If there was anyone inside, they never came. Scout moved around the house, cupping a hand to each window and trying to make out what was inside. It was hard to see because thick white drapes blocked her view.

A gravel driveway curved around the house. There was an old broken-down Ford truck with a flat tire. To her that was a good sign. It meant someone lived here. She hurried up the wooden side steps to the main floor and looked through a set of large French patio doors. Finally, she could see. Inside, it was clean, tidy, orderly. The complete opposite of where she'd come from. Every room she'd lived in was full of feces, dead animals and clutter, an endless array of junk.

Scout rapped her knuckles against the glass but got no answer.

Her stomach dropped at the thought that what they'd told her might be right.

There's nothing out there. No one will help you.

What if they were right? What if she had blown her only chance of a life?

A life?

No, it was no life being cooped up inside, chained to that bed.

She rubbed the bright red marks around her wrist then looked over the porch balcony and got an idea. After checking that none of the windows were open, she went back down and collected a large rock. She reared back her arm and threw it straight through the glass.

Without a moment to lose, she scanned the tree line for them and then cautiously climbed inside. It was anyone's guess whose place it was, but inside she was safer from those hunting her out there.

2

Later that morning
Deadwood, South Dakota

The fight started outside Sunshine Diner. It was only ten fifty in the morning. John Sheridan felt privileged to have a front row seat to the brawl-filled mess while scooping eggs into his mouth and drinking black coffee. He already was fortunate to have slid under the eleven o'clock cut-off wire and nab the seven-dollar special but entertainment — now that was a bonus.

He was going to miss *seeing* this. All of this.

The small diner crouched at the corner of Lee Street and Highway 85. There was nothing fancy about it, but it was clean and the food they served wasn't greasy or undercooked. The inside was channeling the 1950s with black-and-white checkered floors, retro diner wall decor and a bright red Coca-Cola machine near the cashier. There was a busy kitchen out back and leather booths lined the far side of the wall.

It had once been a favorite of Katherine's. They would visit on Saturdays. He felt it was only fitting that he should sit in the same spot they always did — on one of the four high stools set in front of the main window. Off to the side was the usual stack of newspapers. He scooped up the *Black Hills Pioneer* and thumbed his way through it to catch up on local news. It was always the same. In a town just shy of sixteen hundred people, the focus was usually on what was happening in Lawrence County. Today, the front page was the Sturgis Motorcycle Rally.

Beyond the window an ominous grey sky stretched over the land, fulfilling predictions that there would be thunderstorms later that day. It wouldn't have been the first time in August. The weather was as unpredictable as the event itself.

Only moments earlier he'd seen two of Deadwood's boys in blue fly by, only to circle back around and swerve up outside. The light bars were flashing red and blue. Doors burst open and officers dove into the midst of an angry knot of Hell's Angels and Reapers who had decided to tussle over something. John had only just been reading about how outlaw motorcycle clubs and gang colors would be banned at some of the establishments in town.

The cops extracted extendable batons and a Taser and

began bellowing commands but it was nothing but noise falling on deaf ears.

A red-faced Deadwood police officer slammed a rider up against the window, revealing a patch — a grim reaper, the emblem of the motorcycle club. Flipped around, his cheek was pressed up against the pane of glass as the officer cuffed him.

The rider snarled, hurling profanities.

The Reapers were just one of countless clubs that gathered annually for the biggest motorcycle rally in the world. Held in the town of Sturgis, thirteen miles east, the rally was a mecca drawing in riders from all over the nation.

Every year for ten days in August the population swelled as over a half a million riders, concert fans and street food connoisseurs descended upon the vast craggy mountains of the Black Hills region. It was like a hillbilly fashion show, a Mardi Gras of sorts for custom bikes, ear-splitting music and scantily clad biker chicks shaking their goods.

On the opening day, a slew of Harley-Davidsons would rumble into small towns in the region, each rider trying to one-up the others. Many of the bikers were sporting weathered leather, ink and dripping in more silver on their hands than any man should. The term less is more didn't apply here.

Of course, there was the comradery of brotherhood and listening to bands at the Buffalo Chip Campground, but for the most part it was a whole lotta wasted folks trying to act badass.

John crammed another forkful of bacon and egg into

his mouth. At one time he might have come to their aid, but with the uptick in stabbings and police shootings and age creeping up on him, he figured it was better to just let the cops handle it.

It didn't take long. Backup from state police and the local sheriff's department arrived. Multiple cruisers. Doors flung open before cops dove into the fray.

Right then, the bell above the door let out a shrill.

"Son of a bitch!" A blonde bombshell entered the diner, holding the back of her head. She was a little over five foot four, athletic with deep blue eyes. "Maggie, can I get some ice?" She stopped at the counter, leaning against it.

Tom, the cook, spoke to her through a window into the kitchen.

"Another wild one, chief?"

"What's that saying... out of the frying pan into the fire. Yeah, some days I wonder why I put up with this crap. Police a small town, it will be easy they said."

John chuckled, taking another sip of his coffee. Steam spiraled off it.

"Didn't they remind you in the academy to watch your six when you handcuff?" John muttered, staring out the window and not looking back.

"Excuse me?" the woman replied as she ambled over.

He glanced her way with a big grin.

"John?" A broad smile formed as she recognized him.

"Sarah. Or should I call you chief?"

Sarah Olsen was the new chief in Deadwood. A department that consisted of twenty-three members and a couple of reserve officers. John and her father Frank went way back. He'd met him through his wife, Katherine, who was friends with Frank's wife, Gloria. They'd bonded over their interest in motorcycles. It had been Frank who had invited him to join Deadwood's own motorcycle club called the Pagans, but that was many moons ago. He hadn't ridden his Harley in a long time.

She leaned in and gave him a warm hug. "Call me a fool if you like," she said with a laugh. "I can't believe you're back. Dad will be over the moon. So, are you here for the rally?"

"That and to finalize the sale of the house. Sale by owner didn't go too well."

"Well, I could have told you that. It relies on you being here."

He chuckled. He'd actually left it in the hands of another good friend of his and although they'd had a few couples show up to take a look at the place, there were too many comments about it needing some work. It was true. His cabin on the mountain had fallen into disrepair. Nothing major but it needed the flooring replaced, and new front and back doors with sidelights, but getting them was a nightmare. Companies were backed up six months and when he got quotes, they wanted anywhere from five thousand to eight thousand dollars. He didn't have that kind of cash on hand. He'd told the guy on the phone before hanging up that those doors had better be gold plated. It was absurd. He wouldn't have minded if the bulk of the quote had been labor, but that portion had only amounted to about a grand. It was the glass and supply and demand.

He'd planned to pay a local guy to create him a couple of doors from wood but since Katherine's death from cancer a year ago, he hadn't had the gumption to do much except meander through his day like a ghost. She'd been the guiding light in his life, the one person that had kept him anchored, especially after the accident. Now he felt lost without her.

"When did you get back?" Sarah asked.

"I flew in a few days ago."

"You look well." She pointed. "I like the glasses."

John touched the black frame. "Ah... I wish I could say I'm doing it for fashion but my damn vision is on the way out. The doc said I could be blind in the next six months. I'm already classed as visually impaired."

"The TBI?"

He'd suffered a traumatic brain injury in Iraq when he was exposed to an IED blast that hit his vehicle. For the first few years after he couldn't see a damn thing, then slowly his vision started creeping back in. The doc had said it was something that was common with those who'd suffered TBI. Vision issues were different for everyone. He'd asked all manner of questions. Would he go blind? When would he go blind? Why had his eyesight returned after a year and why was it getting worse now? Why did he get tunnel vision while driving after so long? The doc couldn't give him a straight answer.

TBI affected people differently based on the injury. His had affected his eyes, leading to what the doc called traumatic glaucoma, which was caused by an injury to the eye. The symptoms could show up immediately or years later.

Then there were the symptoms of TBI. It could fade in and out throughout the cycle of the day. He never knew when he might need to lie down. He could feel fine for several hours then come down with a vicious headache or his vision would go blurry. And that wasn't the worst of it. He struggled with motion sickness, memory loss, sensitivity to light and sound, anxiety, and would at times feel like someone was pulling on his eyes. And all of that was only compounded by his tinnitus — an incessant ringing in his ears. Meds wouldn't touch it. At home in the silence, he had to turn on a radio, the TV or a fan, anything to create some form of white noise just so he didn't lose his mind. Many with it had been driven to suicide and he was damn sure he wasn't going out that way.

"Yeah, that and the accident," John replied.

Just when he thought things were getting better, his vision had crapped out on him at the worst time surrounded by the best people. He wouldn't ever forget that day. His daughter wouldn't let him even if he wanted to. That's when they took away his driver's license.

John felt an ache in his chest.

Sarah nodded and the smile faded. Most folks in town knew about the crash. It had happened right here in Deadwood at Christmas of all times. There was still a blue ribbon tied to the tree years later. That was another reason why he didn't want to stay. He didn't like to talk about it as it only dredged up painful memories. "Anyway, what with my tinnitus and my brain going on the blink, I'm thinking it's time to retire my ass to the old folks home."

"So, you're definitely going to stay in the Sunshine State?"

"That's what Laura wants. She thinks I need someone to look after me in my old age but I keep telling her I'm fine. At least for now."

Sarah placed a hand on his shoulder and squeezed it. A long time ago, when Frank had a motorcycle accident, John had stepped in and helped out. He'd taken Sarah out for ice cream, taken her fishing and to the cinema just to take a load off Gloria. It had given him a chance to get to know her. Even back then when she was in her early teens, she'd had her mind set on becoming a cop, following in her father's footsteps. It seemed only fitting she would wind up as chief.

"How is she?"

"Laura is Laura. Overworked, underpaid. The hospital has her doing all manner of hours. It's kind of ironic really. When she was growing up, I wasn't around that much because of the military and now the shoe is on the other foot. I can see now why she used to get so mad at me."

"And Charlie?"

He got a smile on his face. He sure loved that kid. His only surviving grandson.

"Oh, you know, sixteen going on thirty." He chuckled. "He just got his driver's license. You should have seen him. Ecstatic. All proud. I bought him a used Jeep Wrangler. He loved it. Laura didn't like it. Especially when Charlie dropped the comment that it would be the last she would see him. It was a joke but of course she never took it that way. I got the brunt of that. She thinks I've contributed to keeping him out of arm's reach."

"It's her baby boy. After what happened, it's natural to be clingy."

"Yeah, I guess. So where is Frank?"

He quickly shifted the conversation away before she delved too deep into the past.

Sarah glanced out the window and made a gesture with a wave of her hand. "Oh, out there somewhere. Probably swigging beers in a saloon or riding the back roads with my mother. You know, they got matching tattoos just this past week. Ugh. They still think they're teenagers." She shook her head, laughing. "Hey, why don't you swing around this evening? I'll tell them I bumped into you. I'm sure they would appreciate seeing you."

"Chief, your ice!" a large-breasted woman with fiery red hair yelled before tossing a bag over.

Maggie O'Neil was a Scottish transplant. A lass with a wicked sense of humor and one hell of a right hook. He couldn't count how many times he'd heard about her turfing rowdy bikers out of her café without an ounce of help. She'd knocked one of them out with her broomstick, and gave another a serious case of nut pain with a swift kick to the family jewels. Rumor had it she kept a small frozen haggis in the back tucked inside a thick stocking for special occasions when she needed to go all William Wallace on someone's ass.

"Oh, you're a star, Maggie," Sarah said, setting it on the back of her head and breathing a sigh of relief.

Looking back at John, Sarah waited on an answer.

John's eyebrows went up. "This evening? Um. Yeah. Sure."

Looking past Sarah, John noted the flat-screen TV above Maggie's head was tuned into the national news. There was a reporter standing in a news room, providing updates. Behind him it looked as if he was out on the street but that was the magic of CGI. He was holding a microphone up to his mouth as the green screen showed a close-up of Florida on a map. At the bottom of the screen scrolled *BREAKING NEWS - HURRICANE FIONA MAKES LANDFALL IN LESS THAN 24 HOURS.*

John got up and made his way over. "Hey, uh, Maggie, do you think you could turn up the volume? My daughter is down there."

"Aye," she muttered, taking a remote off the counter and aiming it at the screen above her. As the volume increased, the reporter's voice came in clear.

"The extremely dangerous Hurricane Fiona continues to close in on the southeast of the United States and with it will come a significant storm surge. Okay, behind me you will see a variety of maps created by the National Hurricane Center that will give us an eye-opening view of the kind of damage and water we will see above dry ground."

He turned and pointed to the southernmost regions. *"Take Miami-Dade, Broward, Monroe, Palm Beach, Collier and Lee counties. These are just some of the areas that we think will get significant storm surge. The areas shaded in red, yellow and orange could see water rising from ten to eighteen feet. For example, Marco Island, Naples, Cape Coral and Fort Myers* could see water rise above twelve feet and even further northwest than that. Remember that the direction could shift at any time. This storm surge will find its way inland."

At which point the green screen changed and began showing water flooding around the anchor and rising up as he continued to talk from the safety of the news room.

"It looks so real," Sarah said.

"The beauty of green screen and CGI."

It was an effective way to bring home the danger. It was one thing to tell people, another to show what it would look like as water rose behind the anchor on a street full of cars. It soon swallowed the front bumpers and continued to rise.

The anchor continued. *"So, let's see how this plays out. We know for sure that a hurricane at a lower category level will bring at least five feet of inundation in many locations across the west and east coast of Florida. That alone is enough to stall cars, knock people off their feet and flood lower-level structures. But we know that Fiona is going to rise far above that. Let me show you what that looks like."* The water rose even higher behind him, now covering cars, carrying them away, flooding buildings and turning ordinary objects into battering rams. *"If it makes it above ten feet, many one-story buildings could be underwater completely. When it rises this high, there are few places which are safe and that includes hurricane shelters in your local area."*

John felt a shot of fear.

It was one thing to hear it, another to see it. The noise of the wind, the thrashing of palm trees, SUVs being carried away by flooding and buildings buried below.

"Right now, Fiona will come up through the Keys, but with a second hurricane approaching from the northeast, that's sent many into a spin since warnings only came out 72 to 48 hours ago. For many that was enough time to get out of Dodge but not for everyone. For the old, the vulnerable and those with special needs, the road ahead is daunting."

The anchor flicked to a different screen showing lines of vehicles and people fueling up. Gas stations had posted notices that they were no longer open. "Many have gotten out ahead of time to stock up on fuel, water and get what they need to evacuate, but there are many that have not left. And with I-75 and I-95 backed up, well things could get really dire. So please follow the advice of all local officials and heed any evacuation orders. Remember it can take twice the amount of time to evacuate. Stay tuned to this channel to be notified of what zones will be evacuating."

John hadn't heard from Laura. She would have called him if she was worried. He was well aware that the months of June through to November were hurricane season. Before he left he'd heard that there was a tropical storm but that had been downgraded to a tropical depression. How did it develop so quickly?

"Anything to be worried about?" Sarah asked.

"Ah, it should be fine. It's not like she hasn't ridden out one of these before." Her work as a first responder at the local hospital meant she would likely shelter in place and Charlie would go to one of her friends who lived further north. That was always the routine. There had only been one time she'd headed north, and that was to escape Hurricane Irma back in 2017, but she was prepared for that.

Most Floridians were. They were a different breed of people down there. Tough as nails. Battle hardened by mother nature and weathered by the brutal sun. By the time most storms made landfall, windows were already covered with shutters, patio furniture was safely stored away in garages and anything that could fly around was firmly nailed down or set out of the way. And supplies. Well they usually had a good stock of candles, flashlights, food and fresh water on hand.

To be on the safe side, he took out his phone and made a call.

It went straight to voicemail.

"You okay?" Sarah asked.

"Yeah, she's probably on shift. I'll leave her a text."

He thumbed one out and then pocketed the phone, trying to stay calm. John had a lot of confidence in her.

As he was about to turn to collect his coffee, Maggie hit the remote to check the other channels. On the screen multiple broadcasting stations presented more of the same, except these storms weren't just occurring off the coast of Florida, they were happening all around the world. "What the hell...?" Maggie said. "You ever seen anything like that before, John?"

"Not in my lifetime," John muttered. "I mean of course they're known to form in seven basins but not all at the same time." He squinted at the screen; it went slightly blurry. Like a TV that wasn't working well. John patted the side of his head and opened his mouth a few times. The pressure behind his eyes caused his vision to go funky. It soon cleared. He resumed watching the TV.

Hurricanes weren't restricted to just the Eastern Pacific and North Atlantic, they could occur in different places. They were referred to as tropical cyclones in the South Atlantic and Indian Ocean, or typhoons in the Western Pacific. But this was far beyond the seven basins. There was one that had formed off the United Kingdom, others around Australia, the Mediterranean Sea, the Arabian Sea, east of China and even as high up as the Arctic Ocean above Russia. That was impossible.

Maggie flipped to a local news channel that was reporting heavy thunderstorms by evening with crushing winds of up to 90 miles an hour. That was enough to knock down some smaller trees.

John thumbed off some green and left it on the counter. "Thanks, Maggie. I should get going."

"How did you get down here?" Sarah asked.

"Uber. I know, I never thought I would see the day. Which reminds me, do you think Frank would be interested in buying my Harley?"

"You're not going to sell it, are you? That's your baby."

He shrugged. "It was. Won't be of much use to me soon. And right now, I can't ride it because I don't have a license. It's just been sitting up there in the garage gathering dust."

Sarah leaned against the counter. "Look, I'll give you a ride home."

"You sure?"

"Of course." She turned and thanked Maggie again for the ice and they ventured out into the madness.

The street was buzzing in the aftermath of the scuffle. Cops were patrolling the sidewalks, moving curious onlookers on. All around them were Victorian structures that had been tastefully restored. Walking down Main Street felt like stepping back in time to the 1870s, when gold mining was as big a gamble as any card game. Even now with modern edifices, the small town was full of casinos, museums, tattoo parlors, spas, antique holes in the wall, vintage stores, saloons, hotels and mom-and-pop gift shops. It had something for everyone. History dripped off the streets with the ghosts of Wild Bill Hickok, Calamity Jane and Seth Bullock and those looking to hide from the law or seek out their fortune. The community had already survived three major fires and almost had become a ghost town before 1989.

And yet despite its past, there was something about the town that he loved. It reminded him of Katherine.

Getting into Sarah's black SUV with a gold police department emblem on the side, John piped up. "Are the rallies getting worse?"

He'd missed the last three.

"No, actually that's the first bit of action we've had in a while."

Although American bikers had gotten a bad rap and become synonymous with the modern-day outlaw, those who descended upon the annual gathering were far from it. Sure, the Hell's Angels were there and many others who wouldn't back down from a rumble if one broke out, but most of the black leather-clad folks were just there to enjoy a concert, ride the back roads and rub shoulders with their own kind.

"You serious?" John asked.

"All right, we still have some unlawful activity brewing underneath the surface. But it's not like we're overwhelmed by drug deals, gunfights and brawls every day. Most of it involves helping inebriated sweaty bikers back to their hotel room to sleep it off. The age of the folks showing up at the rally is in the upper level, John."

"You mean they're old." He smiled.

"I didn't want to offend." She laughed. "Anyway, they're pretty mellowed out. We were getting a lot of assault calls but the past few years have been good. Nothing to call home about. Certainly nothing for newspaper fodder. It's been DUIs, a few minor traffic infractions and misdemeanor drug offenses."

"And the rest?"

She smirked. He knew the town well enough to know that they were very cautious about what they printed in the *Black Hills Pioneer* out of fear of scaring away tourists. That was the lifeblood of the town. When they weren't catering to them in August, they saw a steady flow to the Terry Peak Ski Resort or Mount Rushmore an hour south.

As the SUV wound its way out of the brick streets and through the busy town into the dense Black Hills of the National Forest, Sarah continued. "Okay, so we've seen a few felony drug charges, assaults and some trafficking recently but it's rare. In fact, we come across more youngsters trying to use false IDs than anything else."

He smiled. "Oh the days of trying to get served a beer underage."

John had grown up in Deadwood. Born and raised. The place was in his blood. That's why the thought of leaving it behind didn't sit well. It wasn't just the memory of Katherine, but it was the years of living in a town where he'd gotten to know a lot of people. They were good people. Hard-working. Honest. Folks who knew the value of a dollar but would gladly hand it over if it meant helping another out. "Most of the people here now are just looking for a good time. They all have the same passion, and act the same way," she said.

She knew it. Locals did too. The biker culture had been for the most part unfairly maligned. But as someone who had ridden in a club, and seen the steady influx of bikers showing up, he knew there was always one or two looking for a reason to act up. The morning had been proof of that and that was only at a small level.

They drove for a good five miles outside of town into a remote area nestled in dense forest. His nearest neighbor was over a mile away. He liked it that way. Peaceful. His home was at the end of a long gravel road where there was no chance of anyone building behind him.

"Here we are," she said, smiling. "It's been a while since I've been up here."

"Thanksgiving. 2016."

"Has it been that long since she's been gone?"

He nodded. "Afraid so."

Gravel crunched below the tires as the SUV swerved in front of the cabin. "Well, remember to see him before you leave. Dad would be devastated if he knew you were here and he didn't get to see you." John opened the passenger side door, thanked her for the ride and promised he'd be in touch. When that would be was anyone's guess. He had a way of making plans and then dropping them at the last minute because of his eyesight. Before she pulled away, she brought down the window. "John. You forgot something."

He turned back and she handed him his wallet.

"Oh. Thanks. I would lose my head if it wasn't screwed on."

She honked the horn and peeled out. His memory loss was becoming more frequent. Leaving things behind. Forgetting why he came into town. It frustrated him to no end. John fished into his pocket for his key and then let himself in.

The first sign that he wasn't alone was when he smelled toast.

He paused at the door. His immediate instinct was to reach to his waist where he had a handgun. The kitchen was at the back of the house. Deep. Far inside. He clutched the .45 in hand and made his way in. His vision blurred as his heart sped up. It happened all the time. Stress brought it on.

John kept his back to the wall and moved quietly down the hallway. He figured by now they would have heard him and run out the back door but to his surprise when he stepped into the kitchen, he was met by the sight of a young Native girl shoveling cereal and milk into her mouth with her bare hand.

Despite her untidy appearance, she was strangely beautiful.

Her dark hair was braided.

Her face dirty.

Her clothes soiled and torn.

She reminded him of a street urchin.

The girl froze. Deep brown eyes grew as wide as dollar coins. Like a deer in the headlights, she stared at him.

Milk sluiced between her fingers, a steady dripping. All over the kitchen island were boxes of cereal, empty packets of cheese and ham, and the leftovers from the previous night's pizza were gone. Nothing but crumbs.

The girl's gaze darted to the back door then back at him. She was weighing her odds. Considering how long it would take and whether or not she would make it. Then, she noticed the Glock.

Now whether she liked her chances of escape or didn't understand the predicament she was in, it was hard to tell as in an instant she burst away from the kitchen island, gunning for the back door.

She was fast, that's for sure, but not fast enough.

John darted sideways, cutting off her route.

She dodged right, hoping to go around him, but he caught the back of her collar.

"Get off me!" she bellowed. "Please."

John dragged her back to one of the chairs. "Sit!"

She continued to struggle like a wild animal, thrashing in his grasp. "Stop it," he said in a calm voice. When she wouldn't listen, he bellowed, "STOP IT!" The moment he said that, she froze. He released his hand, expecting her to take her seat or run again but she didn't. She just remained unmoving, almost like a statue.

That's when he noticed a puddle forming at her feet.

She was peeing herself out of fright.

"What the..." he muttered. "Oh geesh. Hey, hey!" He

turned her around so she would look at him, her face was a mess of tears and snot. She cowered back as if he was going to strike her. He put out a hand toward her and she flinched, turning her face away, closing her eyes and clenching her fists. On the side of her neck, John saw a deep red mark, and multiple bruises that disappeared below her T-shirt.

"Look, I'm not going to hurt you. Okay? Just... just stay here."

He crossed the kitchen and scooped up some paper towels and some disinfectant spray all the while keeping an eye on her. He thought she would bolt again but she didn't. She was standing beside the stool he found her on, not making any sound as tears continued to streak her cheeks. Her eyes were closed as if expecting the worst.

"What's your name?" he asked.

She didn't answer.

"Do you have a name?"

No answer.

"Mine is John."

He crouched and wiped the urine from the floor, grimacing at the smell. It stank badly like someone had held it in for too long. A quick spray and it was all clean. He tossed the paper towels into a green trash bag and tied it off before setting it out the back door. As he returned, her eyes were open.

"You want to tell me where you come from?" he asked. Again, nothing. "Look, if you don't tell me who you are or where you're from, I'll have to call the police," John said, pulling out his cell phone.

"No. No. Please don't," she said. Her mouth opened then closed. Her hands were still balled tightly. So tight that it was making them bleed. A few droplets of blood dripped onto the floor. It was so odd. She wasn't wearing any footwear and her ankles were red and raw.

"Give me one reason why not?" he asked.

She hesitated then replied, "Mother and father."

3

Florida

A clap of thunder rattled Laura awake, followed by an explosion of light filling her home. Steady rain and howling winds battered the storm shutters on the three-bedroom house in the suburbs of Cape Coral, reminding her of the impending threat. She was glad to have gotten them up a couple of days ago. All she had left to do was the front door.

Advance preparation was everything.

She rolled over on her couch, pawing at her eyes, still in her blue scrubs from the night before. She'd gotten in just after seven that morning. Bleary eyed, she'd written out a to-do list that she had to get done before her next shift but instead of plowing her way through it, she'd collapsed in a heap.

"Ugh," she groaned, swinging her feet onto a large scrap of paper, her to-do list. Her iPhone was on the table nearby, set to wake her up if she slept past four. She glanced at the digital clock on the wall. It was a little after three in the afternoon. She had to be at work by seven that evening for a grueling twelve-hour shift. Nights were brutal. For her it always meant two things — bags under the eyes and comically large cups of coffee. Her body adjusted after a couple of nights but by the time her internal clock got into the swing of it, she would be back on mornings.

But this day would be different.

It was the final twenty-four hours before landfall.

With Hurricane Fiona bearing down, many hospitals along the southern coastal regions were involved in partial or full evacuations of critical patients further north. So far in Florida alone four hospitals and eleven nursing facilities had closed completely. The evacuation decision was made by officials, driving over seven million people out of their homes before the storm unleashed. Many were still stuck on I-75 and I-95.

Others had chosen to stay.

What made things difficult was that Fiona's course had changed multiple times over the course of the past five days; that uncertainty had driven hospitals from the tip of the Florida Keys all the way up the coastal barrier islands of South Carolina to move patients out. Now with an additional hurricane that had formed seemingly overnight, there was now one making its way around the Gulf of Mexico and the other coming from the northeast. The media were talking about the kind of devastation that occurred back in 2004 when four hurricanes hit over the course of six weeks — except this time, it looked like two would hit within days of each other.

It was unprecedented and only made worse by multiple hurricanes occurring simultaneously around the world. Of course it had provided fodder for conspiracy theorists and news channels that stirred the fear pot even more by announcing that it was some kind of geological terrorist attack.

Laura didn't think so.

It was easier to shift the blame than to admit that humanity had screwed up the planet and perhaps now mother nature was about to dish out a few hard slaps.

The plan that evening for Cape Coral Hospital was to continue to evacuate some patients over to Lee Memorial in Fort Myers as it was the only state-approved level II Trauma Center between Bradenton and Miami. The rest would go further north.

While both hospitals had solid structures, Cape Coral only had 221 beds while Fort Myers had over four hundred.

Still, the proximity of both hospitals to the coast meant that those plans might change today. Laura would go with the flow. Adapt. That was her motto.

Despite the strength anticipated for Fiona and the closing of some hospitals in the region, the hospital association had opted to keep many of the biggest hospitals open and keep staff on hand to run the emergency rooms.

She was to be part of that skeleton crew.

Laura yawned.

Emerging from the fog of sleep, she ran her hands over her face just as the lights in the house flickered then blinked out.

Outages were expected. All day yesterday across the state the power kept going out and backup generators would kick in.

Shrouded in darkness, Laura scooped up her phone and turned on the flashlight. She crossed the room and activated multiple mini-lights and solar lights she had dotted around the house in preparation to shelter in place.

Days before, she'd already done her due diligence of filling up her vehicle with gas and getting a few more cans of gasoline to have on hand. She'd bought five days' worth of supplies, candles, flashlights and batteries. She had dug out her battery-operated radio, and had several coolers for ice ready to go.

After that she'd put away all the patio furniture and outdoor decor in the garage. She'd emptied some of the water from the pool and turned off the filtering system. She'd gotten out her two Bluetti Solar Generators and made sure they were powered up and ready. She had a portable gasoline-powered one in the garage for the heavy-duty appliances.

The night before, she'd filled the bathtub and sinks with fresh water. As August was the most humid month of the year, Laura had purchased a substantial amount of water bottles — some of which she'd frozen to combat the heat. She'd learned that tip from an elderly neighbor who had weathered far more storms in her thirty-plus years in Florida than Laura had. Jillian would sleep with these frozen bottles around her to keep her body cool and by morning they were ready to drink. She'd also take out all the shelves from the fridge and pack essential foods in a cooler, then put the cooler in the fridge and pack ice around the cooler. That way it would last at least three days longer. She swore by that trick.

Beyond that, Laura had a disaster kit in her car, and her reentry tag ready to go.

She wasn't a survivalist. These were just the basics. Simple things that most Florida folks did. Still, despite all her preparations, her gut told her she'd be sleeping at the hospital by the end of her shift. The weather would probably be too bad to drive back and who knew by then how much water the land would have taken in.

A loud metallic bang outside got her attention.

Beyond her door, trees were bending down, bowing under the strength of the first wave of winds. Litter and debris sailed through the air, scattering across the roadway and colliding with homes. This was mild and just the beginning; it would get far worse.

If it wasn't for her job, she would have gone north with her son Charlie. He'd gone to stay with a family friend up in Orlando, of course not without him protesting.

He never used to be a handful but after losing his father and sister, and then turning sixteen, it was like he'd become another person. He'd always been a happy-go-lucky kid. It pained her to see the change in him.

The power blinked back to life again. Off, on, off, on, if she threw on some music it would have been a disco. Knowing it could shut off again as crews battled to repair downed lines, she opted to take a shower while there was still hot water. After that she would have a bite to eat, finalize what else she had to do and then head for the hospital.

∼

LAURA PUT her plate of crumbs into the sink and washed it before setting it on the counter. She turned on the TV and let it play in the background, keeping her updated on the unfolding situation. Two anchors hashed it out, trying to make sense of the global hurricanes and tropical cyclones. There was no new update, just exaggerations. While the Weather Channel had a tendency to use fear tactics and go overboard with sensationalism just to scare people, she had to wonder if they were right this time.

She flicked through the channels while heating a frozen meal.

"It's unquestionably the strangest sight we have ever seen, Doug."

"I bet you now wish you'd bought that bunker."

The two of them laughed like it was some game. It wasn't. Lives would be lost. Injuries would be seen in the ER. They wouldn't be the ones to deal with the influx of people who couldn't or wouldn't evacuate and ended up injured — no, it would be first responders like herself.

People didn't always leave in the face of a storm for numerous reasons: disabilities, not hearing warnings, fear their home would be looted, financial stress, refusing to leave pets behind because many shelters wouldn't take them, and one that only a Floridian would understand — those who felt they could ride it out.

Laura changed the channel to local news, anything but the hurricane, while she prepared a meal to take with her for work. In the background she could just make out snippets of it.

"New video has emerged of the chaos that unfolded in a Monroe County courtroom when a murder suspect managed to slip out of his shackles and escape two days ago. Local 12 Mark Jenkins has more in this new video."

Laura briefly turned and looked at the screen but then turned back as the microwave dinged. She took out some food, juggling it. "Hot, hot, hot," she muttered, dropping it on the counter. The news continued to play out.

"The latest video out of the courtroom shows the moment when murder suspect Carlos Rodriguez took off."

Laura turned for a second and saw the backs of multiple accused people being led into a courtroom.

Focused on scooping food into a Tupperware container to take to work, she didn't watch but just listened. *"Several bailiffs rushed out of the courtroom. Everyone else looked confused, unsure of what was happening. The escape happened forty-eight hours ago when Rodriguez was awaiting a hearing for the murder of his girlfriend and child, when somehow the 33-year-old managed to get free from his shackles and run out of the courtroom waiting area. One of the bailiffs tried to capture him but Rodriguez escaped through the west wing of the building, leaving his jail jumpsuit and shackles behind. Cameras outside caught him getting into a getaway vehicle. It's believed that three of his accomplices were in the courtroom and helped* him. This led to a two-day manhunt but due to the weather from the approaching hurricane, Rodriguez still remains at large. Extreme caution is advised. If you see him, contact your local police department or Monroe County Sheriff's Office."

Laura's phone jangled. She set a sandwich down and glanced at the caller ID. It was her father. Their relationship had been strong up until the day she lost Michael and Libby. While it was an accident, it didn't lighten the blow that rippled out and affected each of them in different ways. She stabbed accept and put him on speaker phone while she packed a lunch bag. "Hey Dad."

"Been trying to get hold of you for the past few hours."

"I was asleep."

"You and Charlie okay?"

"Of course. Charlie should be in Orlando by now. He drove there," she said, shaking her head. He must have caught the worry in her tone.

"Alone?"

"No, Gareth and Julie came down to pick him up. He kicked up a fuss and said if he was going to be trapped there for a week, he wanted to be able to get out. Which was a whole other conversation. Dad, I know you were just being kind." She sighed. "But I really wish you hadn't."

"Well, what's done is done. He'll soon be eighteen, Laura. You can't keep a boy his age locked up forever. Speaking of locked up—"

"Look, Dad, sorry to cut you off but I'm running late. I've got a lot to do before I head into work. I'll call you later."

"Oh. Okay. Um. Be safe."

"Always."

She clutched the phone tight.

~

BY EIGHT O'CLOCK, Cape Coral Hospital, the 221-bed facility centrally located on Del Prado Boulevard, was in a tumultuous state. Staff were frantically working to evacuate patients as new ones were coming in. They'd been given instructions that unless EMTs brought them in, they were to turn everyone else away.

As the first of Hurricane Fiona's heavy winds blew out windows across the street and stripped surrounding buildings of anything that wasn't nailed down, many doctors, nurses and care workers were outside, trying to get cell service and contact loved ones.

It was fear.

A sense that they might not see them again.

As Laura helped two EMTs load a patient into the back of an ambulance, she caught wind of a commotion near the front entrance between security and several people asking for medical care.

One guy in particular caught her attention. He was a rugged fella, with a Miami Marlins baseball cap and a thick beard. He wore a Nike jacket, blue jeans and what looked like brand-new white sneakers.

"I've been in an accident. I fell off my bike. I need someone to take a look at my head. Where else am I supposed to go?"

Roger, the lead security guard, kept a hand out in front

of him. "I'm sorry, sir, but your best bet is to head to Lee Memorial or one of the hospitals further north. We've been given strict instructions from the governor that the remaining patients in this hospital are to be evacuated."

The man waved an arm at the main doors. "But you're still open. This won't take two damn minutes."

Laura jammed her hands into the pockets on her scrubs, the wind blowing her dark hair all over the place.

"Lift!" one of the EMTs said to the other while she eyed the man and listened in to the conversation.

"I'm sorry," Roger said.

"But I might have a concussion."

"Sir, if we let you in, everyone else will want in."

"So let me get this straight, my head is busted up and you are refusing to treat me?" He took off his cap to show them his matted blood-soaked hair. There was a streak of blood down the side of his face. "I already went to Fort Myers and they turned me away. C'mon man, my vehicle was ruined by a tree that fell on it, and I'm looking for my family right now. Help a brother out."

As several people nearby pushed forward, the two security guards had to get physical and push back. It was then the man with the matted hair tried to slip into the hospital. Roger grabbed him by the back of the collar. "Sir. I told you!"

Laura intervened, hoping to calm the situation.

"It's okay, Roger. Let me deal with this," she said, motioning to the guy to follow her into the emergency entrance while security dealt with the others.

Roger stuttered. "But... we..."

"I'll handle it," she said before turning to the man. "What's your name?" she asked.

"James Bauer," he said, looking back over his shoulder at the commotion. "Hey, look I really appreciate you doing this. A tree came down on my vehicle a few miles from here. I was lucky it didn't crush me."

A tree? He'd said a bicycle, Laura thought. She shook her head. People lied all the time to try and get treatment. She let it pass.

"It's not a problem."

He thumbed over his shoulder. "So, what's the deal with the overbearing security guards?"

"They're just doing their job, sir. Following orders. All of them are," she said, leading him back through a sanitized hallway past multiple gurneys of people waiting for transportation. They had shuttle buses for those who could walk, several ambulances and four helicopters from the region to assist.

"Yeah, well, they should tell them to mind their manners. Karma can be a real bitch."

Of course, every patient that came through their doors thought they should be seen immediately. While the hospital did its best, sometimes it could take hours to get around to treating a patient.

As they ambled through the hallway, he struggled to keep up with Laura. She was in the habit of moving fast. They didn't pay her to dawdle. "Seems like a big endeavor to try and move everyone. Shouldn't they have done this days ago?"

"There are a lot of patients, sir, and we didn't get the

order to start moving patients until yesterday. These kinds of things are very much touch and go. Up in the air until they have a firm idea of what's happening."

"Seems like what's happening is pretty clear."

She ignored him, sensing he was still angry. In her nine years as a nurse, she'd encountered her fair share of patients who couldn't control themselves. As good as security were at handling them, the attacks on staff usually occurred before help arrived. She'd gone home once with a black eye, and had her hair pulled another time. Though that had occurred in Albany, New York, when she lived there. However, Cape Coral still suffered from a few outbursts from the mentally ill or those in pain.

Laura led James over to one of the many beds and pulled a pink curtain around him. "Okay, take a seat and let's get a look at that cut."

He perched on the edge of the bed and removed his cap.

"That's a nasty gash. You say you got that from a bicycle fall?"

"It's windy out there," he said in a defensive tone. "Damn near broke my neck. Signage flying across the road struck the front of the wheel, sent me over."

"Huh. And yet you said you were driving when a tree came down."

She noted the inconsistency in what he'd told Roger and what he'd told her.

"Yeah, I meant before that. I went home and got my mountain bike."

"Because your family are missing," she said.

"That's it."

Squinting to get a better look, Laura got near his face with a light. A smile formed and she backed up. "Right, well stay here, I'll be right back."

"Doc."

"Ah, I'm not a doctor. I'm a nurse."

"Oh, well, what's your name?"

"Laura."

"Thank you, Laura."

She went out, closing the curtain behind her, and made her way to one of the many supply carts where they kept antiseptic wipes. She collected Steri-Strips, otherwise known as butterfly bandages. The cut was shallow and small, nothing that couldn't be solved by one strip. Amber, one of her colleagues, was eyeing her with a wide grin. "I thought we were turning patients away. Or is that only the ugly ones?" She cackled.

"Oh, lay off," Laura said in a joking manner, fishing through medical supplies. "It's only a small gash."

"Well, he certainly is a dish," she said, popping a plump green grape into her mouth. "Maybe you should take some of these over and see if he will feed them to you." She was always the joker, sometimes to a fault. It had gotten her in a lot of trouble.

Laura straightened up, holding some supplies to her chest. "Aren't you meant to be working?"

Amber leaned back in her seat with a big smile, her blonde locks pinned up off her face. "My shift's nearly over."

"Nice for some."

As Laura was gathering what she needed, her phone buzzed in her pocket. She took it out and noticed it was from Julie. She hit accept and brought it up to her ear while she continued to search for what she needed.

The line was crackling.

"Laura, Charlie is…"

The noise of rain and wind in the background was deafening.

"Julie. What? I can't hear you. You need to speak up."

Julie continued talking but the line was breaking up. It kept going in and out. She caught snippets of it, something about Charlie, his Jeep and then the line went dead. She glanced at it and tried calling the number back but it went straight to voicemail. Figuring she'd call back, Laura returned to her patient. When she pulled back the curtain, James was laying on the bed.

"Sorry for the delay. We are run off our feet here."

Laura set the supplies down and began to clean the wound.

"So, is all the staff heading to Fort Myers or one of the other hospitals?"

"Some are, some will be here."

"You?"

She stopped cleaning and gave him a glance. "I'm staying."

"Not sure I would with that hurricane coming."

"Well, someone has to be here. Not everyone will evacuate. And this hospital has weathered more than one category five storm before…" she said, tossing bloody pads into a steel tray. "And it's still standing."

Laura turned to collect a few more supplies.

"So, you're not married?"

"What?" The question caught her off guard. Over the years patients had flirted with her and some had even sent her flowers but those were few and far between. Most were respectful.

"I just noticed no wedding band on your finger or don't they let you wear jewelry?"

Some wore wedding bands, others put them on chains around their neck, but most would choose to not wear them while on the job. It depended on what they did. No one wanted to tear a sterile glove, scratch a patient or get a ring stuck in equipment. "Oh, I take mine off," she said without hesitation. It was a lie; she hadn't worn it since the funeral two years ago. It was too painful.

"Kind of figured you'd be married. An attractive woman like yourself."

She felt her cheeks flush red, not from the compliment but because it felt awkward. "Let me guess, your husband is a doctor?" James asked.

"No."

"A security guard? Yeah, that's it. Roger outside."

She laughed at that. "No, Roger is happily married to a good friend of mine."

James nodded. "Well then... what does your guy do?"

At one time when Michael was alive, she would have told him outright. That he was a firefighter, and yes, she'd met him while on the job. He'd come into the hospital with burns and she was the one who treated him. One thing led to another and after Michael was discharged, he sent her flowers with his number and asked her to call him if she felt comfortable doing so. She'd waited four days. A friend had told her to let him stew a little. Make him work for it. Eventually she called, and after one date the rest was history. After three years together in Albany, and the birth of Charlie, they'd moved to Florida to escape the brutal winters. Not having grown up in Florida, they didn't think they would be exchanging one bad weather for another. Still, the two of them had settled into married life and for the next fifteen years until his death they'd built quite a life for themselves.

"You happy?" James asked.

"What?"

"Content with your marriage?"

"Why would you ask that?"

"Well, most married people aren't. They act like they are but if you dig a little deeper, they live quiet lives of desperation. She wants this, he wants that. And somewhere along the way whatever they had in the middle just seems to disappear."

Laura bit down on the side of her lip. "And you would know this because?"

"I was in a serious relationship." He paused. "Once."

She didn't like to pry as it wasn't her business.

Unless the conversation was about work, or small matters like the weather or such, she steered clear of personal topics. Keep it professional. In and out. He noticed. "Aren't you going to ask how it ended?"

"That's not my business."

He laughed. "Probably smart. The less you say…"

"The less trouble," she added.

Both of them chuckled.

Silence stretched between them.

"Well, I'll tell you how it ended. She cheated on me and after I gave her a baby. I never wanted one but she did." He shook his head, staring off into the distance. His eyes were growing cold. "Yeah, I gave that woman everything... and then just like that... one day she thought she could do better. Can you believe that?"

He was probing for an answer but Laura wouldn't give it. Instead, she quickened her pace and he continued. "Anyway, she and I ended up having a little conversation and we straightened things out. Everything's good now. Really good."

Laura smiled politely. "That's good to know."

Her phone buzzed in her pocket.

She ignored it.

It stopped and then buzzed again.

"Aren't you going to take that?"

"Right. Um. Excuse me," she said, stepping away and pulling the curtain around. The caller ID revealed it was Julie again. Answering it, she was met this time with less noise. Her voice was clear. The panic even more so.

"Julie. Are you okay?"

"Laura. There's a problem with Charlie."

Her stomach sank. All manner of thoughts came rushing in. Was he sick? Had he had an accident?

"Like what?"

"He drove off."

"What?!" Her voice rose, panic gripping her. "But you were with him."

"Yeah, we needed to stop for gas. I went in and paid for it and then had to use the washroom. When I came out, he was gone."

"But what about Gareth?"

"He was in the store paying for his own gas. Look, I've tried calling his cell phone but he's not picking up. It just goes to voicemail."

The news hit her so hard that her brain couldn't comprehend.

"Wait. What? He's gone? Where?"

"I can't be sure but I think he's heading back to where you are. He said something about his girlfriend and having plans."

She immediately knew what that meant.

They'd had an argument several days ago. A close friend of his had a father that was a storm chaser. Dawson Jackson. What a guy. He'd instilled the same crazy love of capturing storms into his son Seth, and Seth of course having no fear of being killed had asked Charlie if he wanted to join them. They were planning on turning it into one big party. A party? If that could even be believed.

It was so stupid.

Of course, Charlie told Laura and she said it was insane and put her foot down, telling him he wasn't staying and he would be heading to Orlando. And that was it.

Obviously, he'd decided to do the complete opposite.

Laura gripped the phone tight, she was fuming. She couldn't fault Gareth or Julie as they had been kind enough to take him while she worked. All of this extended back to him losing his father and sister. It had destroyed both of them and left a hole that couldn't be filled. Everything reminded her of Libby and Michael. Two years and they were still grieving.

"So let me get this straight. Charlie, my son, told you he was going to leave?"

She laid it out again. Hoping that maybe Julie was mistaken or that this was some kind of dream. It wasn't.

"No. No. He'd mentioned that he wished he could have stayed in Cape Coral because he had other plans. I swear, Laura, if I had known he was going to do this, I would have stayed with him, but…"

"It's okay. I'll phone around and see if I can locate him."

"We can come back and help."

"No. It's too dangerous now. The hurricane is nearly upon us. Head home. I will be in touch. Thanks for letting me know."

"Again, I'm so sorry, Laura."

She disconnected and stood there dumbfounded. Laura couldn't believe Charlie would do this. Then again, she should have seen this coming. In some ways it was like this storm. Forecasters could make their predictions but at the end of the day no one could control it or guarantee which way it would turn or how it would play out.

The problem was she didn't have his friends' numbers on her. They were at the house, at least one of them was on the fridge. And a girlfriend? She didn't even know Charlie had a girlfriend. She felt like the world was spinning. A boom of thunder shook Laura's bones. The storm was getting worse. She cut a glance toward the emergency doors and saw a torrent of electricity snake across the sky.

"Problems at home?"

She whirled around to see James standing beside the bed. How long had he been listening? She swallowed hard and tried to act professional when everything inside of her wanted to drop what she was doing and rush out of there. Laura motioned for him to go back to the bed so she could finish tending to his wound.

∽

As Laura finished applying the butterfly stitches, her mind thinking of her son, she said, "Well, that should do it, Mr. Bauer."

"Call me James."

"James. I hope you have somewhere to shelter. Stay safe."

He rose from the bed and put his jacket back on. "Thank you. Listen, I hate to be so forward but I couldn't help overhear. You're searching for your son?"

Caught off guard, she said, "Um. Well. That's a private matter. I'll be handling that."

"You or your husband?" he asked, giving her a disturbing look.

She pulled back the curtain, feeling as though the conversation had now stepped over the line. "Thank you again, James. Stay safe."

Just as Laura turned to walk away, the power went out

in the building, but this time the backup generators didn't kick in. A few cries could be heard from patients. Several people reached for flashlights. Bright lights illuminated the inside, dancing off walls. Laura navigated through the corridor using the light coming from lightning outside. Then, as if by some miracle, the generators kicked in and the lights blinked on.

It was just the storm.

4

Florida

He couldn't wait to stare into the eye of the storm.

Charlie gripped the wheel of the Jeep hard, weathering the approaching storm with giddy excitement. The way he saw it, if he died, he won, if he lived, he won.

Charlie didn't have a death wish, more of a life wish.

Losing his father and sister had caused him to think deep and hard about his existence. People just didn't do that enough in life. They spent their days getting an education, pursuing a career, finding a partner, getting married, going on vacations and one day retiring to a sunny place like the one he lived in. And somewhere in all of that hustle they were meant to be happy and feel alive.

Alive? Was anyone alive?

No, it felt like every decision that people made in life was like rolling over and hitting the snooze button. Society catered to a comfortable life, a safe life, a don't go near the edge life.

Screw that!

He was tired of living that way, especially when it could be taken away in the blink of an eye. No, up until that day, he felt he was living a life like everyone else his age —average, normal, meandering through life playing it safe but pretending to be adventurous. He'd spend hours thinking of ways to capture that unique selfie that would blow up on social media, and turn into a viral sensation with a bazillion likes and followers. At his age, it was all about appearances — fashion, money, gains, haves, one-upping the next person — even if deep down he knew it was all shallow.

That had changed when he got word of the accident.

All that blew away like debris in a hurricane and revealed itself for what it was, meaningless.

No, he didn't want to slide into death at the ripe age of eighty-five having played it safe. What was the purpose of that? So he could stick around a few years longer to make everyone around him feel secure and happy?

No way.

Happiness was fleeting and so was life if not fully lived.

He didn't want to be that guy that turned up at a water park but never went on any of the rides because he was too scared that something might happen. That he might get injured, or die. No, he wanted to jump head first into the fray with reckless abandon and feel every emotion to the fullest. For what was the alternative? Sitting on the sidelines, dipping his toe in? Watching the fun from afar? No. Not him.

He'd seen Seth's videos; he'd talked long into the night with him about storms and what fascinated his father.

Charlie wasn't sure if it was a fascination with storms or jealousy. The Jacksons had created a video channel where they traveled around the country chasing storms. As terrifying as it was to witness, they had survived.

"If you don't risk a little, you lose a lot," Seth's father would say.

He was right. Seth and his father Dawson had taken some incredible shots of tornadoes and hurricanes. Some had made their way into *National Geographic* magazine, others had been picked up by prime media and broadcast all over the country. Hell, even Hollywood had come knocking with the possibility of a TV show called *Storm Chasers* where they would feature four or five different storm chasers around the world.

Seth was pumped. Why wouldn't he be?

This was his ticket to the big time. A way out from a life of normality.

But him? Little old Charlie. Always the one who had to play it safe, even more so now his father and sister were dead. But it wasn't his choice. It was his mother. She didn't want to lose him. God, if she had her way, he would have been smothered in cotton wool and spending his time in a panic room.

No. Something had to change. What did he have to show for his sixteen years on planet earth? A few photos of Mount Rushmore in South Dakota — boring! There were tons of people who had visited there. A guitar he couldn't play even though he'd taken countless lessons. The only good thing that had come into his life since that horrible day was the Jeep. He loved it. Charlie figured his mother would too. It was his ticket out of a claustrophobic world.

Why wasn't she thrilled?

He had a small job working down at the harbor to cover the cost of gas and insurance so it wasn't like she was paying the bill.

But no, owning the Jeep was a mistake.

So, that's why he was thrilled when Seth's father invited him to tag along with them as Hurricane Fiona got closer to the south coast. It was to be the opportunity of a lifetime. A large majority of Florida would be heading north while they would face it head on at the southern tip. He'd never stayed long enough to see one close up. He figured his mother would have been overjoyed to see him expanding his mind and learning something new, especially with someone who was trusted in the storm-chasing community.

But no.

It was always no.

It's too dangerous, Charlie. You'll get injured, Charlie. You're not staying, Charlie.

Like what a buzz kill. Instead, she'd wanted him to head north to Orlando. To spend his days cooped up in some shitty apartment in the city with her two boring pals whose only excitement was crocheting and watching football. He hated football. Throwing a ball around like a moron. He couldn't think of anything duller.

Still, like a good son he'd agreed to go with them, of course with the intention of ducking out the first chance he got. And he had in exquisite fashion.

They'd made it out of Lee County into Charlotte County when Charlie told them that he needed to gas up. With the long lines at gas stations and many turning folks away due to the hurricane, the whole thing had played right into his hands. Charlie said he would pump the gas while Julie paid and grabbed some snacks. Gareth, her husband, was doing the same thing. He couldn't have timed it better. Charlie had kept an eye on them as he pumped the gas. As soon as they disappeared into the rear of the store, he was back in the Jeep, and flooring it out of there. He figured Gareth might follow but since he had to pay for his gas before he could pump it, it gave him enough time to haul ass.

That had only added to the excitement.

He tried to calm his nerves, talking to himself as the rain bombarded his windshield and the wind shook the Jeep. "I know it's getting a little scary out there but Seth's dad says we'll be perfectly fine."

He swallowed hard, wondering if that was the truth.

His destination that evening was one of the barrier islands called Sanibel. The population was a little over six thousand. It was a beautiful place that boasted some of the nicest shell beaches and wildlife refuges in South Florida. His father used to take them there when they wanted to have a family day out. Because the southwest only suffered from direct strikes by hurricanes every twenty years or so, Seth's father thought it would be a great place to witness the storm in a safe location.

Safe?

Was it safe?

A clap of thunder followed, and streaks of lightning lit up the night.

Charlie's hands were sweating as he white knuckled it. Despite making the decision to tag along, he had his reservations. For all the times he said he wanted to die, he really didn't. He just didn't want to die without having lived. And he felt this was a step in the right direction.

Charlie's phone started ringing. His mother's name flashed on the screen. He knew it was inevitable that she would call. Julie and Gareth had sold him out — probably they got on the phone the moment they saw he was gone. He let the call go to voicemail. He received another six calls after that in rapid succession. It was to be expected. He wasn't in the habit of making her worry but he'd tried to convince her. Why wouldn't she trust him? Charlie had shown her the videos of Seth and his father Dawson. He'd told her about the awards Dawson had won. He'd been storm chasing for years and nothing bad had happened. His thoughts shifted back to their conversation.

Charlie: They always make it out. They're still alive. Why can't I go?

Laura: Because I said so.

Up ahead on US-17 Charlie saw a blockade. There was a silver Chevy SUV that had overturned and an 18-wheeler in the ditch. He could feel how strong the winds were but that accident hadn't been caused by wind. It was the rain, the traffic and drivers that were desperate to get out. Charlie glanced up through his driver's side window. The evening was pitch black and ominous. Rain battered his windshield making it almost impossible to see.

Charlie looked up ahead, easing off the gas.

He noted multiple police cars on scene and white barriers. Cops were standing out in the rain with yellow rain jackets, guiding a long line of drivers to a turn slightly further down where they would have to circle back. Horns honked. Vehicles crawled ahead of him at a snail's pace.

Charlie brought his window down just a touch.

He could hear cops yelling, shining flashlights into people's cars. Front and back. It seemed like they weren't just sending drivers on a detour, it appeared as if they were searching.

Somewhere in the back of his mind, he started to wonder if his mother would call the cops. She'd never done that before but with the hurricane and him not answering, there was strong possibility that's what she'd do.

Noticing a few other drivers doing U-turns and heading back to the Brownville exit, he opted to do the same. It would take longer to reach Hannah's place in Cape Coral but if it meant avoiding the police, then so be it.

No officer batted an eye as he followed three other vehicles.

Using Siri, Charlie called Hannah Lambert. He'd only started dating her two months ago. He'd met her at high school after they were partnered in a science lab. At first it was uncomfortable, then they hit it off. Unlike his mother, Hannah's wasn't the caring type. Wendy Lambert had struggled for many years with drugs, so much that her attention to what Hannah did with her time was next to none. As long as she didn't have to cook or clean for her and she was out of the way, Wendy didn't care if Hannah was walking head first into a storm. Both she and Charlie had suffered deep wounds from the past. Hers from being abused by her mother's boyfriend before he was sent away to jail, something she felt her mother held against her, and his from the loss of his father and sister.

Charlie floored it. The engine roared as he overtook vehicles.

He was meant to swing by her house and pick her up before heading over and he was running a little late.

The phone rang and her face popped up on the screen. He tapped accept and it turned into a video call.

"Where are you?" Hannah asked.

"Sorry, I might be ten minutes late because I had to avoid the cops, but it's all good." Something about those deep green eyes and full lips of hers drew him in. She had this wicked sense of humor that was second to none and a unique way of just knowing what he was thinking.

"Your mother will go mental when you get back."

"When has she not?" he replied. "What about you?"

Hannah turned the camera and showed her mother asleep on a ratty couch, with several bottles of pills on the floor.

"Hannah, you should probably call her sister to come and get her."

"Why? If she wanted to be safe, she wouldn't stick needles in her arm and swallow pills all day. No, screw her!" He heard what sounded like disdain in her voice but it wasn't that, it was pain over having a mother that cared more about getting high than anything else.

Although Charlie's mother was overbearing, at least she cared.

His phone dinged, alerting him to an incoming call. "Hey, listen, I got to take a call. I'll be there soon," he said. Hannah blew a kiss at the screen and he smiled as he took the next call coming in from Seth. Seth had ginger hair buzzed short and a round face with lots of freckles. Although most wouldn't consider him the kind of guy that would attract the female species, somehow he seemed to magically pull it off. They didn't see a nerd interested in a storm, they saw something else, what that was, well, that was a mystery. He liked him because he had a good sense of humor.

"There's my boy! Please tell me you are on your way?" Seth asked.

"Of course."

"Then why do I see a sign for New York behind you?"

Charlie rolled his eyes.

"Look, I had a few things to work out with my mother."

"So, she was cool with it in the end?"

He hesitated for a second before reeling off a lie. "Oh, for sure, she was thrilled. Wanted to come herself."

In the background, Dawson, Seth's dad, shouted, "She

should have. The more the merrier." He was setting up all manner of equipment and checking readings on an iPad.

"All right man, well, we'll see you when you get here. Make it quick though, Charlie, the causeway is looking pretty bad. I would hate to see you get stuck on the other side and miss out on all the fun." Charlie gave a nod, hung up and drove the accelerator up a few notches, racing to arrive. Within minutes he slowed as he noticed up ahead, the roadway quickly turning into a waterway as flooding occurred. As much as he trusted the tires on his Jeep, that vehicle wreck had unnerved him.

~

It took almost an hour to reach Hannah's place just off Tamiami Trail. She was peering out the window of her 80-foot-long dilapidated trailer in the northern part of Cape Coral. It was a run-down park with old trailers and weathered fences. The place had a reputation for cheap digs, and folks on welfare and drugs. It was also one of the worst places to be in a storm.

Charlie parked outside the single-wide trailer and hopped out.

Hannah was all ready to go, decked out in a blue Puma windbreaker, tight black jeans and brown riding boots that went up to her knees. "You look prepared," he said, pointing to her boots and laughing.

"Hey, my feet will be dry and toasty warm while you'll be complaining when yours are soaked." It was a good point. All he had on was Converse sneakers. As she went to close the door, he saw her mother on the couch and couldn't help wonder if that was his mother what he would do.

"Hannah, we should call your mother's sister."

"I told you—"

"I know you did but... well... I'd feel better if she was safe."

Hannah studied him. "Some days you really surprise me, Charlie."

He shrugged. "I just know what it's like to not have a parent around."

"So do I," she said, tutting as she pulled out her phone. Even though Hannah's mother was physically present that didn't mean she was there for her. "Aunt Dottie." She stuck a finger in her ear as the wind howled. "Yeah, I'm still here," Hannah said, rolling her eyes and smirking. "I need you to come and get her."

Charlie held the door as it was pushing against Hannah's back.

"No. I'm going out." Another pause. "That's none of your business. Come and get her or don't. I don't care." And like that she hung up. "All right, let's go." She crossed to the passenger side of the Jeep while he locked the door on the trailer.

Back in the Jeep, Hannah brought the visor down to adjust her hair in the mirror.

Charlie waited a second to start the vehicle.

"What?" Hannah asked, smiling at him.

"Nothing."

It wasn't nothing. He wished he could click his fingers

and make life better for the two of them but life wasn't like that. What had occurred in their life was like a ferocious storm that showed no preference to whatever got in its path. It blew in and rolled out, leaving them behind, victims of its merciless barrage.

5

Hours earlier
Deadwood, South Dakota

The fear in her voice was undeniable.

As she perched on a stool at the kitchen island, nursing a glass of orange juice, the tale Scout told him was shocking, almost unbelievable. John listened intently as she recounted the harsh treatment at the hands of her parents. His stomach roiled with every detail. The violence, the deprivation of food, sleep, hygiene, education and health care. It was the worst case of abuse he'd ever heard. How could anyone, especially a parent, do that to their children?

She wasn't the only one. She had four siblings, each of them vulnerable and held captive. Scout was the second oldest of five sisters. She had a brother but he was no longer with them — murdered by his own father.

At least that's what she believed. She didn't know for sure.

John shook his head, wondering how it had gone unnoticed.

As Scout continued to bring him up to speed, it started to become clear.

Scout told him that Elijah was the only one that had attended school, though only for a short while before he was yanked out and all of them were homeschooled. Owning a home in a remote area, out of sight, away from prying ears only made it easier. They'd also been told that if anyone visited the house, they would wear long-sleeved sweaters and long pants to hide any bruising. They were to act as if nothing had happened. If anyone said anything, they were told they would be taken away. Taken to a place far worse than the one they were living in. It was a form of manipulation through fear. They were kids. They knew no better. The only guiding light in their lives was their mother and father. Why would they question them? Still, no one from child welfare ever ventured in to check on them as there were no neighbors who heard their cries or who saw them awake at all hours of the night. That was the strange part; their parents had kept them awake at night and they would sleep in the day while her father went out to earn a living, a living working no less than as a social worker.

The irony wasn't lost.

No wonder no one showed up.

When he thought it couldn't get any worse, it did.

They weren't sexually abused by her parents, however, what they had in store for Scout — if it was to be believed — was the reason why she fled.

By the time she finished telling him, he only had one question at the end of it.

"Why?"

She shrugged, a shell of a girl, as if she had asked that question every day of her short life. "I don't know."

"How did you know it was wrong then?"

"What do you mean?"

"The way they treated you. You said that you've only ever seen the inside of your home, only known what they've told you." He paused. "Scout, we learn by comparison. We know what is up by what we know is down, and we know what is wrong by what we know is right. How did you know?"

Scout took a sip from her drink, relishing every drop. She'd never had orange juice. It was like watching a child taste ice cream for the first time. All she'd been allowed to have was water, bread, peanut butter, rice and pasta, occasionally some green beans. It wasn't because the family didn't have enough food or good food. No, they did but only the parents and her uncle were allowed that. The rest of them were given scraps, barely enough to keep them alive. She didn't look sixteen. Maybe thirteen at the most. John had told her to drink and eat slowly otherwise she'd throw up. Her body wasn't used to it.

"I learned from my brother Elijah. He was two years older than me. He stole my father's old cell phone. It didn't have any service. But we could connect to... I think he called it the intern or something."

"The internet."

"That's it," she said. "He hid it in the wall and at night when they were asleep, he would collect it and show us videos of the world outside." The way she formed words was awkward, unusual. "It looked so different. Kids happy. Nice clothes. Eating burgers. Leaving behind food on trays in school. Music, movies and so on." She reeled off an array of things that he or anyone would take for granted. "Elijah wanted us to know that everything they were telling us about the outside world was a lie."

He nodded. "Why didn't your brother call emergency services? Even if you don't have service on a phone, you can usually still call 911."

"We didn't know that. He didn't, I mean... it was new."

"And so you never left a comment online or sent anyone an email?"

"A comment? Who would have believed us? And mother and father said people would hurt us. That someone would take us from them. Kill us."

They had been leading such a sheltered life. It was a form of brainwashing. Using fear to keep them in a state of submission. It was almost like Stockholm syndrome.

"We didn't have the phone long. A couple of days."

"Why?"

"Mother and father."

"And what about your brother? What happened?"

She dipped her head. "One night we heard arguing. Mother and father were speaking with Elijah. I couldn't hear what they were saying. They would keep us in our rooms. If we misbehaved, they chained us to our beds. That's where I got these from," she said, showing him the bright red circles around her wrists. "Anyway, after that night I never saw him again. Days passed and I asked mother and she said that Elijah had left home and that people had taken him and he wouldn't be coming back. And that we weren't to ask again." She gave a pained expression as if reliving it all in her mind. "I know it wasn't true. I went to collect the cell phone from the wall but it was gone. I think they found it and hurt him."

"Hurt him?"

She shrugged.

"Did they hurt any of you?"

Scout nodded. "Many times."

She didn't give details and he didn't pry. Just getting her to open up to him after finding her in his house was a miracle in itself. John got out from his seat and set his empty glass inside the sink. He knew the right thing to do was to contact the police department but Scout was scared they would take her back there. It had happened one time before, years ago when they weren't living in South Dakota but were in New York. Elijah had managed to get out and flag down a vehicle. But his babbling account was so incoherent that the cop thought he was on drugs or suffering from some mental illness. He'd taken him home and their parents had convinced the officer that he was autistic and that running away happened frequently.

A month later they moved to South Dakota.

"Why did you risk escaping?" John asked. Though he

understood why anyone would run. He would have done the same but with so little knowledge of the outside world — except videos — and the fear of being taken back and punished, he was curious.

"They were going to exchange me for drugs and beer money."

"What? Where?"

"At some gathering. Mother said it was a motorcycle rally. I overheard them. I knew if I didn't get out then that would be it. I would probably vanish like my brother."

"And your sisters?"

"One is one year older, the rest are younger than me." She reeled off their ages. It was unfathomable to imagine that anyone from the rally he had associated with for so long would have anything to do with such a heinous crime.

The Sturgis Motorcycle Rally attracted hundreds of thousands of bikers from across the nation for a week-long rally. Most of them were there to tour the natural beauty of the Black Hills, drink, enjoy the outdoor concerts and spend their hard-earned money at vendor tents, bars and restaurants. However, there were rumors of drug and human trafficking, but those were just that, rumors.

John had always notched it up to bullshit because the Hell's Angels and other notorious biker groups attended, but in all his years, he'd only ever seen a few brawls. Of course, he wasn't naïve enough to think that it was impossible.

John nodded, pondering.

As he was thinking, he heard footsteps crunching

gravel outside. He turned and looked out the back window to see a tall man emerging from the tree line. He was rugged-looking, with a heavy overgrown beard and wearing a blue plaid shirt, jeans and construction boots. He was carrying a long, thick walking stick that he banged against the ground with each step he took.

"SCOUT!" the man cried out, scanning the area.

John heard the stool screech behind him. He turned to see Scout ducking down.

"Hey. It's okay."

She shook her head, her body trembling. "No, it's not. That's my uncle."

John looked back out the window and then told her to stay put, he would handle it.

Scout pleaded with him. "Please don't tell him I'm here."

"I won't. Don't worry."

"Please."

"Scout, it's okay. No one is going to harm you." John made his way out of the kitchen and got to the back storm door before the stranger reached the cabin. The rusted hinges groaned as he pushed it open.

"Can I help you?" John asked.

"Ah," her uncle said. "Glad to see someone is home. I'm looking for my niece. She's about yay high, dark hair. Braids. Have you seen her?"

"Can't say I have. I don't get many visitors up this way."

The man's face screwed up as he dug his thick walking stick into the gravel and leaned against it to catch his breath. He removed a bandanna from his pocket and wiped his forehead. The humidity was brutal.

Her uncle looked around, scanning the area.

"I didn't think anyone was living here anymore. You the new owner?"

"Current. I'm selling," he said. "The name's John Sheridan. You are?"

The man nodded with a smile but never replied. Nothing about him seemed nefarious. He just looked concerned. But having grown up around here, John knew it was uncommon for anyone to not introduce themselves. Her uncle still hadn't.

"Well, if you see her, tell her we're concerned and searching for her. We live a few miles from here up at the Miller estate."

"Will do."

The man turned to walk away. He had taken only a few steps when he stopped and cast a sideways glance. He had this puzzled look on his face. He glanced back at John, narrowing his gaze.

"Your lower window is broken."

John wasn't aware as Scout hadn't said how she'd broken in, but it made sense as he'd always locked the house up tight. He was anal about things like that. Security and whatnot. In a cabin so remote, he'd even installed cameras on the property so that while he was away in Florida, he could keep an eye on it remotely. For anyone to make their way up there, they had to have good reason. There was nothing surrounding his cabin except forest for miles. John didn't move or even look that way.

Calm and cool, he replied, "Yeah, been meaning to fix that."

"That's going to cost you. How did it happen?"

He was digging.

"Renovations. I'm here to get the cabin up to scratch. A lot of work to be done. A lot of mistakes to be made. That was one. My eyesight isn't what it used to be."

"Huh." The man nodded, still looking at the broken window. "Well, you have a nice day then." He ambled away, stepping back into the tree line. John felt relief wash over him as he stepped back inside, closing the storm door. He peered around the kitchen but Scout was nowhere to be seen.

"Scout. He's gone. You can come out now."

The pantry door opened ever so slightly and she peered out.

"It's all right. Come on." He waved her out. "We need to discuss your future." Hesitant, she padded out. "And we need to get you cleaned up and some better clothes. I think I have something you can use. Oh, by the way, there's a shower in the back. You can use that."

She gave a nod. She looked so pitiful.

"Go on then," he said.

She didn't move.

"All right." John turned and collected a large steel bowl from under the sink and turned on the faucet to fill it up. He wasn't going to push her into any situation that she felt uncomfortable with. Even though he'd managed to get her to open up to him, she still had reservations about him and a shower. "All right. If you don't want to use the shower.

Use this. Soap. A sponge. Clean your face and hands, and I'll get you something to wear."

As he was about to walk out of the room, she muttered, "Do you have children?"

"Yeah. But I have some old clothes left over from when my granddaughter used to visit."

He went to turn away and she asked again.

"Where is she now?"

"Dead."

Her jaw hung and he was quick to clarify.

"Oh, not like that. She passed away in a vehicle accident. She was sixteen, about your size. Well, I should get those clothes. Go on, clean yourself up." John walked out; the memories of Libby rushed to the surface of his mind. Her infectious laughter. Those long dark curly locks. The way she brightened the room every time she entered. She was the light of his life. John felt a lump form in his throat as he made his way up the stairs and down the hallway to the spare room. He hadn't stepped inside there since the accident. It was left the same way from the day Laura, Michael and the kids had visited. There were even a few Christmas lights above the single bed with a pink duvet. In the corner, a small Christmas tree that Libby had wanted. He stood there for a second, hearing her voice.

"*Grandfather, what do you think?*"

"*It's beautiful, Libby.*"

"*One day I'll have a huge tree in my house. So big I'll have to cut a hole in the roof.*"

"*Then how will you put the star on top?*"

"*I won't need to; it will reach the stars.*"

He laughed.

The memory faded as John made his way over to the closet and picked out a pair of jeans, some underwear, socks, a T-shirt and purple hoodie. Her white Converse sneakers were on the floor. Holding them in his hand, he smiled. Right then, the sound of something metallic hitting the floor in the kitchen reverberated with a clatter followed by a muffled sound and then a high-pitched scream. John dropped the clothes and burst out of the room, hurrying down the hallway just in time to hear the rear storm door close with a steely thud.

John hurried down the stairs.

Through the glass of the rear door, he saw Scout's uncle holding her with both hands. He had her hoisted up over his shoulder, her legs flailing around as she thumped on his back with both hands.

Removing his sidearm, John pushed open the door and fired a round into the air.

"That's far enough!"

The man froze, his back to John.

"Put her down."

"You'd be wise to stay out of this, old man."

"Are you deaf?" John asked.

"She's coming home with me."

"She's staying. Put her down."

The man turned and looked at him. "You know the punishment for holding someone captive?"

"No, but I expect you do. I won't ask you again."

"You're making a big mistake." He took a few steps back so John fired a round near his feet.

"The next one goes in your head."

"I dunno, old man. Is your eyesight that good? You might hit her."

"It's good enough."

"Look, I don't know what she's told you but this isn't the first time she's run away and told some sob story. My niece is autistic. She has problems."

"You're going to have a problem if you don't put her down!"

He nodded. "All right. All right. Just go easy. Lower your weapon."

John just stared back. The guy knew he wasn't going to walk out of this alive if he didn't follow directions. A high-pitched ringing in John's ears made him feel like he wanted to vomit. His eyesight blurred for a second or two and then snapped clear again. It was stress. Blood pumping through his veins elevating his blood pressure, messing with his heart and head.

Her uncle lowered Scout.

Just as her feet hit the ground and her uncle went to straighten up, he reached behind his back for a knife. It happened so fast in one fluid motion. The knife soared through the air and clipped John's shoulders, sending him back.

The gun went off and her uncle came barreling toward him.

As quick as a flash, John stepped to one side and used the forward momentum of her uncle to lock his arm and throw him to the dusty ground. His other hand, the one with the gun, was now pointing at his face.

Her uncle groaned.

"All right. All right. I'll leave," he said.

"Get up!" John bellowed.

John stepped back and the man rose to his feet, scowling at Scout. "Get off my property, now!" Her uncle nodded as he shuffled away, but then sneered looking over his shoulder. He didn't say anything more, he made no threats but John knew that this could only end badly.

6

Scout trembled.

In the kitchen John pulled off his jean jacket to check his shoulder. He pulled his white T-shirt down at the collar. Nothing. Just a little red. Fortunately, her uncle had a lousy aim or John had shifted just at the right time as the only pain he felt came from his back where he'd twisted it.

"You shouldn't have done that," Scout said.

Distracted while looking in a mirror, he glanced over his shoulder at her. "Yeah, well you shouldn't have broken in so I guess we are both prone to make mistakes." He shook his head and got a glass of water, then fished through his cupboard for his back medication. He winced as he placed a hand on his lower back. John turned on the fan, a radio and his TV just so he could drown out the ringing in his ears. Tinnitus tended to get worse when a person was under stress and he was swimming in it right then. He gripped the counter, feeling dizzy. His vision doubled.

"Are you okay?" she asked.

"Just dandy," John replied. "Do you want a drink?"

"No. I'm good. You know he'll come back, and next time it will be with father and mother."

"Great, a family reunion."

John tossed a few pills back and swallowed some water. He needed to tackle this head on. "Look, I know you are worried about the police but I have a good friend who is chief. You can trust her. But that means we need to go into town."

"No. I'm not doing that."

"Scout. They're there to help. If what you're telling me is the truth, your sisters need help as well."

"You don't believe me?"

"I didn't say that."

"You believe my uncle. Don't you?" She shook her head and made a beeline for the back door. John was quick to cut her off.

"Can you just stop? Stop running and listen. I want to help. But I can't if we don't involve the police."

She stared at him with an incredulous expression. He went to take hold of both her arms the way he used to with Libby when he wanted to make something clear to her. Scout backed up, folding her arms. She looked like a scared animal. Cowering back.

"All right. I won't touch you. But I need you to…"

An engine rumbled, drawing near. Both of them

turned toward the front of the house. He looked at Scout again as fear masked her face. "It's them."

John crossed the room and peered through the living room and out the window.

"No, it's not, it's Eddy. An old friend of mine. He said he would bring lumber and give me a hand renovating my place." She didn't look as if she believed him. "He's a friend, Scout. Just give me a minute. Don't run off. Okay?" He paused and repeated himself, eyebrows raised. "Okay?"

She nodded and crossed the room, disappearing into the pantry. Why she thought she was safe in there was beyond him but it was clear she had serious trust issues. John took a deep breath, locked the back door just in case, then made his way through to the front door. Heading out into the dull grey afternoon, he glanced over his shoulder just to be sure Scout hadn't taken off.

"So, I got the two-by-fours you wanted. Man, they have really jacked up the price," Eddy said, hopping out the back of his F-150 truck. Eddy Johnson was black, mid-fifties. An old friend from high school. A large burly man with a laugh that could rattle a person's bones. He always had a grin on his face. Eddy had grown up in Deadwood but had ventured out to California for four years before returning and starting his own construction company. That day he was wearing sand-colored dungarees and a black T-shirt with tan suede work boots. Around his waist was a tool belt. "What's the deal?" he said, motioning to John's attire. "Shouldn't you be wearing some old clothes?"

"Change of plans."

"Oh. You don't need help?"

"Believe me. I need help just not with renovating right now. I've got bigger things on my plate. We'll unload the wood and maybe get started on this tomorrow."

"Sure." Eddy went to the back of the silver Ford and brought down the tailgate. The two of them slid out two-by-fours and carried them over to the garage. "So, what's come up? You worried about the weather? I heard it's going to be brutal."

"No. Just my tinnitus is acting up and my vision is wonky again."

"You know, John, you really should go back and get that checked. Hell, I'm surprised you lived through that blast."

"You and me both. Listen, you ever done work down at the Miller residence?" he asked. As someone who knew the area well because of his frequent work at residential homes, Eddy was all too familiar with families, and the ins and outs of neighborhoods.

Eddy wiped sweat from his brow. "Know it well. I built a barn for them. Ray and Tammy Miller. Religious folks. Not your typical kind though. Not churchgoers. They gave me bad vibes. I saw all this kids' stuff outside their home but in the week I was there, I never saw any of them come out. And I was there at all hours. A little weird, to be honest. Her cousin Jethro is associated with one of the motorcycle clubs. Which one was it, she said..." He stood there tapping his chin for a second before pointing at him. "Vipers. That's it. Vipers MC."

John had heard of them. Seen them around. Their reputation preceded them much like the Hell's Angels for the trouble they caused. Though their membership was nowhere close to the scale of the larger motorcycle clubs. They were local. Based out of Sturgis. A few times they'd tried to lock heads with the Pagans. Though that wasn't new. Clubs were fickle. It didn't take much to set them off. A wrong glance. The wrong colors. Riding through the wrong district.

As they came around the back with the wood, Eddy remarked on the window. "You got squirrels throwing nuts at the cabin?" He chuckled. John was about to reply when his phone buzzed in his pocket. The caller ID was for Deadwood Police Department.

He lifted a finger and stepped away so he could take the call.

"Hello?"

"John. It's Sarah. We've got a problem. The Millers showed up here claiming you have their daughter and that you roughed up Ray's brother. That true?"

"The part about roughing him up or their daughter?"

"Look, can you come down to the station? I'm sure this is just a misunderstanding and we can get this cleared up. I was going to send a patrol car up but figured you're not the type to run."

"Where would I run? I'll be right over."

"Oh, and John, if you have the girl. Bring her too."

The chief hung up. John took a deep breath to steady himself. "Hey, uh, Eddy, you think you can give me a ride into town?"

"Where we heading?"

"The cop shop."

"Three days back and you're already stirring the pot?" He laughed. "It wouldn't be to do with that window, would it?"

He chuckled and told him he would be right out. John went inside to speak with Scout. Based on what she'd told him, he hadn't thought that the Millers would take this route. Too much to risk, especially if their daughter told the truth and showed her wrists and ankles. Then again, they could blame that on him. Had they told the cops a story that he'd kidnapped her? He wouldn't put it past them. The only way out of this now was to take her down and hopefully they would listen to her. His relationship with Sarah and Frank would count for something. They'd known him over twenty years.

Opening the pantry, John found Scout sitting on the floor, tucking into a packet of all-dressed chips. "You like those?"

She answered by showing him the empty bag.

John smiled as he crouched, setting his forearms on his knees. "Look... I have to go into town. Seems your parents have decided to show up and speak with the cops. I know you don't want to go, but if you don't there's a chance they might try to blame me for taking you. Now you wouldn't want that, would you?"

She shook her head but didn't respond verbally.

"Now the chief is a good friend of mine. I'm sure once they see those wounds and hear your side of the story, your parents will have to come clean."

"No, they'll just blame me. Say I did it."

"Well the cops would want to see your home."

She snorted. "Been there, done that. They won't find anything. By now they will have removed the chains from the bed and told my sisters what to say."

"Scout, if they find chain marks on your sisters, it's going to be a little hard for your parents to say they had done it themselves."

"They won't find anything because they weren't chained. Only I was."

John exhaled hard, studying her. He tapped his lower lips with his finger. "Well, I can't leave you here. If your uncle returns while I'm out, that would be problematic."

"I'll hide. I won't make a noise. He won't find me."

John grumbled, running a hand around the back of his neck. "And the cops?"

"You can't tell them I'm here."

John snorted. "You want me to lie?"

"Why not? Mother and father will."

John tilted his head back and glanced at the ceiling. Paint peeling. Another reminder that he needed to get cracking on work around the house. He was too old and too busy to be dealing with all of this. He wanted to come home, do the improvements the real estate office suggested and then place it back on the market. After, he'd return to Florida and live out the remainder of his life soaking up sun before his eyesight finally went and his world turned dark. He groaned. That was all beginning to seem like a dream.

John had considered having Eddy look after Scout, but dragging him into this was the last thing he wanted to do. "I'm going to regret this. But okay. You can stay here just until I speak with them. I can't guarantee anything, you understand?"

She nodded, a smile forming.

"Follow me," he said, leading her up the stairs to the second floor. John pulled on a cord and brought down the attic trap door. "Head on up."

She looked into the darkness then shook her head.

"Scout, it's for your safety."

She shook her head again.

"Why not?"

"They would lock us in a dark room when we were really bad."

"And by bad you mean?"

"If we tried to take food out of the trash."

His heart shattered. If this was true, these people were worse than animals. "Well... look, I don't have anywhere else to hide you."

"I'll be fine here. I could hide under the bed. In a closet. I'm small. I've done it before. Or..."

"Run away?" He asked.

"No. Hide. So mother can't find me."

John looked at her in disbelief, trying to grasp her existence. "What on earth happened to you, child?" he said in a quiet voice.

Eddy honked his horn impatiently. John groaned looking over his shoulder. "Okay. But don't touch or break anything else," he said. "And if anyone shows up. You don't answer the door. If they break in, you hide or get into the forest. You understand?"

She nodded.

Driving away that evening as the sun began to wane behind the trees, John looked in his side mirror and saw Scout looking out the living room window. What are you doing, John? he asked himself quietly as the F-150 rolled out of his property.

∼

DEADWOOD POLICE DEPARTMENT was located off Sherman Street. The one-story, red-brick structure housed the police and City Hall. It had three flagpoles outside, the one in the middle was an American flag flapping in the breeze. It had been a while since he'd stepped foot inside. Sarah's father Frank had been chief there until his retirement two years ago.

Outside was a parking lot full of vehicles, with additional space in the rear.

After thanking Eddy for the ride, John headed in, ready for the onslaught of questions. He still wasn't sure what he would say. If Scout's allegations were true, the parents would counter with lies.

Almost immediately he heard loud angry voices as he walked through the lobby. Mabel Davis, the officer manager who had worked there for as long as he could remember, was manning the front desk from behind plexiglass. She was in her mid-fifties. Her hair was short and curly; her face — overly round with a sharp pointy nose. "Hey John."

"Mabel," John answered with a nod. He was about to say why he was there when she buzzed him in.

"She's expecting you. You know where her office is."

He nodded, pulling on the door as the buzzer rang out. The bright fluorescent lights overhead hurt his eyes.

A loud female voice bellowed, "He's kidnapped my daughter. I want him arrested and put behind bars today."

"Look, calm down, once we..."

"Don't you tell me to calm down. You should have sent multiple officers up there. You want to see what he did to Clay again? Because I've taken photos. His face is a mess."

As John got closer, he knew that was a fat lie. He hadn't touched that moron other than to bring him to the ground.

A male voice chimed in. "Calm down, Tammy, Sarah's going to handle this but you're not helping. I'm sorry about this, chief, my wife tends to..."

"Tends to what? Huh?" the woman bellowed gruffly.

John knocked on the door and all eyes locked on him through the glass window. Sarah approached, telling Tammy to stay calm. She opened the door and thanked him for coming then shouted for Lieutenant Gary Howell to take over. "Sorry, John, but I can't bring you in here. Not right now. I'll be in to see you once I..."

"You! You did this! You got my little girl. You pervert!"

Sarah rolled her eyes and closed the door.

Howell approached. "Mr. Sheridan. If you want to come this way." Howell was an oversized man, five foot ten, late fifties with dark hair and salt and pepper flecks at the side of his temples. He wore extra thick black glasses. He led John into a back room. "Take a seat."

Howell sat across from him. "Sorry about the dramatics. Tammy Miller can tend to be a bit of a handful. The family keeps to themselves for the most part but the few times they do come into town, she's known to be a little outspoken." He paused. "So... Sarah has told me a lot about you. Friends with Frank, right?"

"That's right," he replied, distracted by the ruckus Tammy was making.

"So, you just came back to town?"

"A few days ago. To do some renovations on the house and get the right person to sell it."

"And your wife?"

"No longer with us. Died a year ago."

"Sorry to hear that. My wife is still with me but is sick."

"You're new here," John said, looking around. The interview room was bare. No one-way mirror. Thick cream-colored paint coated the cinderblock walls. There was a clock on the wall.

"Well, sort of, I guess. Or you haven't been here in a while."

John inhaled deeply and leaned back in his seat. "Yeah, it's been some time since I've been in town. My wife was raised here. She wanted her ashes spread here. And well..."

Before he could say any more, Chief Olsen entered the interview room, shaking her head. "What a woman," she said, closing the door behind her. She glanced at John, leaning back against the wall with her arms crossed. "Seems you've got a lot of people riled up, John. You want to tell us about it?"

"Sure. But what did she say?"

"She said that her daughter disappeared from outside

her home. Her brother Clay showed up at your house and saw Scout and tried to get her back but you stopped him. Said you pulled a gun on him, and messed his face up."

"Really?"

Sarah crossed the room and took out a phone and showed a photo of Clay. His nose was bulbous, red and bleeding, and he had one hell of a shiner on his right eye. "So what's the truth, John?"

"Well, I can tell you that isn't. He'd look far worse."

She snorted. "Do you have Scout?"

John wiped off dust from his thighs. "She's at the house but I didn't take her. After you dropped me off, I found her in my kitchen. She'd broken in and was helping herself to food. That child was starving, dirty and her wrists and ankles are raw. Told me she'd been chained to a bed, kept inside. Told me she never gets out. She and her siblings have been deprived of basic essentials. When that sorry excuse for an uncle showed up, he said she had run off which I guess kind of goes counter to what Tammy has told you, right? Anyway, he entered my house without permission, scooped up Scout while I was in the back. I pulled a gun on him. You're damn right about that. Told him to put her down. He threw a knife, and then came at me. I put him on his ass. But I didn't touch that ugly face of his. Look, I planned on bringing her down here and getting to the bottom of it. That's all."

Sarah cocked her head to one side. "So where is she?"

"At the house. That kid is terrified... of them, and you all. She thinks you'll send her back to them."

"That's possible. She is their daughter."

"You got confirmation of that?"

"They've registered their kids to be homeschooled."

"Yeah, and has anyone ever checked in on them in that time?"

Sarah glanced at Howell.

Truth was it was easy for a family to fall off the radar if kids weren't showing up at doctor's offices, involved in a school or if neighbors weren't within spitting distance.

"We've had no previous contact with them, John. Child protective services hasn't been called to their home," Sarah said.

"Well, I wonder if that's because her father is a social worker."

"Listen, John—"

"That's not all," he replied, cutting her off. "Scout told me they were going to exchange her for drugs and booze at the rally here. Human trafficking. Seems to me you might want to pay their home a visit, talk to her siblings before you go giving Scout back to them."

Sarah nodded. Before she could reply, an officer opened the door. "Chief, we have a big problem. A huge fight has broken out between two rival motorcycle clubs."

"I'll be right there," she said to the officer before looking back at John. "Stay here for now. I'll send an officer up to the Miller house and I'll go with you and see Scout." She paused at the door. "You should have brought her with you, John."

As Sarah went to exit, suddenly the lights blinked a few times and then the power went out and the department was cloaked in darkness.

7

Thirty minutes earlier...
Florida

It was an emergency.

All she could think about was where her son was. Laura tried to call him but it just went to voicemail. "Damn it!" *You wait until I get my hands on you,* she thought. She'd never been physical with her son and she didn't plan on it but there were some days, days like this that she wanted to wring his neck.

If she didn't have enough to contend with, now this?

Standing outside the main doors of the hospital, taking shelter under the awning with her phone in hand, Laura glanced up into the dark sky. The weather was getting worse. Sheet rain bombarded the earth, soaking the ground and transforming the roadways into mini streams.

Powerful winds beat trees into submission and brought an endless flurry of debris across the landscape. "Ma'am, you really shouldn't be out here," Roger said from inside the safety of the hospital doorway.

"I'm having difficulty getting a signal inside. Just a few more minutes."

Laura thought she'd be able to get through to him and resolve this herself but with the storm getting worse and the chance of being locked in the hospital for the night, and not knowing where he was, she had to get someone to help. She opted to contact 911. What good it was going to do was anyone's guess, but it was a gut reaction. A mother's instinct. At least she knew the color and make of Charlie's Jeep and his license plate. If she gave that to the cops and he tried to drive through one of the many roadblocks, they might be able to stop him.

She made the call.

"911, what is the address of your emergency?"

"Yeah, I'm at Cape Coral Hospital. I work here. My son Charlie who is sixteen is out in the storm and I need police to be on the lookout for his vehicle because…"

Before she could finish, the dispatcher cut her off.

"Okay. Is he in trouble?"

"He will be if doesn't get to a shelter or evacuate."

"Do you know where he's heading?"

"That's the thing, I don't. He was meant to be heading to Orlando with close friends of mine but he drove off. Left them behind. I think he's heading south to a friend of his down here in Cape Coral to go storm chasing."

She heard the dispatcher grumble. She wanted to join

her. It was absurd but then so were those who chose to go towards a storm when others were running in the other direction. While she knew his friend Seth and his father were into this, she had to wonder if Charlie didn't have some death wish. He had suffered a great deal of depression after losing his father and sister.

"Ma'am, what do you want me to do?"

"Can you get emergency services to be on the lookout for his vehicle?"

"Emergency services are spread thin right now but I will alert them."

Thin? Ugh, she groaned. That's right. Laura thought back to a week ago when the news did some piece on the local police department. With Cape Coral having over 180,000 people outside of peak season, most would have assumed there would be lots of cops patrolling. There wasn't. They were operating at the same number of officers as cities half its size, leading to only one police officer for every 12,000 people. That meant only fifteen officers per shift to cover the north, central and southern zones. To see them was a rarity.

And now with the hurricane bearing down on them, the number of officers responding to calls for help would be even fewer. Most would be manning roadblocks and turning people back.

"All right ma'am, give me your details."

The dispatcher wanted the make, model and color as well as the license number. She reeled it off. Laura knew she was going out on a limb expecting them to do this when there was so much need and chaos occurring, but at least it would give her some peace of mind while she tried to find him.

"It's very possible he'll be turned around," the dispatcher said.

"I understand but I don't want them sending him off until I reach him."

"Ma'am, have you tried your home?" dispatcher asked.

She hadn't thought to call home yet. The landline they had at the house wasn't used much. All their calls went to their cells except for a few. "I will give it a try but please can you just request them to be on the lookout for my kid? He's only sixteen."

"Do you think he might go to his father's?"

"No, his father isn't in the picture anymore."

The dispatcher took her name and contact details just in case. Laura thanked her and hung up. She'd been so distracted by the call, she didn't see her patient exit the hospital. James was standing only a few feet behind her, smoking a cigarette, foot up against the wall and observing her.

"I thought you said you were married?"

She frowned, finding his question an invasion of her privacy.

"No offense but it's none of your business," she replied, about to walk by him while trying her son's phone number again for the umpteenth time. Laura was determined to get his attention. Even if she had to phone him every few minutes. Eventually he'd get annoyed and pick up. If Charlie thought he was going to coast out of this without an earful, he was sorely mistaken.

"No, you're right. You're right. I was just trying to be friendly. I should mind my own business. But... well, you could say I've had one hell of a day."

"Yeah, haven't we all," she snapped, as the phone rang and reached Charlie's voicemail again.

James continued. "I'm sorry. Is there anything I can do to help?"

"No. I'm fine," she said, texting her son.

Charlie phone me now. This is urgent.

"You don't seem fine," James said.

She ignored him, hoping he would just walk away. But no, he was persistent.

"I'd be willing to help you find your son, just like you helped me — just say the word."

"It's fine," she said in a stronger tone.

"It's no skin off my nose. It's not like I've got anywhere to go."

Laura shut her eyes. "Please. Enough."

James chuckled. "It's strange how back there you were all smiles and politeness but I guess that's how it is, right? A façade. Nothing but a masquerade of false pretense hidden behind a uniform," he said, flicking out his almost finished cigarette into the roadway. "You are all the same. Nothing but lies unless it benefits you. Now someone goes out of their way to offer to help, a kind gesture and it just gets slapped back in their face."

"I never asked for your help," she said, outraged that he was turning this around on her, trying to make her look like an asshole.

Laura glanced at him out of the corner of her eye.

The alarm bells were ringing. His tone. His posturing. She'd seen it before in those that were mentally ill. She glanced at the doorway, but Roger was no longer there. He was inside his booth. It would take a good minute before he could reach her. That could be a minute too long.

"You know, humanity is like the weather. All sunshine and rainbows one minute and then a mean, dark brooding cloud the next." He glanced at her, locked onto her gaze. Laura swallowed hard as she felt his eyes bore into her soul. "You think the storm's bad? Let me tell you something, lady, Mother nature hasn't got anything on human nature. That's for damn sure. But I guess you'll have to wait and see." He chuckled, wiping the side of his face and spitting on the ground in some kind of revulsion. "You should do what Roger told you and take up shelter inside," he said. "It's not safe out here."

He glared at her, an ominous icy stare.

And just like that he stepped off the curb, yanked up his collar and ambled off into the driving rain. Laura let out a breath not realizing she'd been holding it.

~

TEN MINUTES LATER, inside the hospital, Laura glanced up at the clock. Time was ticking and the weather wasn't getting any better. Once the storm made landfall and the eye passed over Cape Coral, there would be no hope for anyone outside.

Laura didn't want to abandon her post. Leaving the

hospital short-staffed wasn't on the agenda when she woke up that day but then neither was this situation.

"You okay, Laura?" Amber asked, collecting her jacket as she got ready to leave. Her shift was over. Laura knew it was now or never.

"Amber, would you do me a huge favor?"

"Of course. Anything. What?"

"Do my shift."

"Oh hell no. I just got off a twelve-hour. I've got plans." She flipped her long locks over her shoulder.

"The only plan you have is to seek out a shelter. You can do that here."

"What, so you can go home and snooze?"

"Amber. It's my boy. Charlie. He's in trouble. I need to find him."

"Find him?"

"Uh. It's a long story. Look, I don't have time to go over it. You would be doing me a massive favor. I will cover two of your shifts if you do this for me."

"Two?"

"And I'll pay you two hundred."

"Hmm." Amber loosened her grip on her handbag. "I don't know."

"You're single. Young. Look, I've already done an hour. Eleven hours. That's all I'm asking. Look around you. There is hardly anything to do here. Nearly all the patients have been evacuated barring a few urgent cases that will come into the ER, and by the looks of it they might even turn them away."

Amber narrowed her eyes, looked at the clock and then

the door. They'd covered for each other in the past but that was when they were doing eight-hour shifts. The additional time the hospital had tacked on had made it exhausting.

Amber nodded. "Five hundred dollars, and you cover four of my shifts."

"What?"

"That's the deal. Take it or leave it." Amber folded her arms and got this glint in her eye.

Laura grumbled.

Amber was taking her for a ride. She knew she was in a pinch but desperate times called for desperate measures. "Fine." Amber put her hand out, expecting to be paid immediately.

"I don't have that kind of money on me."

"But..."

"You'll get it. I promise."

"I better," she said, removing her jacket and grumbling.

Laura was going to regret this. Ugh. She thanked Amber, signed out and made her way to the back to get her coat. The first thing she would do was head home. There was a slim chance he'd gone back there. It wouldn't have been the first storm they'd ridden out, as quite often the ones that had blown through had changed direction a few hours in. But if he was there, it could end badly.

From within the safety of the multi-floor hospital, Laura could hear the wind howling outside. Rain battered against the storm shutters.

Scooping up her coat and bag, she made a beeline for the door.

"Stay safe," Roger said. She nodded and thought about what the weirdo had said before he left. Was he out there? Lingering around? No. He would have been a fool to do that. She slapped the paranoia from her mind, staying focused on the task at hand — get home, find Charlie.

The rain was relentless.

As she hurried to her vehicle through a sparsely filled parking lot, her phone jangled in her pocket. Fumbling with the keys and being blown around by the wind, she couldn't answer it until she hit the key fob and opened her vehicle. Inside, she was dry but in no way safe. The wind was like a battering ram, moving the vehicle in such a way that it felt like it would lift in the air.

Quickly checking her phone, she saw she'd gotten a message from her brother Tommy. The black sheep of the family as he liked to say. He lived in Chattanooga, Tennessee, seven hundred miles away. She hadn't seen him in a good three years and for good reason. The last time they'd met he'd convinced her to invest in some stocks that were supposed to blow up. Oh, they blew up — in her face. She lost over thirty thousand dollars. Since then, his calls had been few and far between.

Why was he calling now?

She dialed his number as she fired up the engine on her soul red Mazda CX-5, set her phone in the hands-free holder and then swerved out. Tommy's face came on the screen. He was the spitting image of their father when he was young. A granite jaw, lots of stubble and deep brown eyes. His hair was faded up the sides with it long on top and swept to one side.

Laura tried to act like she didn't care. The truth was she didn't in that moment. Life-or-death situations brought everything into perspective. Money didn't even register in her mind.

"Hey, what's up?" she asked, turning her wipers on full speed. The arms couldn't swipe the rain away from her window fast enough.

"You know, I've left four messages already."

"I worked a long shift last night, and I had to work again." She'd seen his messages but just didn't answer. She figured he'd be asking for more money or had plans to introduce her to another one of his hare-brained schemes. It was rare that he ever contacted her just to see how she was doing.

"Working during a hurricane?"

"Yeah, some of us have to work, Tommy." It was a dig but he deserved it.

"Millions of people are being evacuated."

"Being? They already have, Tommy."

"Have? When was the last time you tuned into the news? They're all stuck on I-75 and I-95. Idiots. I bet you they're Floridians. They're always the last ones to go. Look at you. I figured that's where you and Charlie would be. I wanted to know if you were coming this way. I can put you up."

"Really? And how would you do that if you're living out of a van?"

"I got a place."

Laura narrowed her eyes. Her headlights cut into the

darkness. Her face was a picture of concentration as she tried to avoid unknown objects sailing through the air.

"Yeah, well that's great, Tommy. But I'm afraid I've got a lot on my plate right now."

"Right. Have you heard from dad?"

"Briefly, earlier today. Why?"

"He's another one that's not picking up. What's the deal with that?"

"Uh, I don't know, Tommy. I should ask you the same thing." She cut him a glance and he noted it.

"Figured you'd still be mad."

"I'm not mad about that, Tommy. I was a fool for trusting you. No, I'm just surprised. Three years of no contact. You practically fell off the radar. You didn't even show up for mom's funeral. How could you?"

"I wanted to be there."

"Sure you did." Her frustration shone through. "Let me guess, you had some business venture come up. What was it now? Stocks? Oil? Crypto? Or no, maybe it was NFTs."

He shook his head but didn't elaborate.

"Look, dad usually gets back to me."

"Really?" she asked.

"Would you stop acting as if the family has blacklisted me."

"We wouldn't do that. You've done that to yourself."

Laura suddenly swerved aggressively as a metal sign burst across the road like tumble weed, almost colliding with her vehicle. She cursed loudly. Her heart thumped inside.

"You okay?" He looked stressed.

"Oh, you know me, Tommy. Curveballs come and I keep bouncing back."

There was a pause.

"Where are you?" he asked.

"Still in Lee County."

"No, I meant now. You said you were working."

"Something came up," she answered as her vehicle rushed by others who were heading in the other direction — toward safety. Exactly where she should have been going. She glanced off to her right while passing over a canal that was now full. The water had risen to bank level and was beginning to flood the roadways. Her tires tore through water, forcing it up the sides.

It was hard to see out.

Darkness, rain and debris flying around only added to her sense of fear.

Her house wasn't too far from the hospital, a short ten minutes' ride down into the southern district of Cape Coral. The canals looked very different from the way they did a day before. The hurricane had created one hell of a tidal event. It had drained the shorelines like Hurricane Irma. It was so powerful that it changed the shape of the ocean and sucked water away from the shorelines, leaving many of the bays and beaches almost dry. The canals had been depleted and boats were grounded, manatees stranded in knee-high mud. The news had been reporting that this was setting up for catastrophic flooding and a devastating storm surge unlike anything they'd seen since Hurricane Irma.

"Look, I will try to get in contact with dad later but he's probably busy working on the property," she said.

"What about Charlie? Where's he?"

She knew she wouldn't be able to dodge the question.

"That's what I'm trying to find out."

"Why do I get a sense you don't know?"

"Uh... maybe because I don't," she said in an angry fashion. "But that's not your problem, Tommy."

"I want to help."

"The last time you said that, I ended up thirty thousand dollars lighter."

He sighed. "Laura. I'm sorry. I really am. I will pay you back every cent. With interest. You have my word."

"Your word means very little nowadays, Tommy. But hey, thanks for calling." She hit the red button and hung up just as he was saying hold on. He phoned back but she didn't answer. The last thing she needed right now was to get into it with him.

Glancing in her rearview mirror, Laura noticed she wasn't the only one that was driving toward danger. Bright halogen headlights not far behind made her squint. She figured they had to be in the same predicament or were tourists who'd gotten lost.

Heading down Santa Barbara Boulevard, Laura turned off onto South West 34th Lane and then made her way around onto 1st Avenue. The SUV lurched into the driveway. There was no Jeep outside but Charlie could have parked it in the garage.

Getting out, Laura hung on tightly to the door as shear winds tried to knock her over. Cursing under her breath, she made her way to the front door, jammed the key in and pushed into a darkened house. "Charlie! Charlie!?"

Nothing, just her voice echoing off the walls.

It felt like she had to use all her strength to get the door closed. Laura gasped and flicked the lights on. She hurried into the kitchen and over to the fridge where they kept a list of home phone numbers. "All right. Dawson Jackson. Where are you?" She zigzagged the page with her index finger and landed on a name and number. A spike of hope filled her as she called.

It rang, then rang some more but no one answered.

"Pick up. Pick up!"

Nothing.

"Damn it!" She crossed the room and her gaze roamed. Where had she put the phone book? She dropped down to her knees and looked under the couch, then in a cupboard and finally she found it in a wicker basket at the side of the recliner chair. She spread it out on the table and thumbed through, looking at all the Jacksons in the area. She compared phone numbers to the one she had.

Finally!

Laura circled the address in Fort Myers just off Emily Drive. She tore the page out and took it with her. Seth came from a divorced family, so she didn't expect to find the mother there. With Dawson out storm chasing, there was a slim possibility that one of his neighbors knew or he'd left information in the house on where he was. Laura tried the number again, hoping someone would pick up. Nothing. All calls to Charlie went unanswered.

Next, she needed to get prepared.

She already had a go-bag in the car with all the essentials.

If she did find him, they would have to go to one of the nearest hurricane shelters. There would be no time to flee, especially if her brother was right and the main interstates were backed up. As evacuations were done by zones, she needed to know what shelters would be open. She kept a list in her glove compartment. She was living in the B evacuation zone.

The lights flickered above her as she hurried upstairs and entered Charlie's room. She did a quick search to see if he'd left the location, or a name or number for this girlfriend of his. Why hadn't he told her? She opened his laptop and tapped in the family password. A quick scan of his internet history revealed all manner of searches. Some of it was porn, typical for a boy of his age. Then she came across a few searches of "Good places to party on the barrier islands." It listed nearby Estero Island, Pine Island and Sanibel Island. All three were pencil-thin islands when viewed on a map, but severely dangerous places to be in a storm.

No, he wouldn't go there, would he?

Another search took Laura into his social media which already had him logged in. She scanned through his last messages and noted there were several to a girl named Hannah Lambert. A beautiful brunette with highlights and bright green eyes.

The conversation between the two of them sounded odd, cryptic even.

If the location or a time to meet was discussed, they

hadn't done it over social media. All this revealed was a conversation about going with Seth that evening to capture the storm on camera and that she should come along as they'd have alcohol.

Laura swiped through a few of Hannah's photos, trying to get some sense of where she lived. It said Florida, Cape Coral but no address. And most of the homes looked the same. She certainly wasn't going to waste precious gas hightailing it up and down the streets looking for a house similar to the one in the photo.

For now, she'd have to work off what she had, keep trying the phone numbers and hope to God that the cops stopped Charlie at one of the blockades.

Laura headed downstairs.

An explosion of thunder set her nerves on edge as she prepared to head out. Laura opened the door to leave, but was then stopped in her tracks by the sight of the same truck she'd seen following her. It was at the far end of the driveway, blocking her exit.

Lightning streaked overhead followed by a clap of thunder. The flash briefly lit up the occupant.

James Bauer.

What the hell? He'd followed her?

They locked eyes for a few seconds before he hit the accelerator and zipped away.

Fear caught in her chest.

Laura went back in the house and waited there for at least five minutes, hesitant to leave, before she realized she was burning time.

No, screw him! He was playing with her. Nothing more.

Dashing out to her SUV, Laura got in and tried to still her beating heart. "Stay calm. Stay calm." She muttered the mantra but it was doing little to alleviate her worry.

She pushed down on the vehicle's brake, then pressed the push-button to start it, expecting the engine to grumble to life. Nothing happened. She tried again.

Not even a splutter.

"C'mon!" she said, trying for a third time. No lights. Not even a cough. "What the hell is going on?" Again. One more try.

Nope. It was dead.

8

Ten minutes before blackout
Deadwood, South Dakota

She stared at the large kitchen knife with dark thoughts.

Her wrists already bore the scars of half-hearted attempts.

To die would have been a sweet release from the misery of her life.

Scout moved around the kitchen with the knife in her hand, contemplating, and observing the clock. She still wasn't good at telling the time using an analog clock, but based on where the little hand was pointing when he left, John had been gone far longer than she expected. She tapped the blade against her palm and peered out the locked storm door, thinking about her uncle. He'd always been mean. The worst one in the house.

"Where are you, John?" she muttered under her breath.

Scout started to think about the worst outcome.

She was petrified of what would happen if she was handed back to her family.

As night fell over the cabin, she wasn't sure if she should leave and keep on running or if it was better to stay. John hadn't harmed her. He genuinely seemed interested in helping, which was foreign to her. All she'd ever known was a lack of interest from mother and father. There were no hugs, no kisses, no bedtime stories growing up. She never really knew how they would react or what side of them she would get. One moment her mother could be nice, the next calling her stupid and dragging her across the floor by the back of her hair.

Scout made her way upstairs, observing family photos on the wall.

John was in them as was a beautiful woman, and two children. They all looked happy. A far cry from her existence. She never had her photo taken. There were no family photos adorning the walls in her home, only crosses, a warped version of the Catholic faith, and yet it was the only version she'd known. She'd once walked in on her father nude as he was getting out of the shower, for that she was made to kneel on frozen peas as punishment. Did everyone do that? She didn't know. All she knew was that it burned and it was only one of the ways they made them suffer.

Scout ran her small hands over the photos, longing to

know what that felt like — to be loved, to be cared for, to have a mother and father that defended her. She'd noticed the way John had intervened, put her uncle on his ass. A smile formed. Oh, how many times she'd wished for someone to do that. To make him feel even just a fraction of the humiliation and pain she felt.

Even then as she thought about it, guilt washed over her, guilt entrenched through years of brainwashing. You can't think that way. You must honor mother and father. Honor? Did they deserve to be honored? Had they ever honored their children?

She made her way upstairs, exploring the house, experiencing more freedom in those few hours than she had in the years with mother and father. On the second floor, the hallway divided off to the left and right. Various cabin-style decor adorned the wall. There was a large bathroom at the far end, and two small rooms and a master bedroom to the right. Curious, Scout went into each one, going through a medicine cabinet, pulling random leather-bound books off the shelves, thumbing her way through piles of paperwork on computer tables and lying flat on clean beds, burying her nose in the duvet and inhaling the fresh scent.

Everything was new, clean and beautiful to her.

Her home had been a place of filth. It was covered with mold, dirt and trash. The bedsheets weren't washed nor were their clothes. When she'd asked to have anything changed or new, they would just stare or slam a door. In some instances, they would rebuke her, then cuff her to the bed for days on end using the Bible as a way to explain their behavior — as if twisting ancient words from another culture could free them of guilt.

Her siblings didn't even have to do anything bad to bring down wrath upon them.

And God help them when they did. Scout had been choked, punched, kicked, beaten with belts and sticks, thrown into walls, tossed down stairs and had her hair pulled. The worst was when they placed her in a bathtub of bleach mixed with water and had her scrub her skin until it was raw and bleeding.

It wasn't long before fear became her friend, her default emotion.

As she got older, to make matters worse they had used her to punish her siblings, forcing her to put them into an old dog cage in the kitchen and lock it. Doing that to her sisters had broken her. Seeing their tears, seeing them suffer had been the final straw. She planned to get out even if it killed her.

Scout went over to a closet and found a variety of hanging clothes inside, female, all of which might fit someone her age. *John's granddaughter.* She pulled out a few pretty dresses and put them against her body. As she opened the other closet door, she was greeted by the sight of her reflection.

Mirrors weren't allowed. It was vanity.

Seeing herself was unusual. Scout summoned a strained smile and a pair of dirty yellow teeth reflected back. She closed her lips, feeling a wave of embarrassment even though no one was looking. She tried on a few of the clothes and turned sideways looking at herself. All of them hung off her small frame.

Walking out of that room, she went to the master bedroom at the end of the hall. She touched the door gently. It creaked as it opened. Nervously, Scout looked inside, aware that entering any room that belonged to an adult was wrong without permission. Her sister had done it once at home and wasn't able to sit down for days after that.

The flooring inside was shiny hardwood with scuff marks, the same as the landing and downstairs. There was a large four-poster bed, with small side tables, a long set of drawers, a walk-in closet, a rocking chair in the corner of the room and a set of French doors that led out to a balcony. Above the bed was a huge, beautiful painting of a flowing river and someone in a canoe.

Scout cocked her head and stared at it, imagining it was her.

Something red caught her eye — a bowl of fruit was on a side table. She hesitated before taking a large red apple and biting into it, relishing the sweet taste. It was strange to think that she could do that here and fear no repercussions and yet in her own house she might have been whipped for such an action.

Taking a seat on the bed, Scout picked up a photo of an adult woman with lush blonde hair that cascaded over her shoulders. Beside her, John had his arms wrapped around her. She held his hand, beaming with delight. They both looked so happy.

Nearby was a collection of pills in bottles on the table.

She picked one up as she chewed and tried to read the label. She set it back down and noticed across the way a closet where there were both male and female clothes inside.

Scout ambled over and ran her fingers across the dresses on one side and glanced at what she imagined was John's shirts and slacks on the other side. There were different high heels and flats that were too big for her. Like a curious mouse she fished through different items, until she noticed a partially open box on the floor. Sitting down cross-legged, she pushed off the firm cardboard box top.

Inside was a stack of newspapers. Scout pulled one out. **Deadwood man cleared of all charges in CanAm Highway Christmas crash that killed father and daughter.**

There was a large photo of the wreck. A red Toyota had plowed into a tree and a truck had minor damage and was on the edge of the road.

Deadwood police say that all charges have been dropped in the Friday crash on CanAm Highway that killed a 16-year-old girl and her father. The driver survived.

The two-car crash happened on the CanAm Highway just before 6:30 p.m.

Preliminary crash information indicated that a 1992 Ford pickup truck was traveling northbound on the CanAm when a 2003 Toyota Camry heading south swerved into the truck's lane, clipped the truck and then entered the east ditch, rolled and hit a tree.

The impact of the collision sent the truck onto the southbound lane before it came to a stop on the shoulder. The driver was treated at the scene for a minor injury.

Firefighters extracted the occupants of the sedan, but the 38-year-old man and his 16-year-old daughter were pronounced dead at the scene.

All occupants were wearing seatbelts. John Sheridan, the 59-year-old driver of the Toyota, was transported by ambulance to Pierre Hospital and then airlifted to a Sioux Falls hospital in serious condition. He was later released.

Family have identified the victims as Michael Harlow and his daughter Libby Harlow.

On Thursday, South Dakota's highway patrol concluded their investigation into the crash and determined the cause of the accident to be related to an uncontrollable medical issue. No charges have been brought against the driver of the Toyota.

Scout set it down and picked up another one from a different paper. It seemed as if he'd collected one from every paper. Why would he keep these? She looked down at her clothes, realizing these had to be his dead granddaughter's.

Crash.

The sound of glass shattering caught her attention.

A shot of fear went through her.

It was followed by the crunching of glass below boots.

"Scout!"

No. She'd gotten so sidetracked by exploring the house, she'd forgotten the danger. It was her uncle. He'd returned.

Immediately her mind went into overdrive. She set the half-eaten apple down, picked up the kitchen knife she'd brought with her and scanned the closet. This was too obvious. The bed had room under it but he would look there.

"Come on out, Scout. I know you didn't go with him."

He had to have been watching from the tree line or maybe not, maybe things had gone wrong in town and now they knew where she was and John was in trouble. Rising to her feet, Scout moved quietly across the hardwood floor to the door, listening intently to the sound of her uncle moving things around downstairs.

"I'll find you. You know I will. So why don't you make this easy on you and come on out."

For a second, she actually caught herself considering letting him know where she was. Years of abuse had cracked her mind, made her believe that it was better to take the path of least resistance than to push her boundaries and end up with a worse fate.

It was better to get a whipping than to be thrown against a wall or choked out.

But no, not this time.

She was free and she wanted to stay that way.

Scout hurried over to the French doors and opened them. A gust of wind nearly knocked her back. Thunder rumbled in the distance. A light rain had begun to fall as she stepped out onto the balcony and peered over the edge.

It was too high. She'd break her legs if she attempted to jump.

And forget trying to climb down. There wasn't enough strength in her bandy arms to hold on. Behind her, she heard the sound of her uncle climbing the stairs. Each foot fell heavy as he spoke. "He's not around to protect you now. No one is. No one's coming. So come on out."

There was a confidence to his words. He knew her well enough to understand that she wasn't one to fight back. Being made to kneel for hours on end, experiencing little to no exercise had made her weak. One backhand and she would soar through the air.

As she tightened her grip on the knife, her eyes roamed the room, then an idea came to her. She backed into the room, removed one of the shoes John had given her and set it near the balcony. Scout took off the other one and tossed it under the bed.

After, she slammed the door to the ensuite bathroom and then rushed across the room and entered the closet.

Waiting felt like an eternity.

Scout reached up to turn the light out in the closet but before she could, the power went out and now she was shrouded in darkness. She frowned, clicked the switch up and down, but it wasn't working.

Before she could think about what had happened, the door to the master bedroom burst open and through the slats in the closet she watched as her uncle hurried over to the balcony and peered out.

Two things were clear: She couldn't outrun him or outfight him.

But this, this she could do.

As fast as lightning, Scout shot out of the closet. She crossed the short space between the closet and balcony, gripping the knife with both hands. Her uncle whirled around hearing her approach, only to gasp as she drove the knife deep into his side.

Scout stepped back, shock setting in.

Clay's eyes widened.

His jaw dropped.

A faint gurgling escaped his lips as he gripped the handle of the knife.

He stumbled back and without any effort, toppled over the edge of the balcony and disappeared below.

9

Cape Coral, Florida

Nothing was working.

There was no power. Multiple attempts to start her vehicle yielded the same result. No lights came on. The engine didn't turn over. There wasn't even a click. It was impossible. Immediately after getting no response, Laura had tried to phone Julie back but now her phone wasn't working. She tapped it hard against her hand like a pack of smokes, thinking that perhaps it was a faulty circuit or something. Nope. It wouldn't even power up.

Think, think, Laura, she told herself as the wind continued to batter the vehicle, shaking it violently. She cast a glance over her shoulder to see if lights in the houses on the street were out. They were.

The entire block was in darkness.

Climbing around into the back of the car, Laura fished into her disaster kit, and took out a heavy-duty flashlight.

She got out, rushed into her house and made a beeline for the door that led into the garage. She shone the bright light against the wall, expecting to see her son's mountain bike but it was gone. She didn't own one but he did. Had he sold it? She knew he was saving up for a vehicle before her father bought him the Jeep. Damn it. With the bike, it would take at least fifty minutes to get over to Seth's home in Fort Myers, and walking, well, forget that. It would take hours.

Not wasting any time, she exited the home, grabbed the bag out of her car and shrugged into it. She crossed the small grassy divide between her house and the home of her neighbor Geraldine Shaw. Laura banged on the door. The green Chevrolet SUV was still outside and she'd seen lights on when she'd arrived home.

"Geraldine, it's me. Laura. Your neighbor."

The door opened and she was greeted by a petite woman in her early sixties with a blue rinse. She and her husband, Reginald, had been living in Florida ever since they were knee-high. They were known to ride out the storms like many in the county.

"Power is out again," Geraldine said. "Reginald is trying the generator but that's not working.

"My vehicle won't start and my phone isn't powering up."

"Reginald," she bellowed over her shoulder. "Laura is having issues too." She turned back with a smile. "The air's been blue since his phone shut off. He thinks we're being attacked by aliens."

Laura stifled a laugh. "Look, you wouldn't by any chance have a bicycle, would you?"

"A bicycle. No, dear. We sold it after Reginald fell off and broke his hip. Damn hazard, I say."

Laura nodded, looking down the road. "Great."

"But I know Trudy across the street does. I always see her leading her young ones like a mother duck. Though best of luck getting her to agree. I've been trying to get her to trim her trees for weeks but she won't. She thinks nature should take its course." She got all quiet and leaned in. "She's one of those funny ones."

"Funny?"

"You know, the tree hugger type." Geraldine brought a finger up to her lips, as if anyone could hear. On a calm day no one could hear what their neighbor was saying across the street let alone when hurricane force winds were howling. "I mean, Reginald and I enjoy getting our fingers green but as I was saying to Deloris the other day when getting my hair done. You know how I like to keep it tidy," she said, puffing it up at the back with a couple of pats of her hand.

Laura raised a finger.

"Hey, Geraldine. Sorry to cut you off. I would love to chat but I'm trying to find my son and get out of here before the hurricane makes landfall. You should really consider leaving too. This is supposed to be huge."

Geraldine laughed. "Huge. Reginald, Laura here thinks this hurricane is huge. Do you want to tell her about that time we rode out those three hurricanes that hit back in 2004 or should I?"

Laura waved her off. "It's fine. I believe it. Stay safe," she said, then hustled across the road. She worried about folks like that. Diehard Floridians. The elderly. Those with special needs. They were sweet. Besides, there was a lot of truth to what Geraldine had said about riding out hurricanes, but she didn't want to be here when their luck ran out.

Trudy Cartwright was known on the street.

Her clan, as Michael used to call them, were in the habit of going door to door handing out flyers. They made it a family thing. Her and her four kids. Every time Laura saw Trudy's husband, he had this expression on his face that made him look like he'd been emasculated. He would go to say something and Trudy would shut him down with a voice that was louder than any megaphone.

The flyers varied depending on the flavor of the month. No one knew what they were going to get, it could be anything from Save the Whales to come to our local shindig at some nudist colony. She was very much into the earth and energy.

While some neighbors would position boulders outside their home and make their yard look tidy and aesthetically pleasing, Trudy took the opposite approach. Instead of boulders there was a large salt rock from the Himalayas that was supposed to have energy properties that could ward off bad mojo. The plants in her flower beds resembled something out of *Day of the Triffids*. God help you if you stepped off her driveway into that jungle.

Rumor had it, a six-year-old boy was last seen playing near there and had disappeared only to appear a few years later as a full-grown man. Of course, it was all nonsense — just another tall tale from those on the street like Geraldine who didn't approve of Trudy's lifestyle choices. Laura took it all with a grain of salt.

Right now, all that mattered to her was getting a bicycle and reaching Charlie.

Although her phone wouldn't power on, she kept trying but the screen remained blank. Shining her flashlight beam on the door, she banged hard on the hurricane shutter and shouted. It was the only way to let them know there was someone out there, as with the high winds all manner of debris was hitting homes. "Trudy! Richard! It's me, Laura."

The door opened and Richard beckoned her inside. Richard was a short balding man, shorter than Geraldine which was saying a lot. He had a full face and beady eyes but a big heart. By trade he was an electrician. He'd come over and helped with some of the electrical work around the house after Michael had passed. Right then he was holding a flashlight in hand. He pushed his shoulder into the door to get it to close. "I'm surprised you're still here," Laura said.

"It's Trudy. She's on a roll, talking about energy vortexes and you know, the usual malarkey." Richard rolled his eyes. "Now she thinks she's one with the hurricane. I told her that if we stayed any longer she probably would be and us included." He shook his head. Poor guy, he put up with so much.

Trudy bellowed from the back of the house. "Who is it, Richard?"

"It's the postman," he replied sarcastically while shaking his head.

She believed him. "Ask him if my package has arrived. I'm expecting my namaste pillow and chakra bath salts."

"Dare I ask what all that is?" Laura said.

"Not unless you want an hour's lecture," he replied with a grin. "Look, is everything okay with you and Charlie?"

She shifted from one foot to the next. "Well, that's the thing. Charlie's gone missing. I mean, not missing but... ugh... I need to get to Fort Myers and my car won't start, and my phone isn't working so I have no way to get hold of him."

"Yeah, I thought it was just a power outage but everything is out. It's got me thinking that we might have been hit by an EMP." He sighed. "I knew I should have bought a cabin out of town."

"A what?"

"An EMP. An electromagnetic pulse. It can vary in size and intensity, but in a nutshell it's what occurs after a blast from a high-altitude nuke. Generally, most folks don't really know what would happen. Of course, every dickhead wannabe survivalist online thinks 'they know'," he threw up quote signs with two fingers, "but they don't. But one thing most agree on is that it would fry anything with a computer chip, you know, transformers, phones, power grid, and newer cars and trucks."

"What?"

"I know, pretty wild, huh? Being an electrician, my understanding is that basically the EMP induces a current in circuits, kind of like putting everything close to a transformer. That's why distance plays a big factor in it. I figured that unless you were close to the target, the breakers in our home would offer protection against it but obviously not." He looked up, pondering, like he was trying to figure out a difficult math equation. "Though, it's possible it happened near us. Anyway, China has been touting that they've developed a hypersonic electromagnetic pulse missile that can travel Mach 6 which is roughly six times the speed of sound."

"But wouldn't there be some kind of fallout from that?"

"Not if the blast occurs high up. The only way we would know is..." he raised both hands and she filled in the blanks.

"If the power went out."

"Exactly."

"And what's the distance on that?"

"Well, it varies, it could be more or less. But they say it could have a range of around 1,864 miles. And when it erupts, it's bye-bye to communication and power supply lines. Which in turn spells disaster for everyone but especially for us when a category 5 hurricane is about to make landfall. Now it looks like we won't have any other choice than to shelter in place." He sighed again. "God help those people stuck on I-75 and I-95; they won't stand a chance."

"No escape," she muttered.

"You could say that."

She nodded, contemplating the gravity of it all. Not

only were they dealing with a crushing storm but now they also could be facing a catastrophic event.

"So you think the Chinese are behind it?" she asked.

"Ah, the Chinese, Russians, hell even North Korea. They've all developed EMP weapons. It was only a matter of time before the USA prodded the wrong wasp nest. And something that travels that fast would be hard to intercept."

"But wouldn't our country be able to defend against something like that?"

"Maybe, perhaps. It's all a bit up in the air. Of course, we aren't going to say we can't. Can you imagine the fear and arguments that would cause? No, we're America, the greatest nation on the face of this planet," he chuckled, "or at least that's what they'd like us to believe. No, I mean look... what I heard is that the Chinese are claiming that the blackout bomb can be enveloped in a plasma cloud that would shield it from radar. Something to do with when an object travels through the air at that type of speed, the air molecules..."

"Richard, you're losing me," Laura said, cutting him off "Right now, the last thing on my mind is whether or not some foreign country is trying to invade. I just want to find my son."

"Oh honey, they wouldn't need to invade our country with troops," he said. "And believe me, it should be on your mind. No, this kind of thing could set us back to the 1800s and lead to the deaths of up to 90 percent of Americans. And that's not some scare tactic statement put out by some fake news media, that comes directly from Homeland Security. And listen, we might think we know how to deal with a power outage living down here where the power goes out more times than we care to admit, but it's not just that, it's what comes next out of desperation. Looting, fights, protests, disease, famine — no delivery trucks will get through to grocery and pharmacy stores — and emergency services, forget that. They'll all be hamstrung."

"But the cops would do something."

He laughed. "Darlin', have you seen a cop around here in the last twelve hours? Hell, I don't see them patrolling even when there isn't a disaster."

She thought back to that recent newscast that had mentioned Cape Coral police being spread thin. Too many people. Not enough cops.

One of Richard's daughters poked her head out the door. She had a short black bob that bounced against her tiny round face. She couldn't have been more than six years old. Richard looked at her and smiled. "Dad, are you coming back?" she asked.

"Without a doubt, honey, just speaking with a friend. I'll be in there in a minute."

"You know, Richard, there are hurricane shelters you could take your family to. There's still time. I have a list in my car. I can get it for you. I think the nearest one to use is Island Coast High School or South Fort Myers High School if you have a pet. It might be safer than staying here."

"Thank you. I have that list. We haven't decided yet."

"You should think about it and soon. It's getting really bad out there. That hurricane is supposed to make landfall later this evening. This whole area is going to be flooded. It's too flat to stay."

He nodded. Everyone had to weigh up the risk factor. While millions every year evacuated, there were millions that didn't for numerous reasons. While many took shelter in schools and community centers, others battened down the hatches and prayed to God when the hurricane passed over.

And God help those who tried to travel while it was happening.

"Look, do you think Trudy would mind if I borrowed a bike?"

"No, it's fine, it's just through here," he said, pointing to a side door. He was just about to lead her through when there was a loud crash against the front door. Instinctively both of them turned their heads.

Crash.

Again, it happened.

It almost sounded like a stone hitting the door.

One more bang, then a couple of seconds and it happened again.

"What the...?" Richard said, heading toward the door. Laura lifted a precautionary hand as if to warn him, as if some sixth sense told her something wasn't right. Before the words came out, Richard opened the door.

Outside, maybe ten feet away was James Bauer with a golf club.

In front of him were multiple stones.

"What the hell are you doing?" Richard asked.

"Just working on my swing," he said. "Fore!" he yelled

before firing another rock at them. It came soaring over Richard's shoulder, almost striking Laura in the face. Her eyes widened; fear gripped her by the throat.

"That's it. I'm getting my gun; you better not be there when I get back!"

Richard turned to head back inside. He'd only made it four or five steps when Laura screamed out. "Richard!" He turned but it wasn't fast enough. Barreling in behind him, James brought the 9-iron down on his head with skull-crushing power.

Laura stumbled back as blood splatter hit her face.

James stopped for a second and looked at her. "See what you've made me do!"

10

Deadwood, South Dakota

It was a strange kind of panic that gripped the town of Deadwood.

With the lights out and most officers called away to handle a clash between two biker gangs, Lieutenant Howell had excused himself, leaving John alone in the interview room. He wasn't cuffed as it was an informal conversation. While he'd been accused of kidnapping by the Millers, Sarah knew better than that. Had the power been on, he would have been able to clear up this matter in a quick trip home.

That wouldn't happen.

Drumming his fingers on the table, and waiting for over ten minutes, he unclipped a small EDC Olight flashlight from his pocket and clicked the button on the end. A bright glow filled the room. He got up and wandered over to the door. It wasn't locked. He had his history with Sarah's father to thank for that.

The corridor was quiet.

John made his way down to the main lobby, expecting to see a few officers, but it was empty barring Mabel Davis who was still manning the front desk. "Hey, Mabel, where is everyone?"

"Beside the ruckus on Main Street... something strange is happening with the power. It's just me holding down the fort for now. You all done back there?"

"I'd say so. Not sure if they would." He grinned as he approached the door and let himself out.

"You want me to pass on a message?"

"When you see Sarah, tell her she knows where she can find me."

Mabel nodded. He headed out the main doors to find Officer Williams on his way in. He was red-faced, and looked out of breath as if he'd been sprinting. "Everything okay?" John asked.

"No. No it's not. You should be careful out there, it's a damn minefield. All hell has broken loose." He didn't elaborate but rushed by him, heading inside. Perplexed, John looked out down the street. Every streetlight, business lighting and all the decorative bulbs strung from one side of the street to the other were off.

Making his way down six concrete steps, John noticed several vehicles blocking the roadway beyond the parking lot. One of them was a silver Nissan Titan. The occupants were out, a man and woman. She was kicking the truck and having an argument with the guy across from her.

As John got closer, he recognized her. Tammy Miller.

"This is a piece of crap! I told you, Ray, to buy a different model."

"It's not my fault. It's affected all of them," he said, gesturing down the road. John glanced in the direction he was pointing to see a number of bikers examining their Harley's. There were trucks with hoods propped open, and most folks were holding their phones up as if that could give them power. He shook his head.

In the distance the sound of gunfire erupted.

Several couples hurried down the street away from their vehicles.

He got a sinking feeling in his gut. There were only a few things that could have that kind of impact on vehicles. Reaching into his pocket, he pulled out his cell phone and hit the button to check. Sure enough. Unresponsive. The screen remained black.

"You've got to be kidding me," he muttered.

Tammy looked his way. "Oh, there he is, the pervert." She nudged her husband and the two of them seemed to have some disagreement before Ray Miller made a beeline for him. John put a hand on his sidearm and Ray noticed. Ray stopped ten feet away and his eyes bounced between the gun and John's eyes.

"Outside a police station?" Ray asked.

John shrugged. "If I have to."

Ray smirked and jabbed a finger at him. "You know, I've heard about you, old man. Ex-military. Living in that shack by yourself. Lost your wife, right? All alone. That's gotta be hard especially after that accident. Was that what caused the problems with your head and eyes?" He smirked, waiting for a reply.

John said nothing.

Ray cast a glance back at his wife who had her hands balled and was gritting her teeth. "You see, my Tammy wants you strung up by your balls, but my brother Clay, he thinks Scout entered your house while you were out. That you had nothing to do with her going missing." He paused. "Now, I know you could press charges for trespassing, and we could go through the hassle of hiring lawyers, but I get a feeling that you don't want to go down that road, am I right?"

John shook his head.

"Because here's the thing, old man. We could follow through with our accusation that you kidnapped Scout and with you being some oddball military recluse, they'd probably notch it up to PTSD. So I figure we'd come out of it better than you would."

"You must be delusional," John said. John slowly strafed sideways, considering heading north, away from the lot, though all the while keeping his eyes fixed on them.

"Personally, I don't give a crap how it went down or why she's there. But I expect her back. So, why don't you just make this easy for everyone and hand her over?"

"I will…" He nodded.

A smile flickered. "Good."

"To the police."

He sneered at John. "That's really the way you want to play this?"

"After what I've heard you do to that girl, it's the only way."

Ray ran a hand over his eyes and down his face and nodded slowly, a menacing smile forming. "You're making a big mistake, old man."

"Sounds like you've made some of your own."

Ray put a finger to one nostril and blew snot out the other, he wiped it away with the back of his hand then pulled up his shirt to show him a handgun tucked into his pants. John noted a tattoo below his shirt. It was familiar, though he couldn't see it entirely. It was certainly unusual for a man who was supposed to be religious. "C'mon man, you don't want to do this. Things can get really ugly."

"Am I supposed to be frightened?" John asked.

Ray chuckled, looking around. "She doesn't belong to you."

"No, that's right. I have to hand over money if I want her, isn't that how it works?"

Ray narrowed his eyes. "We just want our daughter back. We don't have any problem with you."

"What, are you deaf?" John replied.

Ray's hand slowly slid down to the gun as if he was going to pull it.

"You go for that, it will be the last time you take a breath," a familiar voice said from off to John's right. Out of the shadows, his old friend Frank Olsen emerged, a Winchester rifle up and pointing at Ray. "Don't do it. Back away, Ray."

Ray replied, "Stay out of it. This isn't to do with you, Frank."

"It is now."

There was a long pause as if Ray was thinking it over, then he lowered his shirt.

"This isn't over. You hear me!" Ray shouted, returning to his truck to get an earful from Tammy. She pointed away from the lot, south, as if they knew someone who might be able to give them a ride. As soon as they were out of sight, John glanced at Frank who sidled up to him.

"Back in town a few days and you're already causing shit," he said, laughing. "Just like old times, right, John?" He reached for him and gave him a hearty pat on the back. "Man, it's good to see you."

"Yeah, it's been a while. I see things haven't changed much around here."

"Oh, you know Deadwood. We have a history of trouble," he replied, looking off in the direction of where Ray and Tammy went as if expecting them to return. "Sarah told me you were back. Figured I'd be seeing you tonight."

"Not exactly how you imagined."

"Never is with you." He took a deep breath. "So, you want to tell me what that was all about?"

"Didn't Sarah fill you in?" John asked.

"I spoke with her earlier today."

"You should speak with her again," he said. Although he was good friends with Frank, he didn't want to rehash it all.

"Right. So, looks like China followed through on their warning."

"I'm not sure if this is China's doing."

"Well, it sure as hell wasn't North Korea. Those assholes don't know their ass from their heads. But I am curious. Why don't you think it's them?"

"Too much on the line."

"C'mon. All the trade wars, and those steep tariffs on Chinese-made goods. They've been biting at the bit to snap back at us. Then again with Russia threatening to go to war with Ukraine, we aren't exactly on good terms with Mother Russia."

"I didn't mean that." John glanced at him. "Were you following those hurricanes happening around the world?"

"No. But I heard about the one making landfall in Florida. That's why I was glad to hear that you were back." Frank looked up and sucked air between his teeth. "Though, it doesn't look like we're going to escape. They say we are in for one hell of a thunderstorm."

"It's not just that. When was the last time you heard of multiple tropical storms making landfall around the globe at the same time?"

Frank studied him. "Never. What... you think someone is manipulating the weather? That it's some precursor to an attack? What about the EMP?"

John shrugged. "I don't know. I just know it's not good." He took a deep breath and looked off down the street. "It will get worse before it gets better. You should head home."

"Is that where you're heading?"

"I was."

"Look, John, word of advice. Whatever you've got yourself involved in. Rethink it. For the most part the Millers keep to themselves. And Ray... well, he's the least of your troubles. It's who they're associated with that concerns me." He paused. "Jethro Gatlin. He's a close cousin of Tammy and Clay."

Jethro Gatlin was infamous in the world of MCs. He'd heard the name multiple times over the past twenty years. Involved with the Pagan Motorcycle Club for many years, John had rubbed shoulders with the good and the bad. They'd attended many motorcycle rallies around the United States, and he'd come to know which MCs were dangerous. A longtime member of the Hell's Angels, Jethro had splintered off and started his own club called the Vipers. It had grown in size and established itself in Sturgis, buying property so they could be assured the best for the club members.

"And?"

"I'm just saying whatever feathers you ruffled, it's not too late to smooth things out."

"And I intend to, through the police. That's why I'm here."

Frank nodded. "Because of the girl."

"So, you do know."

He nodded. "She mentioned it on my way over."

"Which is why you came."

"Figured I could help. Sarah has lot on her hands right now with that clash. I help out from time to time, unofficially, but the department allows it because of my ties with the community." He pointed north. "You were about to head back, yeah?"

"I was."

"I'll go with you. Besides, you might need someone to watch your back. It will give us time to catch up, maybe make sense of this blackout."

"It's a long walk."

"No need. I've got us a ride. You've got to see this," he said with a glint in his eye, jerking his head in the direction he'd come.

John glanced over his shoulder, eyeing a rowdy crowd of bikers further down the road.

Trouble was brewing.

John followed Frank. Once he was around the corner of the First Baptist Church, Frank led him into a parking lot.

Frank shone his light on a vintage pickup truck with large 33-inch BF Goodrich tires. It was old school without computer chips. That's why it would work. Generally anything that was older than 1980 had a good chance of not being affected.

"Is that my 1969 4x4 Ford F-100?"

"That it is. Custom rebuilt. I had it restored to breathe some new life into it. What do you think?"

It was gorgeous. After having trouble with his eyesight, he'd sold it to Frank, thinking he would get more use out of it. When John owned it, it was just one color, a baby blue, but it had received a paint job since then. The top half was a royal maroon, the lower half white though it looked more like cream. It was stunning. "I changed out the engine too. It's got a 460 horsepower Coyote V8 engine and whiskey distressed leather interior." Frank laughed. "Had to get rid of that old fabric you were rocking." Frank walked around it, shining his flashlight on it. "I upgraded the suspension; it's got a brand-new 10-speed transmission. Not bad, huh?"

John opened the passenger side and hopped in. He breathed deeply, smelling the fresh leather.

Frank continued, "I would have been rocking my Harley but after this shit storm, damn, I'm glad I've got this. It's got all the bells and whistles," he said, pointing to the dashboard. "Certainly helps lugging things around," he said before starting the vehicle. Frank revved it a few times.

"You might not want do that too loud," John said, noticing they were attracting attention. A single vehicle working in a town where every other had died must have looked like gold. Frank waved off the curious onlookers who were making their way over, no doubt to ask how his vehicle was working when their souped-up shit wasn't.

"Ah screw them. But yeah, we should get going,"

He reversed and gunned it out of there, leaving those crossing the street toward them in a plume of dust and grit. The truck roared past a group of confused bikers. Most would be that way, here and throughout America. A power outage was a temporary inconvenience to many. Millions had weathered hours, days, even weeks without the lights on, but this was a whole other kettle of fish.

The lights weren't coming back on, at least for a long time.

Which meant getting prepared, being ready for what would come next.

No more deliveries of food or pharmaceuticals.

Looting, fights, overpowering law and order, deaths as the elderly and medical-reliant patients were the first to go.

"Five hundred thousand bikers at a rally, in our neck of the woods, and many of which are rivals and then this happens." Frank shook his head. "Could the timing be any worse? God help us," Frank said as he flipped on his bright headlights and lit up the hilly region of evergreen forest.

11

Sturgis, South Dakota

The brawl between the Vipers and Nomads was planned.

It was misdirection, nothing more than what a magician might do to keep an audience distracted. It had worked perfectly. The Vipers hadn't managed to stay one step ahead of the law without knowing a few tricks to outsmart cops. Everyone knew there were undercover DCI agents and other law enforcement officials conducting sex sting operations at the motorcycle rally. It happened every year. The mistake those egotistical pricks had made was making that known to the media a few years back after a string of arrests.

Now logic should have told the Vipers to cut their losses, find other ways to make money but Jethro Gatlin, the chapter president, had said nothing brought in more cash than sex.

And he was right.

They varied the ways they made coin — drug trafficking, violence and intimidation — but drugs were problematic on so many fronts. Not only did they have to put their necks on the line dealing with the Colombian cartel, but then they had to run the risk of being caught transporting drugs to venues like this, then selling them to someone who could be a cop. And, if everything went well, stock always needed to be replenished which again meant more upfront costs.

Not so with trafficking women.

That was a commodity that could be sold over and over again.

And when they were done with them, they could throw them to the curb or put a bullet in the head. With MC chapters all over the country, transporting goods for sale was getting easier. The only risk they ran now was someone speaking out, tying it back to them or having guys found in the act.

But that wasn't their biggest problem, oh, no, it was those who were trying to steal business out from underneath their nose.

While many in society thought that all MCs were outlaws involved in trafficking, that wasn't the truth, there were more clean and wholesome guys just wanting to ride than there were those looking to cash in on the market.

But tonight, they were dealing with an upcoming biker gang, no more than twenty-eight members called the

Regulators. Those assholes had bitten off a bit more than they could chew this time. For that reason alone, Jethro had put a stop to it.

Under an alias, the Vipers had put the word out that one of them was looking for a girl for the night. It didn't matter what ethnicity, hair color or age. It wasn't long before they got a time and a location from the Regulators.

That was a rookie mistake.

When conducting business, Jethro never allowed anyone to see his line of ladies without vetting them first. Who were they? How had they heard about the women? How had they made contact? He would then observe them from afar over a period of twenty-four hours. He'd also have one of his guys follow them. It was a lot of work but better that than to wind up in jail. He'd caught many an undercover cop that way. They were notorious for trying to arrange to have a woman at their hotel. It was an environment they could control. Usually there would be cops in the next room, monitoring everything. Cameras, audio, the works. Once cash was exchanged, the room would be raided by armed police.

But cops wouldn't risk coming out to some trailer in the backwoods where there were multiple ways for bikers to escape and multiple ways a sting operation could go south.

As the newest member of the Vipers, Danny Baker knew he might be involved in illegal activities, but he figured it would amount to no more than drugs. That evening he'd stripped out of his leathers and was to be the john for the night. He rode in an old truck, the only one they had that was working. His story was that he wasn't affiliated with any MC. He was just in town for the rally, looking to have a good time. The truth went far deeper than that.

The rendezvous point was a trailer in the middle of a forest a few miles outside of Sturgis. While the Regulators weren't smart enough to go through a vetting process, they had been wise enough to stay clear of the regular campgrounds that were used for the rally. Undercover cops browsed those.

No, these shit birds had picked a forest just off Yoke Road. A narrow dirt road wound down into the wooded area, one way in, one way out. They must have thought that was a good thing. It wasn't. Jethro's locations always provided multiple ways to avoid the cops including holes he'd dug in the ground and then covered with plywood and sod. Unless the cops had a dog, Jethro's drones would see them coming long before they arrived and if they couldn't get out in time, they would retreat into these dugouts. Inside each one had a bed, lighting and enough food and water to last a couple days.

A plume of dust kicked up behind Danny's old rusted-out Chevy as he drove at a relaxed speed toward the meeting point. Not too fast. Not too slow. He didn't want to give them a reason to second-guess. They'd been observing them for the past few days, getting a better feel for the kind of security they had in place. In the human trafficking business, there was always security. A few armed biker dudes were guarding the outside, making sure everything went smoothly. They couldn't have more than that, otherwise it would attract attention. That worked to their advantage.

As Danny got closer, he noticed the road was blocked by several Harleys. He eased off the gas and brought down his window, ready to address three sweaty biker dudes who were carrying revolvers.

He felt a twinge in his gut, knowing this could go one of two ways.

"You Danny?"

He squinted into a bright flashlight.

"That's right."

"Show us your ID."

He took out his wallet and handed it over. The biker shone a flashlight on it and nodded to the other guy to move the bikes out of the way. "We'll keep hold of your ID until you're finished. That way we know where to come looking if anything goes wrong, you get my drift?"

He nodded. "That's fine. I'm just here to have a good time."

The biker looked over his truck. "How is it that this is working and our bikes aren't?"

"Something to do with the age," Danny said. He didn't know for sure but that was what they'd managed to figure out. After the blackout, all their Harleys were dead, the lights were out, no generator was working.

Danny watched the bikers roll their motorcycles out of the way.

The bearded biker stepped back and waved him on through. Inwardly he hoped to God that Jethro knew what he was doing. He was starting to feel like a lamb led to the slaughter. If they didn't kill him, there was a good chance they might steal the truck. The only reason he'd agreed to be the one to go in was so he could work his way up the ranks. Danny had goals. Big goals. His heart was set on becoming a vice president, a sergeant-at-arms, hell even president of the chapter, but that would mean years of gaining their trust, doing dirty work and being the one who put his neck on the chopping block.

Danny bobbed in his seat as the truck hit a few potholes. The location was ideal in that cops flying overhead wouldn't see it from above. With a rise in human trafficking at the rally, DCI agents had pulled out all the stops to try and halt it. That thought stuck with him as he drove onward. What if they were observing him now through high-powered binoculars? Was he really going to risk his life to gain Jethro's favor?

Of course.

There were levels to this shit.

Long before he became a prospect, someone had made it clear that if he had intentions of being a full patch member, he had to be voted in by at least 75 percent of the chapter. Until then he was nothing more than a friend of the club. It was informal, a friendship with Rodney Ford, an old school pal of his. At that point he wasn't sure if he wanted to join the club.

As a friend, he wore no club colors, no patch, and he didn't pay dues. He had kind of liked it that way. He was allowed to join the club on rides and attend some of their club functions but that was about it.

Once he told them he was interested in being a

prospect for the club, they changed their views and he became known as a hang around — someone who spent more time with the club to see if it was something he really wanted. At this stage he had no idea what illegal activities they were involved in. Everything like that was kept away from him. As far as he knew, they were just another motorcycle club. This was done intentionally so they could feel him out, run checks on him and ensure they weren't dealing with an undercover cop. It was all about evaluating. He'd spent a year like that before they'd entertained having him as a prospect.

They wanted to know why he wanted to join, what he hoped to gain and give by being a part of the club, and what he might do if pulled in by the cops.

It always came back to that one thing — loyalty.

And this, this was just another test.

If he did well tonight, he would become a full patch member of the Vipers MC.

Now that was motivation.

Danny weaved the truck through the dense forest until the path opened out to a clearing where there were two more Regulators waiting for him.

In front of a brand new 26-foot Overlander Airstream trailer, two assholes were sitting in folding chairs, drinking beers and smoking, completely at ease as if nothing could touch them. Boy, they were in for a shock tonight. Danny had no idea how far Jethro would take this, but it was clear from their conversation before that he was about to send a message, not just to this club but to others who dared to trespass and operate on his turf.

The heaviest-set individual, the one sporting a scar down the side of his face, rose from his seat and made his way over as Danny killed the engine and got out of the truck.

"Arms up and turn around."

Do everything they tell you, Jethro had said.

So he did. The grizzled biker reeking of alcohol and tobacco frisked him down. It was routine. They didn't want anyone harming their merchandise, never mind trying to pull the wool over their eyes. "Stand over there while I check your truck."

Danny ambled close to where the other guy was sitting with a sawed-off shotgun on his lap. He tapped it in a menacing way against his thigh and stared at him.

Danny watched the biker fish through his truck, looking under the seat, checking the glove compartment and center console. Once he was done, he gave the thumbs-up and his pal thumbed over his shoulder. "Go on in. You get half an hour, no more."

Danny went to climb the steps into the Airstream when the guy put his shotgun in front of him. "You bruise the merchandise, we bruise you. You got it?"

He gave a nod. The biker flashed him a toothy grin. Two of his front teeth were gold in color. Danny went inside the trailer and looked off to his left, expecting to see a woman in her late twenties. Jethro had told him that the women were runaways, drug addicts, the throwaways of society. The kind of women whose family wouldn't notice if they were gone. But that wasn't what he was seeing. Instead, he found himself looking at a drugged-out girl no older than sixteen smoking a cigarette at the far end, waiting for him on a single bed. The inside of the Airstream was disgusting. Empty bottles of wine littered the counters, with drug paraphernalia on the table, plates of partially finished food nearby and a sink full of coffee mugs along with a basket full of used condoms. It stank of sweat and innocence lost.

"How old are you?" Danny asked.

"How old do you want me to be?" she asked in a seductive way, pushing back a strand of hair behind her ear. She was petite with long dark hair. Native. Pretty. All she was wearing was a bra and panties and a black silk cardigan robe. A sudden feeling of guilt washed over him. A sense of right and wrong. Somehow, he was able to reason within his mind that someone over age twenty-five who was drugged out was fine, but this, no, he wasn't down with this. Of course, no matter how old they were, he had no plans of having sex. He was just the distraction, someone to kick up a fuss, an unsatisfied customer. And in that moment, he didn't need to act.

"I can't do this," he said.

"What?"

Danny opened the door and came out.

"Well, that was quick," the one guy said, laughing.

"I'm not doing this."

Scar-face rose from his seat while his shotgun-loving pal looked eager to hear his reasoning. "And why's that?"

"Not satisfied."

"Excuse me?"

"You heard me."

"You asked for young."

"I did, but not that young. I want my money back."

Scar-face scoffed. "No refunds, asshole. Now you either go back in there or get the fuck out of here!"

"And if I don't like those choices?"

Shotgun-lover got up and tapped his piece against his hand. "Well then you can…"

Before he spat the words out, a gun cocked to the back of his pal's head.

"That's it. Don't even breathe."

Both of them froze.

"Danny, Rodney, take their weapons," Joey Tooley said. Joey wore all black, a black vest, black T-shirt and black jeans. He had a blue skull bandanna around his forehead and a pair of shades pushed up on top of his shaved head. He'd silently emerged from behind the Airstream, him and Rodney Ford. Rodney was the complete opposite, his hair hung loose down to his shoulders. He was sporting a full beard and his knuckles were covered in silver. Both of them were packing Glocks.

Rodney pried the shotgun away from the one guy and made them fish their revolvers out of their jeans. He had them drop the revolvers before checking their ankles for smaller handguns.

"Do you know who you are fucking with?" Scar-face asked.

"I was about to ask you the same question," Jethro replied, emerging from the trees. In his hand was a Louisville Slugger baseball bat. Danny shone his light on him and saw that it was dripping with blood. He figured the guys manning the road in were dead.

Jethro was an imposing man usually hidden behind sunglasses and a full beard. He had blond hair that was pulled back into a ponytail. He wore a black leather jacket with club patches all over it, light blue jeans and biker chaps with black boots.

On the side of his neck was a tattoo of a large scorpion, its stinger came up to his cheek with the rest disappearing down below his neckline.

He pointed the end of his bat at Danny. "Good work."

Keeping one eye on the men, Jethro stepped inside the Airstream and smiled at the young girl before exiting. He moved around to the front of the bikers. "Now as for you two," he said before taking a swing. The bat struck Scarface in the kneecap. He screamed loudly, dropping to the ground, curling into a fetal position while his pal put a hand out as Jethro followed through with one more hard swing to the guy's legs.

Next, he turned his attention to Shotgun-lover. "Now I don't know which one of you pissants is in charge of this sloppy operation but I want you to remember something. My name is Jethro Gatlin. That's G-A-T-L-I-N," he said, spelling it out. "It seems you are either stupid or blatantly disrespectful because I can't think of any other reason why you would knowingly operate this business — if it can even be called that — on my turf." He looked at the guy squirming on the ground. "Ah, put a lid on it, you pussy. That was me going easy on you. Giving you a little taste of what will happen if you continue to sell women anywhere in the Black Hills."

Shotgun-lover spoke up. "We weren't aware that we needed permission."

Jethro looked at Danny and Rodney and smiled before looking back at the man. "Well shit. It's obvious you weren't aware. I expect you're selling drugs at the rally, too, right?" He waited for a reply. When the guy didn't answer him, he raised up his bat and that got a response.

"Yeah, we are."

He lowered the bat. "Ah, I can't fault you. You probably just wanted to make some cash and enjoy life, right?" He paused, getting closer to him. "Well, let me lay it out for you. Your buddies back there are now three heads short. If you get my drift. You see, because I've got one hell of a big machete and I will gladly use it again if need be if I ever see you assholes selling women around here again." He wandered over to the guy squirming on the ground. Jethro crouched down beside him. "I really don't want to have to get my hands any bloodier than they are already. So, here's what you're gonna do. You are going to go back to your little MC and tell that president of yours what I just said." He clicked his fingers and Rodney came over and handed him a bloody burlap bag. "And give him this." He dumped the bag in the man's lap. Inside were the heads of the men. "You catch my drift?"

Scar-face nodded, fear masking his expression.

"Good. Now get the fuck off my turf!"

Shotgun-lover helped his pal up and the two of them hobbled away.

Jethro watched them with a look of glee in his eyes. "How do you think I did?"

"That was an Oscar winning performance," Rodney said as they began laughing. Jethro turned and looked at Danny who was standing there with his hands in his pockets. Jethro made his way over and placed a hand on Danny's shoulder. "As for you, Danny boy, you just earned your patch. How's that feel?"

He shrugged. Unsure of how he felt about it now. "Good. I guess."

Jethro scoffed. "You guess? What's up with you? You're acting all weird."

Danny looked at the trailer. "What are you going to do with the girl?"

"Put her to work, what do you think?"

Jethro turned away, about to enter the Airstream. Danny followed him while Rodney lit a cigarette. "Jethro, she can't be more than sixteen."

"And?" he replied.

"I thought you were only selling people who were adults."

"Danny, Danny," he said in a condescending fashion as he turned and placed both hands on the sides of his face. "One lesson you have to learn fast is this. Don't question why. If you want to last, just do what's asked of you and leave the business side of things to me."

"But she's just a kid."

"As were we all. And no one stepped in to stop people fucking us over. Now go and clean up the mess with Rodney."

As he turned to leave, Jethro asked one last question. "Did Tammy do the drop-off?"

"She was a no-show," Danny replied.

He groaned. "With the power gone, we're going to have to rethink business moving forward. Let everyone know to be at the clubhouse at nine."

12
———

Deadwood

It was quiet. Too quiet.

John had expected to see his home shrouded in darkness but he figured Scout would have found one of the flashlights he'd left on the kitchen counter. There was zero light coming from the windows at the front of the house and when he stepped inside, it was silent. Was she hiding? "Scout! Come out. It's just a friend of mine."

There was no reply.

Frank looked at him and then squinted into the distance as they both shone their lights into the darkened corners of the home. "You think she might have left?" Frank asked, shining his flashlight up the staircase while John wandered into the kitchen.

"I told her to stay here but she could have gone into the forest."

"You really should have brought her down to the station, John."

"That kid is scared of everyone," John replied, checking the pantry. It had been the one area she had retreated to twice but she wasn't there now. He double-timed it up the stairs to the second floor with Frank close behind him. As he was checking the bedroom, he noticed the French doors were wide open. Hurrying out to the balcony, he looked over the edge and his stomach dropped. "Oh shit."

"What is it?" Frank asked, sidling up beside him. He took a look. "Is that…?"

"Clay. Yeah."

They made their way down and out the back and John crouched beside him. He touched the side of his neck. It was cold. He was stiff. He'd been dead a while. One of his large kitchen knives was buried in Clay's side and there was a pool of blood around him.

"She must of attacked him."

John rose to his feet, shining the flashlight around the property. He glanced at Frank.

"You sure that's what happened?" Frank asked.

"What other way would he have ended up here?"

"Sarah told me you had a confrontation with him."

"And?"

"Well, are you sure you didn't…" Frank trailed off.

John scoffed. "I might be suffering from traumatic brain syndrome, but I would remember if I had done that.

Besides, Tammy had footage of Clay while he was still alive."

"That was sent to her from his phone. He didn't return home."

John offered him a puzzled expression. "So, what? You're suggesting I killed him? Why?"

Frank lifted an eyebrow; he didn't need to explain, it was self-explanatory.

"Are you implying I did it to keep the girl?" John asked.

Frank put his hands up. "Listen, I'm not implying anything. I'm just trying to help Sarah, and you. These are serious accusations against you, John."

He turned away, ignoring him, and shouted toward the surrounding forest. "SCOUT! SCOUT! If you can hear me. Come on out. It's okay. No one is going to hurt you."

"John."

"Come on now!"

"JOHN!" Frank said loudly to get his attention.

He glanced at him.

"What?"

"When was the last time you saw a doctor?"

"Oh, screw you, Frank," he said, turning around and marching back into the house. Frank was hot on his heels. "You're not the chief anymore."

"No, I'm not. My daughter is and I don't want to see her in the position of arresting you."

"For what? Huh? The only proof that there was a girl here to begin with is a video sent by a dead man, and my own testimony. And why on earth would I willingly go into the department to smooth things out if I had anything to do with her going missing? I can't even believe you would suggest that I had anything but good motivations to help. For goodness' sakes, Frank, I had a granddaughter that was Scout's age." Inside the kitchen he went over to the door that led to the basement and made his way down, shining the light ahead of him. At the bottom he approached a Faraday cage he'd created for some of his devices for a situation just like this. He didn't consider himself a survivalist or a prepper in any way, but over the years he'd collected a few essentials — items that would help out in the event the power went out in a storm.

He wheeled out his Goal Zero Yeti 6000X, a high-capacity power station that was powerful enough to run an RV. It came with four Nomad 200 solar panels, all part of his home backup system. Inside this one device he had enough power to keep a full-size fridge running for up to four days, plus power tools, lights and a lot more.

He set it back against a wall where he had a Yeti Home Integration Kit installed a few years back. He'd had an electrician wire it into the main breaker panel so that he could use four different circuits for his fridge/freezer, the outlets in the living area, his light switches and his garage door.

"I always wondered why you kept that here," Frank said.

John hit a few switches, the Yeti powered on and made a low humming noise and a moment later, lights blinked to life.

"You always were ahead of the curve," Frank said, looking around. "And self-reliant."

"You have to be nowadays. No telling what curveballs will come your way."

His main generator, which was outside his house, worked off natural gas. It would have been fried with the EMP but he also had another regular gas generator he kept inside the Faraday cage. While the Yeti worked off solar power, and could be plugged into an outlet if there was power, the battery power in it would be eaten up in no time, so that's why he liked to keep on hand a regular generator. It would help to power his furnace and keep the place warm. He liked to use it as a dedicated line, that way he could get more days out of it.

Frank watched him going back and forth to the Faraday cage.

"John. We need to talk about this."

"Talk then. I'm getting this place ready for my daughter's arrival."

"Laura?"

"Well, yeah, I'm sure she'll make her way here if this EMP has affected the whole country. In the meantime, there is a lot to do." He moved back and forth, dragging out different electronics, two-way radios, his ham radio unit.

"Where is Scout?"

He replied. "No idea."

"Are you just going to leave Clay outside to rot?"

"Frank, I think that asshole is the least of our concerns right now. This event couldn't have come at a worse time. The Black Hills has over 500,000 motorcycle club members in attendance for the rally, many of which you know are rivals. Now even on a good day, in a regular small town, you are going to deal with the complications of an EMP — a disruption in cell phone and internet service being two massive problems. Most of our world today runs on electronics — banking, the power grid, water treatment plants, our vehicles. You know as well as I do our entire infrastructure is controlled by computers. No vehicles, no deliveries, no internet or phones, no communication, all of which means — no help." He stopped in front of Frank and looked him in the eyes. "Now realistically, how long do you think it's going to take for those assholes down there to lose their shit? Even with all the support of local police agencies that are here right now, it won't come close to holding back what is coming."

"And what is that?"

"Chaos. Pure chaos," John said. "It will be like the walls of Hoover Dam cracking. No one is going to be able to hold back what's about to rush in. Small town or not, with this rally on our backs, we might as well be living in New York."

Frank stared at him, shifting from one foot to the next as John continued to gather what he needed. "Now I don't know about you but I don't have a lot of food here at the house. I might have a couple of weeks, if that. Once people realize what's happened and the gravity sets in, the looting will start and those store shelves will be cleared and I'm not waiting until then to get what I need."

"Hold on, John. Look, I understand but our military will help."

John laughed. "Wake up, Frank. I love my country and I love the military. Hell, I gave twenty-three years of my life to it but even I know its limitations. What we are about to face could mean months or years until things change. No, we prepare for the worst and hope for the best, and right now, we need to prepare." He took stock of what he'd gathered over the past few years. It wasn't much. Packets of seeds, dried goods, a few boxes of MREs, ready-to-eat canned fruits, veggies, and dried meat, peanut butter, non-perishable pasta, high-energy protein bars, toilet paper tablets, vitamins, coffee, a first-aid kit, cordage, sleeping bags, a water purification kit, candles, extra batteries and containers.

A few cases of bottled water and canned goods wasn't going to cut it. Even for those who had stored a lot, there would never be enough. It was important to find alternative sources for water and food. "We can use brooks, lakes, hell, even swimming pools for staying clean. We'll need to have a way to grow food. We'll need a water filtration system, chemicals, boiling water, etc. I'll use the woodstove to stay warm..." John tapped his bottom lip, going over everything in his mind.

He heard Frank sigh. "What about Clay?"

"What about him?" he asked, distracted.

"Tammy and Ray will want to know... and when they do..."

John whirled around, cutting him off. "If Scout was telling the truth which I believe she was, that man got what was coming to him."

"This changes everything, John."

"Maybe for them. Not for me."

"We'll see about that. I can't protect you."

"Never asked you to."

"What's happened to you? How can you be so cold?"

John snorted. "Cold? Cold!? You know what cold is... Frank? Not giving a child the essentials of life, not loving a child and protecting them the way they should be. That's fucking cold. Now unless you're going to help me. You should probably get going. I'll give you a hand getting that fun-loving man into the back of your truck," he said sarcastically, brushing past Frank and heading up the steps with his head now focused on survival and where Scout could be.

13

Florida

Shock gripped her throat.

Pinned to the wall, frozen by fear, Laura couldn't move. The murder of Richard was more brutal than anything she'd witnessed. She could smell his blood on her face and hair. As James rose, his hands and face drenched, she wanted to open her mouth but she couldn't.

"You motherfu..." Angry words gushed from Trudy as she came wheeling around the corner, wielding a revolver. She fired a round striking James in the right shoulder and spinning him away. Like a wounded animal he scurried out of the house, slipping on the stream of rain water that was blowing in through the open door like a heavy car wash.

Pop, pop, pop.

Trudy fired three more rounds into the night before Laura snapped out of her trance-like state and hurried to slam the door closed. She locked it and turned.

Trudy stared down at Richard.

"Baby. No. No." Trudy dropped the gun on the floor and fell to her knees, cradling what was left of Richard. His mangled face was unrecognizable. Her cries were ear-piercing. One by one, their kids gathered at the corner of the wall, each one a different age. Laura rushed over, urging them back into the kitchen.

"Go, go, go," she said.

She didn't want them to see their father like that. Not like that.

There were five of them. Two teens, a boy and a girl, and three younger ones no older than six or eight. "Okay, um, how about we get those candles over there and..." She looked at one of the teens as her words failed to come out. "What's your name?" she finally managed to ask.

"Rachel," the girl said.

"Rachel. Look. You need to..."

Anguished cries continued behind Laura before she heard a door open again. She raced back just in time to see Trudy head outside into the hellish weather. She'd taken the gun. The skies were a dark black, darker than any night she'd seen. The rain bombarded the ground, leaving several inches of water running down drains.

"Trudy!" Laura bellowed.

Scanning the road around her, she raced toward Trudy who was standing in the middle of the road, turning like a psychotic mental patient. Laura ducked; a hand extended toward her as Trudy pointed the gun her way. "Whoa, whoa! Put it down. It's just me. Laura."

Trudy looked like a deer in the headlights. Her eyes wide, her mouth wider.

"I'm... sorry..." Trudy lowered the gun and Laura rushed in and took it from her then wrapped an arm around her and led her back to the house.

"C'mon, let's get you back inside." As they hurried back, Laura glanced around, nervously wondering where James was. He'd been hit, that's for sure. Maybe that would put a stop to the madness. Why he was following her was anyone's guess but now someone was dead and all she could feel was fear and guilt. She'd brought this on them. Brought a monster into their house and now their kids were without a father.

Trudy fell to pieces. Whatever courage and bravado she had before crumbled as she walked past her dead husband. Laura shut the door and locked it then followed Trudy into the kitchen where her kids were waiting. They rushed toward her, tears flowing.

Laura had no words. Nothing to ease her pain. This was a woman that was all smiles in her everyday interactions with people, almost to the point that Laura thought it was fake, but now she was a shell of herself and rightfully so. That bastard had destroyed their world in an instant.

"Can I get you a drink?" Laura asked.

Holding her youngest in her lap, Trudy looked up at Laura. "Why were you here?"

"What?"

"Why did you come over?"

"I wanted to borrow a bicycle."

"Do you know who that man is?"

"I..." she stumbled. If she said yes, it would be admitting that she had brought this upon them. But she didn't know he would do this, that he would go to this extent. Hell, she still couldn't understand why he was following her other than he was deranged. The hospital was a magnet for those types of people, even more so if they were denied service. But she'd helped him. She hadn't been rude. Had she? And even if she had — did that warrant chasing her down, killing a man like he had? Laura took a deep breath. Rain dripped off her face and clothes, creating small puddles on the kitchen floor. "I don't know him. He was a patient at the hospital. I..."

"Get out," Trudy said in a low voice that Laura barely registered.

"Trudy. I didn't know he would do this, I'm so..."

"GET OUT!" she shouted, cutting her off.

Laura looked at each of the kids, her heart breaking as their eyes welled up with tears. Nothing she could say in that moment would ever have sufficed or eased their suffering. Laura lowered her chin and backed out of the kitchen, scooping up her backpack. She still had Trudy's revolver in hand. For a moment she set it down on a small table near the entrance, then as she unlocked the door, Laura took it with her. There was no telling if he was still out there.

Outside the weather was atrocious.

A never-ending slew of rain bombarded her as she hurried east down the street.

JAMES BAUER GRIPPED HIS SHOULDER, his teeth clenched together. The pain was excruciating. He had a good mind to go back in that house and finish what he started.

But that would only waste this opportunity.

James watched Laura as she moved away from the house. Everything about her reminded him of his ex in the early days when things were good. The long, flowing straight brown hair, the way she talked with him at the hospital, for a moment he thought that maybe, just maybe she could be the one, a fresh start, a new beginning with someone that was like her. Hell, he thought it was fate, the way she swooped in and told that dumbass security guard where to go. Oh, he wanted to shut him up and he would have if it weren't for her.

Laura. It could have been good. We could have been together. But no, no, she had to go and treat him the same way his ex had, brushing him aside like he was nothing more than an annoying fly.

So, just like his ex had paid with her life, he'd now do the same with this bitch.

And there wasn't a damn thing anyone could do to stop him.

He glanced up into the sky. It was getting worse. He didn't care. Not anymore.

His life was over the moment he pulled a trigger on his ex and baby.

No, now this was just entertainment. He wanted to scream at the storm. "C'mon, c'mon, give me your worst," he said as if mother nature was against him.

James grimaced, pain coursing through his body.

As Laura blurred in a curtain of rain, James stepped out from behind an RV, keeping his distance, moving in the shadows and using vehicles and homes as cover.

He'd seen the gun in her hand.

Careful. Be careful, he told himself as he pursued his prey.

∼

Although the force of Hurricane Fiona was yet to be experienced, Laura still felt like she was walking inside a wind tunnel. Her forest green rain jacket flapped hard, pressing tightly against her skin. Her teeth chattered from the cold, and water dripped off her hair and nose. One moment it would be hard to walk forward and the next she'd have no problems. The shifting wind pressure was taking on a life of its own. Even if she could find a bicycle there was a good chance she'd get blown off, but that was the risk she'd have to take. It would take hours to reach Fort Myers on foot, and even then, she had no idea where Charlie was heading. No, she needed to get there fast. She glanced behind her, aware that James could be following.

Her hope was that he'd retreated, choosing to tend to his wound rather than come after her.

Laura pushed the image of Richard's pummeled face from her mind.

More guilt hit her hard and she choked up, tears streaking her cheeks.

She wanted to be angry at Charlie but she couldn't. He wasn't just suffering from the loss of his father and sister but survivor's guilt. He was meant to be in that sedan. A last-minute change of plans had caused him to get out.

As she pressed on through a deluge of rain, Laura's mind went back to that night.

Sitting in Deadwood's hospital, waiting for news of her father who was in critical care. Charlie sat beside her while she drank bitter-tasting coffee out of a vending machine. It was two in the morning and both of them were numb, still in shock. She thought that at any moment Michael and Libby would walk in and tell them that everything was okay, that it was just a mistake.

It wasn't.

"Why? Why did I survive?" Charlie asked.

Laura glanced at him. His face was red from having bawled his eyes out.

"I don't know." She'd made a point to never cherry-coat things with her kids. She felt it didn't serve anyone to do that. Honesty was crucial. She slipped an arm around his shoulder and he leaned into her. Laura wanted to reassure him and say that it was meant to be, that there was some divine purpose to it all, but she couldn't see it even if there was.

"If I hadn't gotten out of the car..." Charlie couldn't even form words. She felt his body shudder as he choked up again. It was one thing to lose a parent or a sibling later in life, another to

have them ripped away from you when you were young. She still hadn't gotten the full story at that time. That came later.

A large sign sailed across the street and smashed into a vehicle with a metallic thud, snapping her out of the past.

"Amelia! Amelia!" a female voice cried out.

Laura stopped walking as a woman rushed out onto Santa Barbara Boulevard, looking frantic. As soon as she saw Laura, she made a beeline toward her. "Have you seen a little girl, about yay high?" she bellowed over the growling wind. "Six years old."

"No, what does she look like?"

"She's wearing a red rain jacket, yellow boots. Blonde hair. We have a small dog. A white Highland terrier. I was trying to get the last shutter on. I only looked away for a minute and she was gone. I think the dog might have taken off and she went after it. I live over there," she said, pointing to a one-story yellow house.

"She has to be nearby," Laura replied.

The woman nodded and jogged off, frantically searching.

Laura pressed on for a moment then looked back to see the woman crouched and crying. Laura exhaled hard and made her way back to the woman. "C'mon. I'll help you." The woman's greatest concern was that she'd wandered off and fallen into one of the many canals that hedged in the properties. Laura told her to look down South East 38th Terrace Street while she continued on south toward the bridge, and if she saw her, she would bring her back.

The two of them separated.

Laura ambled down the darkened street, shining a

flashlight around trying to see a dog or girl. Most of the town had evacuated. The homes were abandoned; the streets empty of life. There were no animals out, no lights on in homes. Dust and grit blew directly into Laura's face, stinging her cheeks. Her legs wanted to give out as she pushed forward through the wind. She traipsed around large, deep puddles which had formed on the road while calling out the kid's name. "Amelia! Amelia!"

Her pants were soaked, cold and sticking to her legs.

The kid could be anywhere. The neighborhoods around here were huge with lots of roads and canals for a kid to disappear into. As she turned to head back, something caught her eye. It was movement at first, a white speck between houses. Hurrying toward it, she began to hear a dog barking through the torrential downpour.

"Amelia!"

No answer. In the distance she could see a white dog at the edge of the canal, barking and racing back and forth. Laura sprinted to see the young girl in the water. She was holding on to a tree limb. From what she could tell, it had collapsed and must have fallen on her, pushing her into the water.

"Hold on, honey, I'm gonna help you!" Laura said. She tucked the gun in her bag, and took out some eight-foot cordage. She collected a large rock from a rear yard at the back of the nearest home and tied off one end and then threw it toward her.

It landed with a large splash and disappeared below the water.

The girl was crying hard and looked as if she was slipping.

The canals in Florida varied in depth from a few feet to thirty-five feet. If she went under, even if she was a strong swimmer, there was a good chance she wouldn't come up again. The wind was blowing so hard that it was creating a swift current. Laura contemplated jumping in but then she'd be soaked and...

The girl lost her grip on the tree branch, and let out a scream. She was now only holding on by one hand.

"Shit." Laura reeled in the cordage and tossed it again, this time it landed over a branch and wrapped itself around it. "Can you reach it? Honey, reach the cord."

The girl wouldn't even try. She was too scared. Laura knew what she'd have to do. As cold as she was, she stripped out of her jacket and jeans, kicked off her boots and stepped off the edge into the water.

Laura immediately sank to neck height. Her mouth went agape with how cold it was. "I'm coming," she said, swimming over to her, teeth chattering, her lips quickly turning blue. The wind battered her on all sides, forcing her into the tree. A branch cut her face and she let out a scream which only made the child even more scared. "It's all right, honey, it's all right, I got you," she said, reaching out and taking hold of her. "Go on, let go," she said. The child released her grip and wrapped both arms around Laura's neck.

As she turned to swim back, she blinked water out of her eyes and narrowed her gaze, thinking she saw someone on the land. She blinked again but no one was there. Fear took hold as she made her way back. As soon as she got back on land and set the girl down, Laura turned for her clothes but they were gone.

She turned her head from side to side.

"No, no, no, I set them down here," she said, looking around frantic.

But there was nothing. Had it all blown away?

She looked further away, into the distance — that's when she saw him — between the houses, holding the bag up with a grin before he vanished around a corner.

14

Florida

The iron giant with four legs stood defiant in the face of the imposing storm.

Sanibel Lighthouse was a sight to behold. One of the first lighthouses to be erected along Florida's Gulf Coast, it stood 98 feet above sea level. At the eastern tip of the thin crescent-shaped barrier island, the iron skeleton with a light on top and a central spiral staircase beneath towered over two white buildings owned by city employees.

"We're lucky we made it across the causeway," Hannah said. "By the looks of it that's going to be under water in less than an hour. Are you sure Seth's dad thinks this is safe?"

"This lighthouse has weathered every hurricane to hit

Florida since 1884," Charlie said with confidence like he knew, but all he was doing was parroting what Seth had told him. In that moment, his mind wasn't on the storm, it was distracted by his Jeep which had given up the ghost several miles back.

Out of all the places it could have died and it stopped on the causeway, a thin stretch of road that spanned three miles across the bay to the tip of Fort Myers. It had been built to replace the ferry and was now the only means of getting on and off the island by car.

Hearing Hannah say that it was going to be under water soon was a crushing blow.

They'd tried to push the Jeep but neither one of them was strong enough and it was even harder with the wind battering it on every side. As large waves splashed over the causeway, covering it in debris, they had no choice but to abandon it.

"Come on, Charlie!" Hannah bellowed over her shoulder as they approached the lighthouse. The white sand beneath them was waterlogged. The mangroves, palm trees and sea oats swayed as they hurried to avoid the worsening storm.

They were just about to climb up a rusted ladder which would take them to the center staircase doorway, ten feet above ground, when Seth called out.

"Hey!" He was standing in the doorway of one of the two Cape Cod-style dwellings. "Over here," he beckoned them.

Hannah kept a firm grip on Charlie's hand as he led

the way. Seth roared with laughter. "I thought you two would never make it. Pretty wild, huh!"

"You can say that again," Hannah said, shaking rain from her body.

"Damn it!" Seth's father said. "There's no generator. We'll have to use flashlights for now." Dawson emerged from a rear room wearing blue jeans and a black North Face jacket. His mousy brown hair was covered by a beanie. "Oh hey, Charlie. Great timing. We were just about to go into the lighthouse."

"How did you pull this off? Doesn't the city own this?" Hannah asked.

"Helps to know a few people," Dawson replied, shining a light in her face. "And you are?"

"Hannah."

"Well Hannah, I hope you are ready for the night of your life."

"So, they let you use the lighthouse?"

"Something like that," he said, brushing past them to a stack of equipment. "Well, this isn't going to be much use anymore."

Charlie thumbed over his shoulder. "Yeah, my Jeep gave up on me back at the causeway. I had to leave it there. Is your vehicle working?"

"Haven't tried it yet," Dawson said, standing before his equipment with his hands out, shaking his head in disbelief. "I've been too busy trying to get this crap going. Not even our phones are working. Are yours?"

Charlie shook his head.

Dawson groaned. "How the hell am I supposed to get footage?"

"I think footage is the least of our concerns," Charlie said. "That causeway was nearly covered when we came over. Not to be a buzz killer, but maybe we should think about evacuating while we can."

"Evacuating?" Dawson laughed. Seth joined in.

"Chill, bro," Seth said, slapping his chest with the back of his hand. "My pops and I have weathered worse than this, and besides, we've got the iron beast out there to protect us. A hundred and thirty-six years of battling mother nature and she still hasn't been able to topple him. So no worries."

"And waves?" Charlie asked.

"It's 98 feet high. Even if we get twenty-footers, we'll be fine."

"I hope so," he said, glancing at Hannah who also looked doubtful. They waited inside while Seth's dad scurried out to his Bronco to see if it would work. All of them waited on the porch but the engine didn't turn over. Dawson got out and popped the hood to take a look.

"It's not the engine," Charlie shouted.

"What?" he replied, cupping a hand to his ear. Against his better judgment Charlie made his way over as Dawson continued to poke around, thinking it was a loose cable or something.

"I said it's not the engine. I think it's an EMP."

For the first time in all the years he'd known Seth's father, he got this confused expression on his face. And that was saying something as this man knew everything there was to know about storms and weather. Before Dawson could ask what that was, Charlie filled him in. "I don't know for sure but my grandfather used to talk about this event that could happen. Something about the power grid going down and computer chips being fried. Because your vehicle and mine are newer, they would run off computer chips or are controlled by them. I mean that's the only reason that both could have stopped working."

"Now I wish I'd brought my other vehicle," Dawson said.

"What is it?"

"A restored 1949 Chevy Truck. A pet project of mine. I only take it out to local truck and car shows these days but that thing could have come in handy right about now."

The wind was so loud and sharp that Charlie was putting a hand up to the side of his face to stop it from stinging his cheek. Dawson directed him back to the house where they retreated into the unsafe thin walls. As soon as the door was closed, he stared at Charlie. "It's a nuke that causes the EMP, right?"

"I believe so."

"I've heard of it but I didn't think it was possible."

"Oh yeah, countries have been developing all kinds of missiles that could take down the power grid. It would destroy communications, water and sewer services, transportation systems and other key infrastructures. Planes would fall from the sky and whatnot. Basically, the country would be screwed."

Seth glanced at his dad, his face pale. "I told you."

"What?" Charlie asked.

"Earlier, I saw several planes come down further out in the Gulf. I mean it was far out but I'm pretty sure that's what I saw."

Charlie nodded. "There are thousands of planes in the sky at any given moment. It makes sense, right? I mean, who needs to bomb the country when you can just hit us with a pulse, knock out the power and fry computer chips. Planes would nosedive bomb the earth. Some of the decent pilots would try to manually control them and set them down in the water, to avoid further loss of life, but..."

"We'd be screwed," Dawson added.

Charlie nodded.

Seth looked stunned. The night had taken on a very different feel.

"So, we're at war?" Hannah asked. "With who?"

"No idea but I would imagine they wouldn't just employ an EMP by itself. It would probably be used in conjunction with cyberattacks, physical damage and maybe something non-nuclear."

"Like a weather system," Dawson added, looking at his son. "I told you it was peculiar."

"What was?" Charlie asked.

Outside the wind howled hard, battering the sides of the flimsy building. It sounded like a jet engine. It was so loud Charlie imagined the roof would tear off at any second.

Dawson took a deep breath and let it out. He crossed the room and took some paperwork out of a briefcase and brought it over to a round table and smoothed it out. It was a large map of the world. "Before the power shut off, I'd been following the formation of the hurricane, then I started getting emails from friends of mine around the world, telling me about tropical storms forming all over the planet."

"Is that normal?" Hannah asked.

"I mean it can happen in the seven basins but some of these are occurring in cold waters."

"You're losing me."

Dawson pointed to the map. "Hurricanes require warm water to form, usually around 80 to 85 degrees Fahrenheit. Usually, the surface water in these parts," he said, pointing to different areas of the map. "Those will remain at that temperature well into November. That's why we tend to get them around here as it's so damn hot and muggy. Now the advantage we have is that hurricanes don't usually come out of nowhere without a warning. We are able to monitor them, take readings and see days ahead if a tropical storm has hurricane potential. And because our technology today is so advanced, we can usually predict when and where it will make landfall. From there everyone can figure out if they are going to evacuate or shelter in place." He pointed to other areas. "Elsewhere tropical cyclones are occurring here, here, here, here... and here."

"And they shouldn't?" Charlie said.

"No. In these places over here, yes, but even still, they shouldn't all be happening at the same time."

There was a pregnant pause.

"You think it's some kind of coordinated attack?" Charlie asked.

Dawson shrugged. "Maybe. But here's the part I don't

get. If China, Russia or North Korea was behind it, why create cyclones and hurricanes off their own shores?"

The four of them stared at the map without answers.

"Do you have a hand-crank radio?" Charlie asked.

"That I do have." Dawson turned. "Seth, run out to the Bronco and get it. It's in the trailer with the equipment. Oh, and grab my smokes. They're in the center console."

"What do you need it for?" Hannah asked Charlie.

"Well, we know these storms are happening all around the world, right, but what about the EMP? Have other countries been hit? I think that would tell us a lot."

Dawson leaned on the map and it crumpled below his hands.

"If they have been hit, I doubt anyone would be broadcasting," Hannah said while Dawson studied his readings under flashlight. She gripped Charlie's arm. "I'm starting to think I shouldn't have come."

Before he could reply, there was a loud crash. Dawson charged across the room to the main door and rushed outside with a panicked cry. "SETH!"

Charlie hurried out to see a large tree had come down on top of the Bronco, trapping Seth inside. "Stay here," Charlie said, sprinting out to help Dawson. The wind was whipping his clothes into a frenzy. Trees around them bowed and creaked as if they were about to break at any minute.

"Seth. Seth!" There was no reply. Dawson tried to get in the side where the door was open but the way the tree had come down, it had buckled the metal, making it impossible. Charlie scrambled up onto the hood and shone his light inside through the broken windshield. He caught sight of Seth. He was unconscious or dead. There was blood streaming down his face. "Shit."

As Charlie slid off the hood to go around, another tree came down, crashing scarily close to him. A huge updraft of grit, sand and dust made him cough. Charlie brought his forearm up trying to see, but sand had gotten in his eyes.

Dawson waved him back. "Charlie, get back to the house. It's too dangerous."

"No, you'll never get inside there. I'm thinner than you," he said, feeling his way out and pulling himself through the shattered window in the rear of the vehicle. He cut his hand on the way in, grimacing as he wriggled his body into the cramped space. The first thing he did when he reached him was to place two fingers on Seth's neck to check his pulse.

It was beating. Steady.

That was a good sign but if he didn't get him out of there soon, he could die.

"Dawson!" he bellowed through the howling wind. "A little help."

"What do you need?" Dawson shouted over the gong of a bell ringing out nearby and the wind screaming in their ears like a jet engine.

"Come around this side. I'll try to free his legs and then you can pull him out."

"Careful."

"Trust me. I'm trying to be," he said before lowering his head and burying it into a ton of branches and leaves.

Charlie reached into his pocket and took out an EDC Leatherman. He extracted the saw and began hacking through some of the branches. As each one fell away, he passed it back so Dawson could take it out.

Blood rushed in Charlie's ears as he kept the small flashlight in his mouth so he could see. As he was hacking away, Charlie noticed one of the branches was embedded in Seth's leg. He was bleeding pretty badly. "Damn it." Being as cautious as he could but working fast, Charlie hacked through the spiny branch until it came away. From that point on he was able to maneuver Seth's leg. "All right, he's free. Take hold of his arms and pull."

Dawson began tugging his son while Charlie made sure the tree didn't collapse any further. He pressed his back into the seat and used both legs to keep the largest branches off Seth.

"All right, he's out. Come on, Charlie. Get out of there!"

Charlie froze as a flashback of visiting the crash site came back to him.

The accident hadn't occurred that far away from his grandfather's. When they had gotten word of the accident, he and his mother had hopped in the SUV and reached the crash site just as the firefighters were using the jaws of life to get out his father and sister.

"CHARLIE!" Dawson shouted.

Dawson's words barely registered. Charlie wasn't there in that moment. He was back in South Dakota, at the side of the road, watching firefighters hack through steel and several of the trees that had landed on the vehicle after it crashed.

Out of nowhere a hand thrust in front of him. "Son. Take my hand."

Just hearing the word "son" snapped him out of it. Charlie looked toward the window and saw Dawson beckoning him. Without missing a beat, he clasped his hand and within a second Charlie was outside, breathing hard. Hannah had rushed out to help, hoisting Seth up. They carried his unconscious body back into the house under the intense and rising storm.

15

South Dakota

The sky finally broke, and a torrential downpour soaked the Black Hills unlike any storm in the past ten years. Claps of thunder sounded as luminescent fork lightning shocked the earth. John pulled down the blinds in his kitchen and peered out into the darkness. *Where are you, kid?*

After helping Frank load Clay's body into the back of the truck, he'd told him that it was probably better that he dumped his body in a ravine than take him home. It would only make matters worse but that wasn't Frank's way. Even retired, he was still a man that lived by the book.

Friend or not, Clay's death was wrong in his eyes. That was because Frank hadn't seen her, or heard Scout's story or peered into those dead eyes of hers. That family had stripped away her soul, leaving her barely a shell.

"What did she tell you?" Frank had asked before leaving.

"Does it matter now?"

"I guess not."

Once he was gone, John returned to the house and went through each room methodically, searching for Scout. He was convinced she was hiding but if she was, she'd slipped out when he hadn't seen.

Peering out that window periodically over the course of an hour, he'd hoped she'd return. She didn't. He'd tried to think of where she might have gone. There was no way in hell she would return home, and she'd been adamant about not going into town, so that left only one other place she might seek shelter from the storm.

Unable to wait any longer, John scooped up his thick army rain poncho and slipped into it. He collected a Winchester rifle, locked up the house and headed out.

He walked away from the cabin, his boots making a slurping noise with each footfall. The weather was getting worse. It made him think of Laura and Charlie. He could only hope they had evacuated or taken shelter.

John squinted into the murky night. He had a basic idea of the terrain. Still, he pulled out a small compass from his pocket and used it to guide his way. He didn't like leaving the cabin unattended, especially after what had happened, but he couldn't go to sleep knowing that Scout was out there, lost, afraid, cold, soaking wet. How long had she been out in this? An hour could seem like four when a person caught a chill. Up in the hills, the temperatures could drop even more so. Add to that some of the animals they had in South Dakota like mountain lions and coyotes, and things could get hairy if people didn't have a means of protecting themselves.

John made his way into the dense forest. Time was ticking. There was no telling how bad the storm would get and he didn't want to be hiking in the dark too long. The risk of injury only increased as rain made the ground slippery.

He'd only been walking for less than ten minutes when his vision started to blur. John brought a hand up to his eyes and squeezed the bridge of his nose as he took a second to let it pass. He thumped a tree with the side of his hand. It was just another reminder that he had no control over what his body was doing. Broken. Beaten down. It seemed to have a mind of its own, turning on him at any moment.

Pressing on, he never called out to Scout. If she had left out of fear, chances were she might have lost trust in him if she had any to begin with. Right now, he was working off instincts. His knowledge of the land, his proximity to the nearest shelter — Mount Roosevelt Friendship Tower.

It was located roughly two and a half miles away from town, to the northwest, nestled in the Black Hills National Forest at the end of a trailhead. He'd taken Libby and Charlie there numerous times when Laura would visit. It was built by Seth Bullock, the sheriff of Deadwood back in the early 1900s, as a tribute to the life and death of his old friend Theodore Roosevelt.

John hadn't decided what he would do if he found Scout.

Convincing her to go with him to the police department wasn't going to be an easy task. Rightfully so, she trusted no one. Every ounce of protection and security had been torn from her life. She must have expected the ground to give out beneath her with every step she took. Social services would take her into the system and while that had served many a child, it had destroyed others. There was no telling how she would cope. And now with the EMP, what little hope she had of a life beyond the nightmare was quickly fading.

John gazed up into the night sky, trying to make sense of who was behind the attack. Without media, it would leave the world guessing. They weren't privy to inside information. That was for the powers that be and right now he imagined they were scrambling to hold on to what little control they had left.

John pitched sideways working his way down a slippery slope, holding onto low-hanging branches with one hand while using his other to keep his balance. His thoughts turned to Ray Miller, his warning and what might have happened if Frank hadn't come along. Would he too have been lying in a puddle of blood?

John coughed hard, wiping rain out of his eyes.

At the bottom of the slope, he took out his compass, shone the flashlight on it and pressed on. It would take a good thirty minutes before he arrived at the tower.

Scout shivered near the opening of the 31-foot stone tower, trying to take shelter from the weather. She had pulled her knees up to her chest and wrapped her arms around them. Even with several layers on, she was freezing, soaked to the bone after getting caught in the downpour.

Although she wasn't hungry, she was tired, tired of hiding, running, trying to avoid pain. She leaned against the cold iron handrail on the lower stone step of the spiral staircase. All she wanted to do was sleep and never wake up again. She'd even contemplated going to the top and throwing herself off. No one would hear her. No one would care. A hiker would one day find her remains or animals would drag her away.

She thought about John.

His kindness, the way he listened and defended her.

But still, she couldn't go back there, not after what she'd seen. Not after what she'd done. The image of her uncle falling over the balcony replayed in her head, torturing her mind. If he had come for her, who else would? She couldn't do that to John. He didn't deserve that. No, she would rest here for the night, shelter from the storm, and if she made it through the night, she would walk out of the forest tomorrow. What she would do from there was to be seen.

Scout's whole body shivered as she closed her eyes.

She wasn't sure how long she had been there when she heard a low growl.

Her eyes blinked open, expecting to see a wild animal at the opening of the door as it sounded that close, but there was nothing. Beyond the tower, only darkness and rain could be seen. The warbled growl sounded like an animal in pain. The growl turned into a screech like a woman screaming. It was a miserable shriek that penetrated and shook her to the core.

There was no door on the tower. Just a wide stone opening. Nor was there a way to block off an intruder if she was to scale up the staircase. Scout squinted into the inky black, trying to make out a shape and get a sense of what was out there. Whatever it was, it didn't sound friendly, and if the sound was anything to go by, it was getting nearer.

Scout stood up, her eyes flitting back and forth as she took a few steps backward. Just beyond the door was a six-foot platform and iron steps that led up to it from the ground. *Move slowly, move slowly*, she told herself. One step at a time. She kept one hand on the railing as she made her way up. *Whatever you do, don't turn your back on it.* The only thing she had to protect herself was a flimsy stick she'd picked up and was using to support her as she made her way down slopes in the forest. It was roughly five feet long, and two inches wide — certainly nothing that an animal would be scared of.

Scout slowly reached into her pocket and took out the flashlight she'd taken from John's place. She switched it on and shone it out into the night.

That's when Scout saw it.

And saw how close it was.

Two piercing yellow eyes seemed to glow under the glare of light. It was already halfway up the outer steps, creeping forward toward her, not making a sound. What the hell was it? Mother and father had cats but this was huge. Fear tried to shut her brain down, make her freeze but she couldn't. That would have been certain death. She didn't know what this was but it didn't sound friendly and it was taking a big interest in her. Scooping off a small bag she'd taken from the cabin, Scout reached inside and took out a can of beans. "Get out of here! GO!" she bellowed but the four-legged beast wasn't fazed.

It continued to make a hideous cry as if it was suffering.

"I said SHOO!" she said. The huge cat bounced forward on all fours into the glow of her light then back into the darkness as if testing her. Its wail sounded like a child one moment, then a full-grown adult the next.

Scout continued to take a few more steps up.

Almost as if the beast knew what she was trying to do, it burst forward again but this time, Scout was ready. She tossed the can as hard as she could. It struck the beast on the snout, sending the wild animal back out into the rain-filled night with a pain-induced cry. Using that moment of distraction, Scout turned and hurried up the steps, her heart pounding in her chest, sweat dripping down her back.

At the top, beneath the roof, she peered over and saw the beast prowling before making its way back. It wasn't going to give up. Scout reached into her bag and pulled out another can. She could hear it growling as it made its way up the staircase. "Get out of here!" she bellowed, shouting loudly, her voice echoing in the stone chamber. But the beast had its eyes set on her and wasn't going to give up without a fight.

As soon as Scout saw it round the final bend, she threw the can. This time, however, she wasn't as fortunate. It barely grazed the top of the animal's head and vanished with a clatter into the darkness.

Using the only objects she had left to defend herself, she took her bag and held it like a shield. She took the stick and jabbed it forward at the tawny-beige animal. Each prod only seemed to anger it more. Half in the staircase and half on the platform she was standing on, it swiped its right paw at her, slicing through the front half of the bag like a knife through butter. She whacked it on the head with a whip-like strike causing it to retreat but only for a second. It lunged forward again, swiping the stick out of her hand.

Panic gripped her tightly around the throat, making it hard to breathe as she crouched down and scooped up the metal flashlight, her last and only weapon to defend herself.

There was no way she was going to be able to get close enough to strike it without being clawed to pieces. She kept the bag wrapped around her arm.

Scout shone the flashlight in the cat's eyes, hoping to blind it.

She peered over the edge. Far below she could just make out the ground, a black nothingness. Maybe this was it, perhaps this was life's final blow, fate's last way of turning the knife inside her. She'd lived as an animal and now she would die at the hands of one.

She wasn't sure what rose up in her in that moment.

Anger.

Pain.

Confusion.

It all swirled together, an emotional toxic cocktail that she was being forced to drink.

"Come on then!" Scout said. "If you're going to kill me. Do it! DO IT!" she said, swiping at its head. It was taunting her. The animal was now fully out of the staircase. Scout circled around the opening, only the outer wall and iron railing prevented her from falling.

And just like that it struck, launching forward.

She no longer felt scared or if she did, she no longer felt worried about the outcome. If she died, it would be a sweet release from this hell called life. The two of them collided as she thrust the flashlight into its powerful jaws and slipped beneath it. The noise it made was horrendous. She felt its claws dig into her side, tearing at her flesh.

Scout screamed.

Whether that scared the animal or it was tired of biting down on a metal flashlight, it backed up, giving Scout just enough room to wriggle back into the opening of the staircase. As she tried to get up again, the animal pounced once more and the two of them toppled down the staircase, rolling head over heels. It felt like she was in a washing machine with fur, fangs and claws. There was a never-ending screeching as they bounced off steps, colliding with the wall and metal railing before landing in a heap.

Excruciating pain shot through her, unlike anything she'd felt before.

Warm liquid trickled down her face, the taste of iron in her mouth.

It felt like every rib in her body was broken.

But even through the pain she was still aware of the danger.

Where was it? Where was the animal?

Scout turned her head ever so slightly and saw a mound of fur just outside the doorway, it was lying on its side, letting out a low growl. It almost seemed comical that this was how she would die.

The world around her started spinning.

In the kaleidoscope of images and sound, she saw the animal get up again, turn and screech one last time before...

Crack.

A deafening sound, and then another.

The animal landed hard on top of her, its chest moving ever so slightly before it stopped and her world turned to black.

16

Florida

The storm bore down on Laura, chilling her to the bone. It took every ounce of strength not to lose her temper in front of that child as she took her hand and guided her back to her mother. Her tiny white dog trotted beside her as if it knew it had been the cause of all of this.

Laura trudged forward, wearing nothing more than a black bra and panties. Rain trickled off her face. She couldn't believe the nerve of that bastard. Taking her clothes, her bag and... as Laura rounded the corner, she found her jeans in a puddle. Not far from that was her T-shirt. It had been purposely placed in a puddle. It had a large muddy boot print on it. She gritted her teeth and narrowed her gaze. Her entire body shivered hard as she retraced her steps back to Santa Barbara Boulevard.

Along the way she found the rest of her belongings.

A sweater now muddied and soaked, and each boot. James had filled them with water to the top and made a smiley face in the mud beside them. She wanted to claw his eyes out, drive a knife into his heart and make him feel all the pain that Richard had.

"Amelia!" the woman cried out in the distance.

The little girl broke away from Laura, running into her mother's arms. The two of them embraced, oblivious to the heavy rain. For a brief moment, she felt good. It didn't last. "Thank you. Thank you so much," the woman said. "I didn't think I would see her again."

"Where did you get that?" Laura asked, noticing she was carrying her backpack.

"A friend of yours gave it to me. Said you..."

"He's not my friend."

"Oh," she replied before handing it over. Laura fished into it, finding everything was still there except for the first-aid kit and the Glock. "Shit. He has a gun now."

"Who does?"

She waved her off as she set the bag down and tried to squeeze back into her clothes. Waterlogged, it was virtually impossible.

"Please. Come with me. I can give you some dry clothes."

She was about to thank her but then she thought of what had happened to Richard, to Trudy and their kids.

Did she really want to bring that upon this kind woman? She shook her head. "No, it's fine."

"It's the least I can do," she said, stroking her daughter's matted, wet hair.

She was stuck between a rock and a hard place. If she didn't get into dry clothes soon, she would suffer from hypothermia. Her body was losing heat faster than it could produce it. Eventually it would use up all her stored body energy and her body temperature would plummet and then she would be of no use to Charlie. Laura looked around nervously, eyeing each of the homes and cars on the street. Was he out there, watching her? He had to be. He'd followed her this far.

"My home is just a block away. Please. Let me do this for you," she said.

Laura nodded. She couldn't help thinking that she would regret this. Her clothes sucked at her skin like a thousand leeches. Her feet squelched inside her boots with every step. "My name is Valerie, and yours?"

"Laura."

Words were kept to a minimum as they hurried to get out of the cold. As they journeyed a block, Laura kept looking over her shoulder, worried that James would pop out at any moment and kill her, or worse kill Valerie and her daughter. They headed south just past South East 39th Street when Valerie gestured to her home across the road. It was a modest one-story abode set back from the canal. There was a white truck parked outside, circa early 1990s. "Go on inside and get out of those wet clothes," Valerie said to her daughter. She took off, and the dog followed.

Once inside, Valerie locked the doors and told her to wait while she collected some clothes. The wind continued to howl. Most of the windows on her home were covered with shutters barring the one she was in the middle of doing before her daughter went missing. Laura stood in one spot, shaking hard, water pooling at her feet.

She looked around her. The whole house had a Spanish touch to it. Doilies on the tables, a couple of crosses on the walls, some framed pictures of saints.

Valerie made her way down the stairs, holding two thick towels in one arm and some folded clothes in the other. "These belong to my sister, she's about your size. I hope they fit."

"They'll be fine, thank you," she said, taking them from her.

"Down the hall on your left is a bathroom. You can get changed in there."

Before Laura walked away, she looked toward the rear of the house. "Is your rear door locked?"

"I believe so."

"Please check it again."

"Are you okay, my dear?" Valerie asked.

"Yeah." She paused. She was tired of lying. "No. Not really. That man who gave you my bag. He's been following me. He killed my neighbor and he took my clothes." It felt good to get it out. To tell someone the truth. She fully expected Valerie to open her front door and kick her out, yell profanities and warn her not to come around again, but she didn't.

Instead, the color in Valerie's face washed out, realizing

how close she'd come to death. "Well honey, you don't have anything to worry about. My husband, God rest his soul, was an avid hunter. I'll grab his rifle. Go on now, get out of those clothes."

As she walked off down the hallway, Valerie shouted up to her daughter, "Amelia. Hurry up now. I want you down here."

"Yes, Mama."

Laura entered a cramped bathroom. There wasn't much inside it. A small toilet and a basin with a mirror on the wall. She peeled out of her wet clothes and began to dry herself off. Every so often she glanced at her reflection in the mirror and sobbed. Laura gripped the sink with both hands and tried her best to stay quiet. She just needed to release the emotion she'd been carrying since Richard and Trudy's house.

Her legs buckled and she dropped to a crouch, placing one hand over her mouth to mute her cries. It was so much more than that. It was the thought of losing Charlie. She'd lost too much already. If she lost him, she didn't think she'd come back from that. She sniffed hard, blew her nose on some tissue and dropped it in the toilet before getting hold of herself and getting into warm, dry clothes. The jeans were slightly bigger in the waist than hers but the belt she'd been given fixed that. Laura pulled a sweater over her head and took a second just to feel how good it was to no longer be damp and cold. It wouldn't stay that way. She had to use her own waterlogged shoes and she couldn't linger as there were still miles to go.

Stepping out of the bathroom, carrying her wet clothes, Laura half-expected to see James holding Valerie and her daughter hostage, a gun to their head, but he wasn't.

"Laura, we're in here," Valerie said from the kitchen.

She found the two of them at a kitchen island.

"I'm using a Coleman stove to boil some water. Can I make you a warm drink?"

"That's very kind but I have to get going."

"You're going back out there?"

She gave a strained smile. "Yes. Ironically for the same reason you did. My kid."

"Is he lost too?"

That was a loaded question that might hold a double meaning as well. Charlie was lost but not in the way that she was meaning. Since losing his father and his sister, he had withdrawn into himself, stopped doing sports, even gave up playing video games which at one time would have been unthinkable.

"He's out there. I'm not exactly sure where but I intend to find him, hopefully before this storm makes landfall."

"Already feels like it has," she said, turning toward the Coleman stove and taking off a kettle and pouring out some of the hot water. "When did he go missing?"

It was bad out there. Far worse than she imagined but it was just the beginnings of something much worse. "He isn't missing. So to speak. He was meant to be heading north to Orlando to stay with friends of mine and he decided to cut ties with them and head back this way."

"To return to you?" she asked, holding out a cup to Amelia. The little girl took it and blew the steam away from the top. She grinned at Laura and that smile made temporarily losing her clothes worth it. Clothes could be replaced, a life, well, when that was gone there was no coming back. She knew that more than anything even years later.

"To his friend, I think. They're storm chasers."

"Oh. Morons," Valerie said.

"My sentiments exactly," Laura replied.

"Well, look, I'll give you a flask to take with you. I hate to send you out there. What about this man? Who is he?"

"I wish I knew. Just a patient."

"You're a doctor?"

"A nurse."

"My eldest was studying to become a lab tech." She gestured to a photo on a wall of a Hispanic female, maybe twenty, in graduation clothes. "She lives in Georgia right now. May God protect her." Valerie paused what she was doing, looking at the photo the way any mother might. It didn't matter how old kids got. Parents still worried. "Anyway," she tapped the air. "Here, you take this," she said, handing her a flask of hot water with a teabag hanging out of it. "And I'll go get that rifle. Oh, you do know how to shoot, right?"

"Yes."

"Self-taught?"

"My husband was a fireman but he used to go to the range when he wasn't working. I tagged along."

"Ah, the same. That's how they sucker us into it," she said. Valerie wandered out of the kitchen and down the hallway, still speaking with Laura. "And your husband now?"

"He's passed."

"Illness?" Valerie asked.

"A car accident."

A moment later Valerie returned, holding a beautiful shotgun. "I figure this might be better than his hunting rifle. It's a lot more forgiving," she said, handing it over with a handful of shells. Laura pocketed them.

"It's a Mossberg 500 pump action shotgun. It holds five rounds in the magazine and one in the chamber. Sorry there aren't any more shells."

"Thank you."

"No, thank you," she said, coming around the back of Amelia and running her hands through the child's damp hair. "I know what it's like to lose someone close."

"Would you have a coat by any chance?"

Valerie smiled. "Anything else you need?"

"A working car."

"Don't have that, my love, but I do have a bicycle." Laura almost wanted to laugh but, in that moment, she couldn't summon more than a strained smile. "Though I imagine you'll have a hard time staying on it. But maybe it will get you where you need to go faster than walking." Laura followed Valerie out into the garage and helped her get down a woman's white mountain bike. Laura tried it out. She sat on it. The seat was a little low but it was sturdy.

It was a ten-speed which would come in handy. Even though the land was flat where she lived, that wind out there was going to make it feel like she was climbing a mountain.

∼

ACROSS THE STREET, James winced as he used a needle and thread to sew up the bullet wound. Nearby in a bowl was what remained of the round — bloodied and bent. Not far from that were the bodies of two elderly people in their seventies. He had to give it to the old man, he planned to put up one hell of a fight. James might have entertained the idea if he wasn't in so much pain. Instead, he put two slugs in their foreheads and set about fixing his wound while watching the house across the way.

He chuckled, thinking of the look on Laura's face when she got out of that canal and found her clothes and bag gone. Oh, he couldn't believe his luck. He'd contemplated killing her right then and there, drowning that bitch in the water, but where would the fun have been in that? He could do that anytime. No, he wanted to drag this out, make her suffer, let her know what real fear was, besides, he enjoyed looking at her — in those black panties and bra. Damn, she was an attractive woman, far better than his ex, and she was at least an eight out of ten.

James winced again with each loop.

He considered going across the street and waiting until the door opened before he popped a cap in that Spanish bitch, and her daughter. After that he'd be all alone with Laura. But that would come in time. He wasn't one for forcing himself on anyone. He wanted her to beg for it. And she would. He pulled out of his pocket a scrap of paper from a telephone book with an address in Fort Myers that was circled. "Is this where your boy is?" he muttered.

Now if he could get to her son before she did, oh the fun they would have. He would have Laura eating out of his hand. A nurse had to be earning good money. No doubt she had squirreled away some funds for a rainy day. Now of course, he needed to think about what he would do once this storm was over. Okay, it was a little strange the cars not working and all, but maybe it was all connected. All he knew was that with the cops already on his ass, it wouldn't be long after the storm cleared that they would be hunting him down again and he would need some coin to get out of the country. She would be his ticket. Her, and the kid — yeah — they would all be one happy little family, at least for a while. That could work.

Maybe he would go north over into Canada, or south to Mexico.

"And what is the reason for your visit?" a border officer would ask.

"Pleasure," he would say, glancing at her with a grin. "Leisure and pleasure, isn't that right, darling." And she would nod affirmatively, smile politely and they would be home free, out of the country and on their way to a better life, a life where he called the shots and she did whatever the hell he wanted. He wouldn't make the mistake he did with his ex.

And... once he was tired of the two of them, well, he reached for the Glock and tapped it against his leg.

That problem could be easily solved.

17

South Dakota

Was this what hell felt like? Mother and father had said that's where she would go if she disobeyed. Typical. Free from life's horrors and she was to endure an eternity of suffering for what? Existing?

As searing hot pain coursed through Scout, her mind replayed on loop her body being slammed into a wall, the taste of a bar of soap pushed into her mouth, and her hair being pulled. Her eyes blinked. Was it just a dream? Light filtered in, stabbing her eyes, making it painful to open them. There was a dull pulsating ache at the back of her head that wouldn't stop, and a sensation that she could only imagine felt like being stung by a thousand bees.

All she could see was darkness. Nothing else but darkness.

Where am I? she thought but no answer came. Somewhere at the edge of the foggy haze she felt someone near her, lifting her head, inserting something into her mouth and then washing it down with liquid. "Slowly, you'll choke yourself."

A familiar voice.

She couldn't place it.

Time slowed.

The smell of burnt wood, the crackling and popping nearby and a warmth that made her feel good slowly extracted her out of the nightmare.

Heavy footfalls, rushing water, someone muttering.

Her brain tried to make sense of it all but it couldn't.

A memory flashed before her, an animal, its jaw wide and ferocious, its claws hacking into her skin. No. No. Scout tossed and turned, trying to escape it but there was nowhere to flee, it was on top of her, its hairy face so close, so terrifyingly real that...

"Hey, Scout. It's okay."

She gasped, her eyes blinked open and she bolted upright into a world of pain.

Eyes bulging, she started hyperventilating as her senses were overwhelmed. Sweat trickled down her back, her hair was matted and pressed to her forehead. Another wave of pain steamrolled over her and she groaned loudly before large hands gently pressed her back into a soft bed. "It's just a dream. You're safe. You're with me."

"John?" she muttered.

Finally, the world snapped into view and she could see clearly. Gone was the image of that animal. Gone was the cycle of pain inflicted on her by mother and father. In its place sitting beside her was John, a heavyset man, broad shoulders, a head of greying hair and a full beard and those kind eyes. He was wearing a blue jean shirt, a white V-neck T-shirt and cream-colored khaki pants with brown boots.

"You came back for me?"

He nodded.

"Why?"

"Because," he said, rising from his seat and crossing the room to get a jug of water from the kitchen. He had set her down on the living room sofa. There was a knitted cover over her body. She pulled it back to take a look at her wounds. Her pants were still on, as was her small bra, not that there was anything to fill it. Her left side had what looked like white bandages attached to it, like huge Band-Aids. She touched it and winced.

"That mountain lion clawed you up pretty bad. It's going to take a while for that to heal," he said, crossing the room and pouring out water. "Here, you should drink. Stay hydrated." He helped her sit up even though it was excruciating.

"Where is it?"

"I shot it. Just in the nick of time by the looks of it. A few seconds longer and it would have had you."

"It nearly did," she said. "The last memory I have was me falling down the staircase with it."

He stood back from her in amazement. "Huh. Then in

some ways you have that animal to thank as it must have cushioned your fall and taken some of the hits. You've broken your left arm. I reset it and put it in a makeshift splint and a sling. You have a nasty welt at the back of your head, a big gash on your chin, and you bit through your lip. One of your lower teeth is missing, I think you might have a broken rib or two and of course there is that nasty gouging in your left side. Damn, Scout. You are one tough kid, that's for sure."

"How long have I been asleep?" she asked.

"Maybe an hour?"

John took a cloth, dipped it into a bowl and wrung it out. He touched it against her head and she stared at him. It felt soft, warm and comforting. Her gaze met his. "Why are you helping me?"

"Why wouldn't I?"

Scout looked off across the room and tried to get up again. "I need to go."

"Go? Go where? You're injured."

"I need to leave."

"Scout, lay down, you're not thinking straight."

"You're with him. You're going to hand me over to them, aren't you?"

"Him? What? No. Don't you remember I tried to help you? Hell, I found your uncle in my backyard. I gather that was you."

"And I would do it again."

"All right, look, just settle."

She pushed up but then felt another searing shot of pain go through her arm. She began crying. John pushed her back on the sofa. "You are in no state to be going anywhere, not until a doctor has seen you, put a cast on that arm and checked you out."

"Where is he?"

"Your uncle? Probably in town now. I helped load him into the back of my friend's truck."

"He's your friend?"

"Frank? Yeah. We go way back. Look, I went into town and spoke with the police and told them what you'd told me. They were going to come up and see for themselves and then..."

"But he's not a police officer," she said, cutting him off.

That caused John to pause. He frowned as he slowly spoke. "No. No, he's not now. But his daughter is the chief. Scout, how do you know he's not a police officer? You said you'd never been out of your house."

"I haven't. He came to the house."

"What?"

"He was the man mother and father had arranged for me to see."

John dropped the towel in his hand back into the bowl and stared at her as if waiting for her to elaborate. She didn't so he probed further. "To see?"

"You know." She averted her eyes, embarrassed.

John shook his head. "No. No. You must have this wrong. I've known Frank for years. He's a family man. Married. He used to be the chief of police. His daughter works for the department. Scout, you've got to be confused. Maybe the bump to your head has..."

"I remember his face, John. That's why I ran away.

When I saw you return with him, I thought you were involved with them."

"With them?"

"The ones who take women and young girls."

"There are others?"

"My older sister. She told me. Mother and father gave her over to them twice. Why do you think I ran away? I was to be next."

John rose from his seat and shook his head, unable to believe it. Not Frank. No. He knew him. He'd known him for over twenty years. He'd eaten in his house. Looked after Sarah when she was a kid. Fished with him. He'd ridden with the Pagans. He'd spent hours upon hours with that man. If he had any skeletons in the closet, John would have known. He would be privy to it. His thoughts swirled back to what Frank had asked him. *"What did she tell you?"*

Frank had wanted to know what Scout had told John.

John tapped his lower lip, thinking. He didn't want to believe it. It seemed too outrageous. Not the part about human trafficking at the motorcycle rally. No, he'd heard that happened but it was rare, or at least seemed that way as each year they only arrested a few people. Then again, it kind of made sense. Having his daughter in the department would keep him privy to who was working undercover and where the DCI agents might be. John ran a hand over his head and to the back of his neck, unable to get a grip on what she'd told him.

He didn't think for one minute that Sarah was involved. No. If there was any truth to this, it was a part of Frank's life that he'd kept hidden from his family. Not even his wife would have known. Especially her. Gloria would have torn him limb from limb. John needed to speak to him, face to face. He needed to look in his eyes. See it for himself. But how? No wonder he was eager to take Clay's body back. He understood now why Frank had tried to make him second-guess if he'd killed him or not. He wanted to make him question his sanity.

It would have been easier to explain.

Easier to deter Sarah from looking at her father or even the girl.

Shit. He had to speak with Sarah before her father did, but with the power grid down, and not having a working motorcycle or a license to drive it, he had no way of getting into town — except for Eddy. Eddy lived two miles from him. If he could reach him, he might be able to hitch a ride in his old '79 International Harvester Scout.

Then of course he needed to speak with a doctor to get them to look at Scout but he couldn't leave her here alone, not after what had happened. If Frank was involved in some way, there would be repercussions for Clay's death.

As he stood there trying to think through what to do, Scout spoke up.

"I saw the newspaper clippings."

"What?" he asked, casting a glance over his shoulder.

"The crash. Your son-in-law and granddaughter." She paused. "Sorry. I was exploring... I shouldn't have."

He nodded and walked over to her. "It's okay."

"What happened?"

He took a deep breath. "You know, that was the first question my daughter asked me. I..." He became at a loss for words. A flash of memory of that night came back to him. Since that day it would return in snippets. Never fully. He'd seen Libby in his rearview mirror, smiling in the back. Michael talking about what he had bought for Laura as he rode shotgun. There was a soft layer of snow on the road that evening, the first of many snowfalls that followed after. He remembered snowflakes, the windshield wipers moving back and forth and bright headlights cutting into the night.

Then darkness.

As his vision vanished.

He didn't even hear their screams as the Toyota cut across the road, sideswiped another vehicle and flipped as it went into the ditch and collided with multiple trees.

"It was a medical problem. Something from my time in the military. I... I have what's called a traumatic brain injury from an IED blast. Long story but I thought my vision was improving and then it just went, everything blurred at first. They think the bright lights may have played a role and..." John sighed, rising again from his chair. "I need to speak with Eddy."

"You're leaving?"

"Scout. He lives about two miles from here. You need a doctor to look at your ribs and put a cast on that arm. And... well I won't be long."

"But he could come back. Please don't leave me."

John balled his fist. Her. The EMP. Now Frank. It was all too much. He wasn't used to dealing with this much stress. Not at his age. Not now. Not with the ringing in his ears and the off-and-on vision loss.

On the far west side of Sturgis, the Vipers gathered in a small one-story clubhouse that used to belong to the Salvation Army. Jethro had scooped it up at a crazy price when it came on the market. Since then, he'd done some renovations. It now had a bar, a pool room, a lounge with leather chairs, lots of storage, a bathroom with showers, a full kitchen with a walk-in freezer out back for yearly events, and a place for meetings where they discussed business.

That evening the atmosphere was different.

Candles flickered creating dancing shadows on the walls. Hand-crank lanterns offered light in darkened corners. Jethro sat at the head of the table, running his fingers over the head of a snake that was carved into a wooden table. "So, all those in favor?"

Hands went up.

"Okay, moving on to the next order of business. The blackout. We have one working vehicle. We're going to need more. Danny here says that most vehicles from before 1980 should be functioning, so I want you all to get out there and see what you can dig up."

"And the cops?" Pete Huxley asked.

Jethro laughed as he poured out two fingers of bourbon. "Who?"

"The cops. What about them?"

Jethro removed a heavy revolver from the back of his jeans and placed it on the table. "Does that answer your question?"

Grins formed on the faces of his men. This was nothing but another opportunity for them to demonstrate their place among the throng of MC clubs that were spread all over the Black Hills. There was always tension even when there was law and order but now, anything could happen. "Never before have we seen a situation like this. What we do in these next few hours will determine who follows who. There's no way of knowing how long this will last or if the lights will come back on again but until they do — it's business as usual." A door opened to the right of them and his cousin Tammy peered in.

"Excuse me, guys," Jethro said, rising and making his way over. He scowled as he forcefully pushed her outside. "I told you not to come around here."

"Yeah, well, we've got a problem."

"Don't we all. Where's my merchandise?"

"Well, that's the problem. She ran off. Took up shelter with some asshole at the Sheridan cabin."

"That's empty."

"It seems not. The owner gave Clay one hell of a licking. Put him on his ass. So, we went to the cops and..."

Jethro pushed away from the building. "Hold on a fucking minute. You did what?"

"We figured they'd intervene. You know, get her back and all but..."

"They haven't," he said, cutting her off and snorting a loogie before spitting it near her foot. Tammy looked disgusted. She was bouncing around, tweaking out. Nearly every woman he knew around these parts was on meth or heroin. It made controlling them that much easier. The things they would do for one hit. His cousin was no different.

Tammy continued to explain, "Well, the power went out and then there was some ruckus in town with your crew and the Nomads."

He grumbled, crossed his arms and spat on the ground.

"Anyway, I figured you could deal with it."

"Like your brother?"

He glanced over her shoulder to where her husband was standing near the gate. Ray gave a nod, and Jethro smirked. He was a fucking idiot. He certainly didn't have any balls. Jethro had a good mind to send Tammy away and let her deal with it but if she was right, this could go south on them. That kid knew far too much about their business. He knew that because they'd caught her listening in. He chuckled thinking of the way Tammy choked her out, put her in her place. When she wasn't all strung out, Tammy was a real firecracker.

The door opened behind them.

It was Joey. "Jethro."

"I'll be there in a minute."

The door closed with a thump.

"You still running your meetings?"

"Why wouldn't I?"

"Oh, I don't know. Maybe because the power is out?"

"And? What am I supposed to be doing? Stocking up on canned goods and all that bullshit?"

"Well, it might help. That's what we plan to do once this is dealt with."

Jethro shook his head, chuckling. "You see, that's the

difference between you and me, Tammy. If I want something, I just take it," he said, getting close to her and running his hand down the side of her face and over her lips. The crazy thing is Tammy would have hiked her skirt up and dropped her panties in front of her old man and let Jethro have his way if it meant getting a free hit of coke. Cousin or not. That was just like her. Tammy sucked the end of his finger and he laughed, looking over at Ray. "You are a fucking walking contradiction, Tammy, that's what you are," he said, pointing to the cross on her neck. He turned to go back inside.

"So?" she asked.

He answered over his shoulder as the door closed. "Yeah, I'll handle it."

18

South Dakota

There were few people John truly trusted but Eddy Johnson was one. John didn't like the idea of getting him involved but he had few options. Scout needed to be seen by a doctor, her siblings were still trapped in the house she'd escaped from and he needed to confront Frank over the allegations. With his eyesight failing him, he couldn't exactly drive into town. Blackout or not, if the cops pulled him over, he'd be arrested on the spot. But sending Eddy, that was a viable option.

The challenges were Scout's injuries and the fear of leaving her alone.

Initially John thought he could take her with him. Eddy's home was only two miles away but that would take at least thirty to forty minutes. She could barely stand without crying out in agony. "Why don't you take the truck outside?" Scout asked.

It was old enough but missing a vital component.

"That old thing needs a transmission. It died many moons ago."

"Then your motorcycle in the garage?"

"No vehicles are working except older ones. That's a newer model."

The blackout had really thrown a wrench in the works. That was part of the reason why he wanted to get to Eddy's: his 1979 International Harvester Scout would still be working. "And even if I could get one working, my eyesight isn't what it used to be." He could see well enough but it was like a faulty TV. He never knew when the signal was going to give out. The last time it had happened was when the accident occurred and he'd vowed never to put anyone else's life in danger like that again. Not that he had taken a chance back then, he thought he was on the mend. And his tinnitus, well, that was just the cherry on the cake.

"Look, I have to leave you."

Scout clung to his shirt sleeve. "Please don't."

"I have to. I'll be back in thirty-five minutes, fifty minutes tops. If I book it, I could be back faster but I have to go. You could have internal damage that could kill you."

A lot could happen in that amount of time. He had no idea if Tammy and Ray were keeping watch on the property. If that incident with Clay had been any indication, he had to believe they were, but he had to go now because Scout could be suffering from internal bleeding. If she died on him while in his care, he didn't think he could come back from that.

It was catch-22. He was screwed if he did, and screwed if he didn't.

"Listen. Here's what we'll do." John lifted her and carried up the stairs. She could stand but not without excruciating pain. He took her into the ensuite bathroom in his room and set her down. He got some pillows from the bed and put them in the bath along with a duvet and then lifted her into it.

"What are you doing?" she asked.

He didn't answer her. He walked out and went to his closet. He reached up and pulled down a gun box and set it on the bed, unlocked it and took out a Glock 22. He collected two magazines and loaded them with 40-caliber rounds. He returned and set it down beside the bathtub. "I'm going to take it you've never fired a gun before in your life."

Her eyes widened in shock at what he had in mind. "John. No."

"Listen to me. I was twelve years old when my father taught me how to fire a rifle, fourteen when I shot a Glock. You're sixteen. You are one hell of a strong girl. You can do this." He looked over his shoulder then back at her. "Now I'm going to lock this door. I'm going to run over to Eddy's, and have him drop me back here while he goes into town to get a doctor."

He took a breath, then continued. "Okay, really simple. The first rule. Never point this gun at anyone unless you intend to use it. Not yourself. Not me. No one. You understand?" He repeated it again. He couldn't emphasize it enough. Any fool could shoot a gun. He wanted her to be familiar with gun safety. "You see this..." he showed her a magazine. "This has bullets in it. It goes inside here," he said. "It's a Glock 22. It holds 15 rounds. When this magazine is empty the slide will lock back like this." He showed her. "To reload just push this button on the side and the empty magazine will fall out. Take this one here and palm it in, then release the slide. From there it's a simple case of point and shoot. But again, don't point this gun unless you know who you are shooting at and are ready to use it. You understand?"

Scout nodded.

"Good. You've got forty-five bullets."

"What if they start shooting at me?"

The bathroom was designed with the bathtub off to the left side out of direct view of the main door. There was a toilet at the far end on the right side along with a wash basin and large mirror. Still, he knew that it was possible for bullets to ricochet.

"Stay low in the tub. I'll be back. Don't worry."

He said the words knowing that it was pointless, she would worry, so would he but what else could he say. He needed her to agree. He couldn't stay. It was as simple as that. He only wished the EMP hadn't occurred. Phones would be working. Vehicles ready to use. Although he hadn't taken her to town when he had the chance, he was glad now he hadn't. Who knows what would have happened to her. If there was any inkling of truth to her story, then she could go missing just like her brother Elijah.

"John."

He paused at the door and looked back. "Yes?"

"Be quick. Please."

"I'll be back before you know it." He closed the door and locked it. It wasn't secure but Katherine had asked him to put a lock on the door so if he was away from home and someone broke in, she could buy herself some time and retreat into the bathroom and call the cops. A lot of the locks on bathroom doors could be opened from the outside with a simple knife. This one required a key to unlock a deadbolt. It was small things that he remembered about his life with her. God, he missed her.

John made his way down, slid into a grey rain jacket and collected his Winchester rifle. He was packing a Sig Sauer. Before leaving he went and hammered in some plywood over the glass window Scout had broken. He knew that if anyone wanted to get in, they could, so before leaving, he created a few simple traps. He took some plywood and hammered in some long nails and set it under each of the windows, then covered the plywood with floor mats. It wasn't ideal but it would give him some peace of mind that if anyone tried to get in, they would be in for a rude awakening. Once ready, he went upstairs and told Scout what he had done just in case.

Thoughts of Frank bombarded his mind as he stepped outside into the dark night and locked the house. He just couldn't believe that Frank would be involved. His old friend. It seemed impossible. Everything on the surface of his life was the opposite of that. He'd seen the way Frank was around women. He was respectful. Everyone spoke of him highly. Throughout his time as chief there hadn't been any sexual complaints made against him. At least none made known. He had to wonder if he'd buried them, if he'd buried anything at all. There was still a chance Scout was mistaken. Frank could have looked like someone else. He thought back to all the biker rallies he'd been at. Most of the guys were middle-aged or in their early sixties, sporting thick beards, goatees and leather. Surely it would have been easy to have misidentified him. Using the glow of a flashlight to light the way, John set his face like a flint toward the rain and headed off down the driveway.

Within minutes his thighs were burning and sweat trickled down his back.

He kept pressing on via the dirt road. At some point he had to leave the road and traipse through the forest as it was quicker. He broke into a run, yet aware that one wrong footing could be his downfall. Hiking through the thick pines was like a maze. Every direction looked the same. If it wasn't for his compass and knowledge of the area, he could easily get lost. The rough and foreboding terrain was a challenge even for the most experienced hiker. Continuing on, he crested a rise and finally saw the familiar sight of Eddy's cabin. There was a faint glow of light coming from inside.

John hurried, breaking through the tree line and dashing across his rear yard before banging on the back door. "Eddy. Hey. It's John. Open up." Beyond the pane of glass, he saw what looked like a floating light coming toward him. Eddy was holding a lantern up, the light illuminating half of his face.

"John?" He opened the door. "What do you make of this blackout?"

"I know," John replied, resting both of his hands on his knees and trying to catch his breath. It wasn't like when he was in his early twenties and serving in the military. Those days were long gone. Pressure built inside his head and his eyesight blurred again. A pitched whine in his ears continued to torment him. "Please tell me your truck is working."

"It should be. Why?"

"I need a favor."

"Of course, anything. John, what is it? You're worrying me."

"I need you to drop me at my house."

Eddy wasn't married. Perhaps that's why they got along so well. When he lived in Deadwood, he would often have him over at his house for a game of cards. They would play long into the night, drinking fine bourbon and smoking cigars. Frank would often join them. Eddy got into some thick clothes to handle the weather, John got himself a glass of water. "So, this kid just showed up?" Eddy asked, walking into the kitchen while zipping up his outerwear.

John gulped then nodded.

"And she thinks Frank is involved?"

"She recognized him."

"I understand but... John, this is Frank we're talking about."

He was as stunned as John was. It was inconceivable

not just because of what Frank had done for a living before he retired but because of who he was or portrayed himself to be — a wholesome, married man with a heart for the downtrodden. Hell, he and the Pagans had raised money for sick kids and even handed out meals in the winter months to those on the street. What Scout was suggesting was so far removed from his character that it was hard to fathom. "I know. I know. Look, we need to get going."

"All right, just give me a minute. You kind of caught me off guard."

Eddy scooped up the keys to the full-size SUV and tossed them to him. "Go start it up. I'll be right there." John headed into the garage, pulled the door open and fired up the engine before getting in the passenger side and waiting with his arm hanging out the window. John waited for what seemed like five minutes before he reached over and beeped the horn. His anxiety was rising as he thought about Scout being alone.

Eddy came out with a backpack, and a rifle which he put in the back before sliding behind the wheel. "Can't be too safe," he said. "Who knows what hell is breaking out in town."

On the way over John brought Eddy up to speed.

"So how many siblings does she have?"

"Four. An older sister, and three younger ones. She thinks they killed her brother."

The truck wound its way around the dark hills, water splashing up the sides as they went over potholes. The weather was atrocious and only getting worse. As they came up to the T-junction and made a left turn onto the final stretch that led up to his property, they were met by the sight of a truck blocking the way. Bright headlights turned on, blinding them. Eddy hit the brakes and the Harvester fishtailed to a standstill in the waterlogged mud. "Who the hell are…"

Before the words came out, another truck came up the rear, blocking them in.

John put his hand on his Sig Sauer. "Don't turn off that engine."

They watched as two guys got out of the rusted-out Ford blocking their way and another two from a classic Chevy behind them. John glanced at his side mirror, watching two of them come up behind. All four were packing AR-15s. The headlights were too bright to notice who they were but he thought he could distinguish biker gear.

"This isn't good," Eddy said.

They were in the middle of nowhere at a time when all communication was cut off, and 95 percent of vehicles were defunct. No help was coming. Ahead of them two silhouettes cut into the headlights, then stopped in front of their truck with a stance of defiance. One of them bellowed, "Turn off the vehicle!"

"Don't shut it off," John said.

"But John—"

"Don't shut it off."

No one went to this amount of trouble if they had plans to just let them walk. This was an excessive display of force, a precursor to something far bigger. One of the bikers made a jerking motion with his rifle. "Are you deaf? Turn off the vehicle."

"Floor it," John said.

"What?"

"I'd say we have less than a few minutes before they execute us."

"Execute? What are you talking about?" Eddy looked behind him. "Okay, I admit this is a little disturbing but we should at least find out what they want."

"Eddy. When was the last time someone blocked you in and were packing AR-15s because they wanted to tell you something?" John didn't take his eyes off the men for even a second. His gaze washed over the side mirrors, keeping an eye on the two at the back who were stationed near the rear tires as if they were prepared to shoot out the tires if need be.

The men raised their rifles at the windshield. "I won't ask again."

"Duck and accelerate."

"But John—"

"Do you want to live or die?" He glanced at his friend. Eddy swallowed hard. He'd never killed a man. Not like him. John had been in situations like this before in the Middle East. They were trained for this. There was only one way this would end and that was in bloodshed.

And this sure as hell wasn't going to be his final resting place.

19

Florida

Huddled together, fear held them as the approaching hurricane swept across the Gulf Coast with winds over a 150 miles per hour. Outside, the ocean roared as impressive frothy waves surged over mounds of white sands, crashing into rocks and forcing trees to creak, bend and break. Seaweed scattered, and boats no longer anchored washed up on shore, destroyed.

Seth's father finished patching up Seth's leg. He sat back and looked at him, running a hand over his head.

Seth was still unconscious but at least his leg was no longer bleeding. There was no way to plan for the worst scenario as a storm chaser. You either lived or died, it was as simple as that.

"Will he be okay?" Charlie asked.

Dawson grimaced. "I hope so." He didn't sound too hopeful. It made Charlie wonder why he agreed to come out. As dark and depressing as his life had become after the accident, something like this had started to make him appreciate the smaller things — his life, his mother, his grandfather, everything.

"Why do you do it?" Charlie asked.

Dawson didn't look at him, maybe it was guilt for asking him to come along, maybe he had spun the wheel one too many times and now he knew fate had dealt him a bad hand. "The feeling. When I was a kid, no older than Seth, my father took me to one of the Caribbean islands so I could experience it. It was the most terrifying moment of my life. But you know what, after that night I no longer associated it with fear. It was more akin to excitement than anything else. So, in those early days it was all about trying to feel that way again, just one more time. Like a drug, I guess. Once you experience it, you either love or hate it. There is no in between."

"And now?"

"Well, I mostly do it to log observation data and assist meteorologists in analyzing storms but I still get a kick out of it."

"And today?"

Dawson dipped his chin. "Look. Seth knows the dangers. It's not like I force him to come along with me. I didn't expect this to happen."

"Don't worry, it's not like I'm going to blame you," he said, pulling out the hand-crank radio from a bag that

Dawson had retrieved from his trailer attached to the back of the Bronco. Charlie wound it up and pulled up the steel antenna to try and get a signal. He walked around inside the shaky four walls, raising it up and hoping to find a signal as he tried a couple different frequencies.

All that came back was static.

"I don't know why you're trying. You won't get anything," Hannah said, looking defeated. Charlie was regretting asking her to come along. "Once the storm hits, no one in their right mind is going to be wasting their time monitoring stations."

"You're wrong about that. There's always stations," Dawson said. He tossed a few out that he knew. "The Florida Public Radio Emergency Network has thirteen stations that will stay on-air and broadcast updates. Mostly weather, safety and evacuation info. They work out of the Emergency Operations Center in Tallahassee. You should know that."

"I'm not native to Florida," she said. "And I meant because of the power outage."

"All my gear is kept in a rubber-insulated steel trailer. Basically, it acts like a Faraday cage. It's to ensure everything is working as there is no telling what kind of electrical storms we could be having. And the emergency operations center has backup generators and I imagine they are heavily shielded because of lightning strikes. Anyway, where are you from?" Dawson asked.

"Kentucky. But my mother moved out here to be close to my grandmother."

"Oh yeah, what's your mom do?"

Hannah glanced at Charlie and he caught her eye. "She's a stay-at-home mom."

That was a polite way of saying she drank and got wasted until she passed out.

"Must be nice having her around."

Hannah scoffed, shaking her head as she crossed the room.

"And what about you, Charlie? Last time I talked to Seth, he said you might not make it. That your mother wasn't too happy about you coming. What changed her mind?"

He snorted. "Um. Well..."

Right then he managed to get a signal. The timing couldn't have been any better.

"This is Rita Gaines and this is continuous coverage of Hurricane Fiona on WGCU. For those of you riding out the storm, this is for you. This looks to be much more powerful than we anticipated. Multiple hurricanes will make landfall, not just one. So, let's start discussing evacuation orders and shelters. Gerald, can you give me a rundown of what color has been ordered to evacuate and where people can go?"

Gerald replied. *"Yes, so let's be clear here. The mandatory evacuation order was issued yesterday by Lee County Sheriff's Office and Lee County Emergency Operations Center but as you know, Rita, most people started to head out sooner than that based on the storm warning. But right now, the evacuation order is for Zone A down here if you are looking at the main evacuation map. It is the red zone. In a nutshell, its all of our coastal areas. Everyone who is south of Highway 98 and along the coast on the west and east. So, if you live in the coastal area* of Lee County, you are under a mandatory evacuation order. We have multiple shelters open in Cape Coral and Fort Myers at some of the elementary and high schools."

He began reeling them off along with street addresses. "These are the ones that have been open since yesterday morning. Please note that these ones are not at full capacity. There's plenty of room there. If a shelter fills to capacity, we will notify everyone and open up a second. We are still taking evacuees."

"Sorry, I just want to cut in. That shelter you mentioned is not full yet, yes?"

"That is what I said, Rita."

Charlie chuckled, he could hear the frustration in his voice. Logic would have told every single person to evacuate but that wasn't practical for many so they had to offer shelters. Whether people opted to go there was up to them but the general consensus was if they decided to stay home and ride it out and they got into trouble, no one was coming to save them. Not until the storm was over. At some point it just got too dangerous for even emergency personnel.

"So, what are you expecting in terms of wind, storm surge and so on?"

"Well, we expect based on our data and briefings in the center that this will be a high wind event."

Duh, Charlie thought.

"We will be expecting at least twelve to eighteen feet storm surge. For those who are near the coast you will have seen how the water receded, the rivers were dry, and the bay water disappeared, but that has now come back and already is spilling over onto land. Again, I repeat, you are looking at a lot of water rushing in so if you are out there, stuck in your house, get to high ground and may God help you."

"And what do you make of these multiple hurricanes that have been reported around the globe?"

"Unprecedented, Rita. I don't have an answer for it. We've never seen anything like it before. But that right now isn't our main concern, it's the blackout. For those who don't know, the blackout is not related to the storm. I know we often see a few days or a week without power, but I repeat, it is not related to the storm. From the briefing that we had earlier, this has fried computer chips in vehicles, and shut down all phone, internet and television communication. The only reason we are on the air right now is because of the shielding here at the studio. Thank God for that."

"And what else can you tell us about it?"

"No idea. Right now, information is vague. It's believed to be some kind of terrorist attack but by who? We don't know. The suddenness has left our infrastructure and ability to communicate hamstrung. Once we hear more, we will update everyone but it's early right now. It could be a week or two before information rolls out."

And that was the truth. Everyone expected to hear an answer immediately. But that wasn't realistic. That wasn't how government operated. Of course, there would be those who would point fingers and jump to conclusions, allowing their own bias, hatred and beliefs to color their opinions, but the truth was no one knew.

The focus would be less on telling people who was responsible and more on sending out the National Guard throughout the states to help those without power. And that would be a massive job. Protection would be at the top of the list as people turned to looting. Even though lots of resources would be thrown at trying to keep elderly people and critical patients alive, millions would still die.

"So, Gerald, do you expect anyone to be able to hear us?"

"I hope so. I like to think that there are a lot of smart folks out there that were prepared for this even if the majority of us aren't."

"Thank you, Gerald. We will continue to provide updates for as long as we can. In the meantime, God help you. Stay safe."

The line crackled back to static as high winds tore something off the roof and a loud metallic bang could be heard on the far side of the building.

"We should move now," Charlie said, feeling as if the walls would implode at any second.

"That lighthouse is the safest place on this barrier island," Dawson bellowed over the howling wind which rattled the side of the building. "Give me a hand carrying him. Hannah, I need you to go out first and unlock the door." She nodded, reached for the key and without any thought to her own safety took a deep breath and sprinted as fast as she could, zigzagging her way. Sand blew everywhere. Debris soared through the air, nearly hitting her.

Dawson took a heavy stone and put it in front of the door to prop it open.

"You ready?" Dawson asked. Charlie took hold of Seth's feet and nodded.

They braced themselves for the high winds as they ventured out into mother nature's wrath.

Laura was distraught. It was just one more hurdle. How many more things could go wrong? Gifted the bicycle by Valerie, she'd felt a smidgen of hope — a chance that she might reach her son before the hurricane hit. But the journey over to Fort Myers was proving to be more difficult than she anticipated, and now she couldn't even blame it on James. He wasn't anywhere to be seen.

She'd spent a great deal of time looking over her shoulder, even circling around the block just in case.

No, what stood between her and the other side was a 3,400-foot bridge that crossed roughly 50 feet above the Caloosahatchee River. Whereas before she was partially protected from the brutal sideswiping winds, now she wasn't and there was all manner of debris soaring through the air.

Out there on the bridge there would be nothing to protect her from being blown off. She wasn't even going to try to ride the bike. Although the bridge was a double lane, it would have been like riding a bicycle across a high wire.

To make matters worse, there had been a multiple vehicle crash after the power had gone out, causing all manner of vehicles on both sides to collide. There was also a huge lamppost resting on top of the two lanes.

As Laura weaved her bike in and around stalled vehicles, she heard someone calling her name. She glanced over her shoulder to see a figure riding toward her.

It took only a few seconds to register who it was.

Her eyes widened.

It was him.

"No. No," she muttered. He was relentless.

Hell or high water, she wasn't going to get anywhere near him. She looked ahead and climbed on the bike and began to pedal with every ounce of strength. The shifting winds made it feel like she was stationary, just spinning wheels. A sharp sideways wind slammed her into a car and she knew she wasn't going to get any further on the bike. The second she got off and released her grip, the bike skittered across the concrete before being lifted into the air and landing on the eastbound lane. She adjusted her bag and set off running, a feat that wasn't easy. The water had risen and the spray of waves was making her gasp with every step.

Laura glanced behind her to see James battling the winds, his body shifting sideways, his head down. She knew she didn't stand a chance of outrunning him. He had a gun. If he wanted to shoot it, he could. And she was tired, exhausted from the miles she'd already traveled.

She took off the shotgun that Valerie had given her and took up position at the corner of a car. She waited until he was closer before she began unloading.

Crack.

Crack.

James darted sideways. Each time he would dash out, she would unload until she ran out of shells. Damn it. Valerie had only given her five. She tossed the shotgun to one side.

That's when she got an idea.

It was all about timing.

Laura looked back and waited until James dropped his chin because of the wind. She tried multiple cars to see if they were open. It didn't take long to find one. She slipped into the back seat, unlocked one half of the rear seating and pulled it down, climbed through and dug around for a tire iron.

All the while it felt like she was inside a fairground ride. The car was shaking hard. Knowing her luck, it would lift and land in the water and she would drown. What a way that would be to go, she thought, pushing the terror from her mind.

When she finally had a tire iron in hand, she got out the opposite side, stayed low and moved up to the front of the SUV. There she would wait, wait for that psychotic bastard to get close. She adjusted her grip on the tire iron and peered beneath the vehicle.

At first there was no sign of him. Just debris.

Then she saw his boots. He was moving slowly, beating a path through the high winds as if he was climbing up the side of a mountain.

Laura swallowed hard, placed both hands on the tire iron and prepared for the fight of her life.

20

South Dakota

Glass shattering with a deafening echo was the first indication that Scout was no longer alone. Her heart skipped a beat, her hand trembled as she clutched the Glock, listening intently. For the past thirty minutes since John had left, she'd been staring at the door. She'd flinched with every creak. The aging house made all types of aching sounds. The pipes. Water.

But nothing compared to the bloodcurdling cry that came next. It confirmed her worst fear — intruders.

They'd stepped on John's nailed contraption.

Loud cursing followed by another window being broken.

"It's the same," a gruff voice shouted.

"Break the damn door down."

A moment of silence then loud thuds.

The whole house felt like it was shaking. She was sure they would gain entrance in a matter of seconds. They didn't. "He must have reinforced the doors."

"Get out of the way. Let me try."

Another series of thumps before whoever was trying to get in gave up. "Here, give me a hand taking this wood. We'll throw it on top." More commotion followed.

Scout took the gun with both hands and tried to remember what John had said. She wasn't ready for this. Tears began to roll down her face. This was how it would end. Either they would kill her or worse — take her back to mother and father. There was little she could do but wait for the intruders to make their way in and find her. If they were going to all this trouble to gain access, a flimsy bathroom door wasn't going to keep them out.

"Whatever you do, don't injure the merchandise."

Merchandise? What did that even mean? There were so many words she didn't understand. All that she'd learned about the world came from her mother and father, and anything outside came from a phone, a phone that Elijah had stolen for two days. A surge of pain went through her, this time not physical but emotional. She missed her brother. She missed her siblings. She didn't want this to happen to them, that's why she took the risk and fled. She'd failed them. Moments from now the door would burst open, men would barge their way in and she would find herself thrown back into hell.

Scout looked down at her gun hand and contemplated doing what she had wanted to do for years. Back then she didn't have the means. One of her siblings had tried to hang herself by removing sheets from the beds. Another had tried to slash her wrists using a filed-down toothbrush. After that mother and father would monitor them in the bathroom.

But here, here she had a tool that could end things in a split second.

Would she feel anything? Maybe? Knowing her luck, something would go wrong and she would be left alive in excruciating pain with half of her face gone.

But still, what was the alternative?

Scout brought the heavy gun up. "Don't point it at anyone you don't intend to use it on." John's words came back to her and she tried to push them from her mind but they were loud and clear, combined with the image of him looking into her eyes. Those eyes. Kind eyes. The first eyes she'd ever seen other than her siblings' that didn't want something from her, that didn't look disappointed or disgusted by her. "I'll be back before you know it," he'd said. He should have been here by now. What if he'd changed his mind? What if he had gone to Frank and not Eddy? What if... her mind tortured her with paranoia.

Scout closed her eyes and brought the gun up but before she managed to bring it to her mouth, she heard a voice that changed her mind. Downstairs, she'd heard footsteps, people going from one room to the next, then a female voice called out, "Scout dear. Where are you?"

Mother.

A shiver went up her spine.

Scout began to grind her teeth. A wave of hatred washed over her.

"Come on now. I've come to get you. I know you didn't run away on purpose. I know you were taken against your will. It's okay to come out. I've got the police here."

The police? That wasn't the police. Or maybe it was. Either way hearing her voice again was like fingernails going down a chalkboard.

"Check the rooms upstairs."

Scout began breathing faster. Her pulse sped up, fear rising in her. Heavy footfalls got closer as multiple people came up the stairs. "I'm telling you she will be worth it," her mother said to someone. Scout brought up the gun with both hands and rested the butt on the edge of the bath with the barrel pointing at the door. It was easier that way. Her arms just didn't have the strength to hold it, and searing pain in her side made every movement agonizing.

"She's not in here," someone bellowed.

The sound of a metal ladder sliding. "Go up."

"Hold on a second."

Silence.

Then footsteps went into the main bedroom and approached the bathroom door. Someone rattled the doorknob. "I think we have a winner." Scout wanted to shoot through the door but she couldn't. What if these people were here to help? What if they were the police? What if they had gotten her mother to confess and now this was them coming to save her? Naïve, perhaps, but Scout wasn't sure if John was out there, among them. Maybe he had convinced them to come.

"Scout. Are you in there? It's mother."

Her throat went dry. Flashbacks of all the times she'd tried to hide from her came rushing back in. Being dragged out of a closet and whipped. Being hit over the head with a hard brush and then pushed down stairs. Though in all those times her mother had never spoken so softly. It had always been harsh. *You ungrateful little bitch. I should kill you now. You know what happens to children who stick their nose in where it's not wanted.*

The doorknob rattled again. "Scout. I know I've made mistakes. I recognize that now. Please open the door. Let's talk. I miss you."

Miss me? The nerve of her. She never once missed any of them. She didn't want to be around them. Scout couldn't remember any of them being hugged or kissed, or having either one of her parents say kind words. It was like they were a burden, a mistake.

"Open the door, Scout." Her voice had an edge to it. Slightly more like the one she was familiar with. "Listen to me. I'm your mother. God would have you obey us. You know what happens when you don't obey your mother and father."

There she was. That was the woman she was familiar with. A spiteful hag.

There was silence for a second then her mother lost it, banging on the door. "OPEN THIS DOOR NOW, YOU BITCH!"

Every suppressed emotion came flooding in like a dam's walls had broken. Before she didn't have the will to shoot, but she now did. Scout squeezed the trigger.

The noise was deafening.

A perfect hole appeared in the door.

"You... you...." her mother said. Outside she heard her stumble, then collapse. "You shot me. She shot me." A commotion outside, her father's voice.

"Keep a hand on it. I'll get you out."

"KILL HER. KILL HER!" were her mother's final words.

Loud thumps on the door as someone tried to kick it open. Scout squeezed the trigger again, once, twice, three times. Someone else hit the floor. Yelling ensued. "I'm not dying for some girl. You want her. You get her yourself."

A loud bang rang out.

"Jethro, no."

Another crack.

"Get him out of here."

It sounded like someone was being dragged across the floor.

There was a long pause followed by low discussion. Scout craned her neck to hear what they were saying but couldn't.

Then.

"Hey kid. I've got to take my hat off to you. Shooting your mother. That was one hellava ballsy move." He laughed. "My name's Jethro. You and I are going to be really close. You see, I've come across girls like you before. Firecrackers all full of spit and vinegar. But you want to know something? Every single one of them eventually breaks. That's right. Now the way I see it, you have two choices. You can either shoot yourself or open the door because if I have to break in, or lose another of my men because of you, I will make it my mission that you suffer worse than any girl that has come before you. So why don't you just..."

Before he could finish, she opened fire, twice.

"Sonofabitch!"

"That's my answer." She chuckled. For once she didn't feel the same level of fear as she had before. This was the first time she had found her voice and now she had something to back it up with.

21

The tension inside the truck was palpable. Eddy crushed the accelerator while at the same time ducking. The two men standing ahead of them didn't stand a chance. The thud of the truck striking their bodies was sickening. One of them disappeared beneath. Eddy had floored it so hard that the front end of his International Harvester smashed into the truck ahead, pinning the second man between the two vehicles. His body slumped over the hood, blood trickling out the corner of his mouth.

A staccato of AR-15 gunfire peppered their truck from behind.

At the same time, John brought the window down, pulled his Sig Sauer and stuck his arm out and began shooting at the two men behind them, using the side mirror. "Stick it in reverse and do the same," he bellowed. The narrow dirt path only allowed enough room for the vehicles. Thick brambles on either side of the road prevented the men from stepping off and taking cover.

Staying low, Eddy jammed the stick into reverse and gave it some gas. The engine whined loudly; the front bumper was tangled up with the vehicle again. The rear tires spun out. "Give it some."

"What the hell do you think I'm doing? We're stuck!"

One of the two men behind them was smart enough to make a dash for his vehicle, the other thought he'd be able to finish them off by emptying his magazine into the back of their vehicle. The biker stayed low, out of the way of the shots John was firing. With the windshield shot to shit, and as Eddy continued to try and free the vehicle, John did the next best thing, he brought his boots up and kicked the cracked and bullet-ridden front windshield until it burst out of the frame. Glass fragments spread across the hood like tiny pebbles.

Then, without any thought for his own safety, John clambered out as fast as he could. There was no way he could have gotten out the passenger side without being shot, and there was still a chance he would take a round, but he had to do something and fast as the vehicle they were in was quickly turning into Swiss cheese. It was only a matter of time before the odds worked against them.

"Keep revving the engine. The tires are kicking up wet soil in that asshole's face. Hopefully that will keep him at bay for a few seconds."

Outside, John slid over the hood. He could see now why they weren't moving. Metal was twisted together.

There was no way they were getting out of that. Taking an AR-15 off one of the dead men, John shot out the front windshield of the truck ahead and climbed in until he was behind the wheel.

Now all he had to do was accelerate.

Although the two vehicles were interlocked, with this truck pushing forward and Eddy's going in reverse, it was like two trains connected. As soon as John crushed that accelerator, the two vehicles moved at lightning speed. The biker at the rear didn't stand a chance. The fool had remained directly behind their truck, using it as cover.

John felt the two vehicles bump over him.

Out of the four there was only one that had the good sense to get the hell out of there. They watched as that truck reversed out at a high rate of speed, leaving nothing behind except thick tracks in the soil.

John made his way back to the Harvester. "I imagine when he returns, he will bring more than three others next time. Listen, we need to get to the house. They've probably gone after Scout, so—"

"I've been shot, John," Eddy said, wincing in pain.

"What?"

John looked at Eddy as he clutched his upper left shoulder. Blood gloved his hand, dripping through his fingers as he tried to stem the bleeding. "Oh, shit. Let me take a look." John tore open his friend's jacket and used his knife to cut the plaid shirt wide. There was a good amount of blood but a quick check of his back and front and it looked like the round had gone straight through. There was no telling what kind of damage he was looking at or if it had hit a major artery as there was blood everywhere. "I've got a first-aid kit up at the house. Do you think you can make it?"

"I'm shot in the shoulder, John. My legs are working." Eddy summoned a smile.

John took a bottle of water and unscrewed the cap; he washed the wound as best as he could before giving the rest to Eddy to drink.

"I could use something stronger."

"I'm afraid you'll have to wait," he said, scanning the inside.

Eddy grimaced. "You know, John. I had to wonder when life would turn on me. Things have been going too good for so long. It's like Murphy's law. What will go wrong, will go wrong."

John didn't reply, he was too invested in finding something.

"What are you looking for?" Eddy asked.

"For now," he searched the truck and found some clean rags in the back. He created a makeshift pad out of the rags, folded it up and gave it to him. "Hold that in place." After that he had him lean forward while he took a strip that could wrap around his shoulder and the top half of his body in a way that it would hold the pad in place. "It's not much but it will have to do."

Eddy clenched his teeth. "Next time you ask for help, remind me to say no."

John smiled and patted him on his good shoulder. "C'mon."

It took some effort on Eddy's part to climb out. They

would have to hike the rest of the way. It was less than a mile up the road. Eddy snagged the AR-15 from a dead guy they'd rolled over. The two of them skirted around the trucks and marched off toward his cabin, hearts full of anguish and rage.

22

Florida

Laura scored a home run.

As rain pounded the earth and unrelenting sheets rattled the tops of the cars like bullets, she unleashed a devastating swing that was felt before she was seen. The tire iron made contact with James's right knee with bone-crushing precision. He didn't have time to react. He was so distracted by the brutal wind and trying to see where she'd gone that it was done before he had a chance to react.

He buckled, releasing an anguished cry.

If he wouldn't stop following her, this would certainly slow him down.

As she'd waited in front of the vehicle for him to sidle up to her, she'd contemplated knocking the gun out of his hand but there was a chance he would punch her. No, she had to disable him first, then when he was in agony, deal with the weapon.

And she did.

The second strike was equally as harsh. Laura brought the tire iron down on his wrist, breaking it and sending the gun flying out of his hand. It slipped across the bridge, disappearing below a vehicle. Yet what should have been enough to stop him wasn't. Furious, he swung his leg into hers, taking her feet out from underneath her. She landed hard and the tire iron clattered, bouncing a short distance away. She twisted over, scrambling to get it, but he clamped onto to the waistband of her jeans with his one good hand.

"I'm going to kill you."

With her heart pounding in her chest, Laura brought up her knee and thrust a foot into his face, freeing herself from his grasp. Like a runner at the starting line, she scrambled to her feet and grabbed the tire iron but when she turned back, he was gone.

Impossible.

Her eyes scanned, then she saw his foot sticking out from the vehicle. He was trying to go for the gun. With him struggling with a broken wrist and possibly a shattered knee, she made her way over feeling a surge of empowerment. As she skirted around a sedan, she pressed her foot down on the back of his leg, then brought the tire iron down on his rib cage. "I gave you every chance to leave me alone. But you wouldn't do it, would you? Why? Just tell me why?"

She released her foot and James flipped over onto his back, groaning. His hand was limp and swollen. "You're just like her."

"What? Who?"

"Trixie. My ex."

Her mind flashed back to the news channel. The one she'd barely paid any attention to before leaving for work that evening. The name. That name had stuck with her. No. It couldn't be. She hadn't seen the face of the person who had escaped the courthouse but she remembered the name of his victim. "Rodriguez? You're the one that escaped?"

He nodded, spitting blood on the ground.

"Then who the hell is James Bauer?"

He laughed. "Some guy who refused to hand over his vehicle."

"The one you crashed."

"What can I say? I have shitty luck."

She stared at him in disbelief. "You killed your ex and kid?"

"Oh, don't look so shocked, Laura. People have done worse things in this world."

"You killed a child."

"No one was going to raise my kid. Not her. Not the guy she hooked up with. No one. I brought that kid into this world, I decided to take him out. It's better that way."

"You're sick."

He laughed. "Of course I am. So is this entire world. We just pretend that we're not so we can live out our boring lives and create our fake wars and justify it under the umbrella of defending our country," he said, giving her a salute. He sang a few lines from "The Star-Spangled Banner" before continuing, "But it's all just bullshit, Laura. Crap we tell ourselves so we can sleep at night. The fact is, Laura, we are all animals. Look at you now. Even you want to kill me. You want me to suffer. Why?" He paused. "It doesn't matter. Because you will come up with some reason. Richard, your shitty neighbor, my ex, me, your kid. But when it's over. When I'm lying here with my brains scattered on this bridge, you will have to live with that and face yourself every day. Can you do that, Laura? Huh? Can you live with that on your conscience?"

"Fuck you," she said.

"You know, after I killed her, I thought it would ease my pain. The way she treated me. The way she tossed me aside for another man. But it didn't. I tried to get the cops to kill me. You know, flashed a gun and whatnot but they didn't. Some asshole tasered me from behind." He laughed. "All those killings on TV of cops taking out innocent people and finally when they are confronted with someone who isn't innocent, they choose to not take me down."

So, while he never said it outright, Laura knew what he wanted. Laura tossed the tire iron, exhausted and tired of playing his mind games. He was right, she wanted to kill him. But then what? Become like him? Justify it in her own mind later? No, that's what he wanted. He wanted her to end his miserable life. Maybe that's what this was all about. Pushing the boundaries of someone until they found enough reason to take him out. That was only confirmed by what he said. She wasn't going to give him that satisfaction.

Laura turned away.

"Don't turn your back on me," James cried out.

She said nothing but crossed to where the car was and ducked down and reached under to collect the gun. Her clothes were soaked, her long brown hair matted and pressed up against the side of her face.

"Don't you leave me here, Laura."

Again, she said nothing but glanced at him and then continued walking back to her bicycle. "You can't do this to me. You're a nurse. You're meant to help people."

A sporadic burst of lightning split the gloomy sky in two like the flash of an old camera. After collecting the bicycle, Laura rolled it past James, leaving him to mother nature. That was far worse a fate than ending his miserable life fast and wasting a bullet.

23

South Dakota

A steady thump of pressure inside John's head made his vision blur. A wave of nausea came over him so he stopped walking and leaned against a wet pine. The sound of Eddy's voice was garbled for a few seconds until it became clear as though his brain had finally decided to tune into the right station.

"John. John. Are you okay?"

Eddy stood beside him, looking up the lane to where it opened to his property.

"Just give me a second," John replied. He swallowed hard and opened his jaw wide a few times, willing his mind to work right. That was all he could do. It was so infuriating. "What do you see?" he asked as he waited for his vision to clear.

"One vehicle. Multiple bikers outside. They're packing rifles."

"Have they entered the house?"

Eddy hesitated then replied, "Yeah."

"Do you see a young girl?"

"No."

"Shit." There was no way he could have avoided this. Scout was in no condition to be slogging it through the dark in the rain. "I'll circle around back; you take the front."

Eddy placed a hand on his shoulder. "Are you going to be okay?"

John managed to summon a smile. "You're asking me after getting shot? Eddy, I've lived with this ailment for some time. Just ensure those assholes don't go anywhere." He broke away as the world snapped back into full color again.

Keep low. Take out as many as you can, he thought.

He didn't want to kill anyone but they had given him no choice.

John needed a distraction and his old friend would be that. If he could get in the rear of the house, he stood a chance but that depended on whether they had Scout or not. He took a deep breath and jogged at a crouch, eyeing movement off to his right. The rain continued to pummel the ground, making it slick and dangerous. As the smell of pine, moss and earth filled his senses, his mind flashed back to his time in Iraq — the siren cries of men cut down under machine gunfire, the deafening explosions around him and the sight of the dead — so many dead.

"Stay focused," he told himself. "You've got this."

As he came around the back of the house he noticed a biker outside, smoking a cigarette. He was a grizzled man, heavyset, slow. The biker flicked the butt to the ground and went inside, back into the kitchen. John hurried toward the house, breaking out of the tree line, only darkness offering any cover. If anyone stepped outside now, he would have to take them down, then all hell would break loose. Reaching the cabin, he pressed his back to the wall and slid along to a window to get a better idea of the threat inside. He took in the scene. There were three guys in the kitchen, two of them helping themselves to food from his pantry, the other drinking his beers.

As John shifted position and crept forward, the tip of his boot touched a steel bowl he'd set outside, water for a stray cat that he'd often see. It toppled over with a clatter. Through the window he saw the men freeze.

"Teddy?"

One of their pals must have stepped outside and not returned. John looked around. Had he stepped off into the forest to take a piss?

"Get in here and stop messing around. We need a hand bringing up this coffee table. Jethro wants it upstairs," the man said inside.

A table? His thoughts shifted to Scout. She must have opened fire on them and now they were looking for a safe way to get in without getting shot. A friend had given him this beautiful brass coffee table as a gift. When polished, it shone brightly and lit up the room on a sunny day.

When there was no response, one of the guys inside

looked at the back door, an expression of concern spreading. He picked up his shotgun from the table and nodded to his other pal. They walked over to the window and looked out. John kept to the wall, staying out of sight. He fully expected one of them to step outside. They didn't.

What he heard next was movement off to his left. It happened fast but not fast enough that he couldn't react. By the time the gun went off, John had already dived out of the way, taking cover behind some lawn furniture.

Almost on cue, Eddy opened fire. He must have thought it was him. His timing couldn't have been better as the three men inside, that he expected to come out, never did, leaving him to deal with just the one.

JETHRO HEARD THE RUCKUS. He immediately crossed from the landing to one of the bedroom windows and glanced out. Muzzle flashes lit up the night from both his men and an unknown assailant hidden in the forest. "It has to be that asshole." He exited the room and shouted as he hurried downstairs, "Everyone outside. I want his head!"

WAS JOHN BACK? Or could it be the cops? Scout heard the commotion. Someone was causing enough trouble for them all to step away from the door. Whoever had shown up didn't know they had bitten off more than they could chew. Scout had managed to keep them at bay, squeezing off a round or two, but she knew it wouldn't be long before they busted through the door and overpowered her. All that mattered right now was they weren't paying attention to her.

"Give me that gun. I'll kill her myself," her father said from beyond the door.

A chorus of gunfire from a fully automatic weapon was followed by splinters of wood shooting in every direction. Scout ducked down in the bath as the air was filled with drywall dust and splinters. She squinted, placing both hands over her ears as the heavy gunfire echoed. When the dust settled, the door or what was left of it was in pieces. "Scout. Scout!" her father said, approaching the door. "You killed her." She caught a glimmer of his face, the man that she was meant to adore and appreciate but she detested. Even when he told her that her mother was dead, she felt nothing.

Not for her. Not for him.

Scout brought up the gun as he peered through. His eyes widened and he turned to run but it was too late. She squeezed the trigger four times and watched him drop hard on the landing. Groans told her he was still alive, barely.

Using what little energy she had left, Scout climbed out of the bathtub, wincing in pain from a sharp ache in her side. There was nothing left to protect her. The door was so badly damaged that she could squeeze her small frame through the opening. Cradling her broken arm in its sling, she lifted the gun in the other hand toward her father — the man that had whipped and beaten her and agreed to let her mother hand her over to these animals. Ray Miller's back was soaked in blood; he turned his face and looked at her. Scout wanted to think that he might say he was sorry, that his final words would be a cry for forgiveness, but they weren't.

"I never loved you," he muttered. "You were a mistake."

Although she knew that already, the painful words stung, cutting deep into her core.

She could have hit back with a snappy comeback about how that made two of them but she didn't, instead, she chose to send him to an early grave.

The gun echoed as she unloaded a round in his skull.

Scout glanced up and saw her mother lying on the bed, hand clutching her stomach, her skin pale and lifeless. She was gone. No longer could these two harm her or her siblings. From outside the room, she heard gunfire, a steady staccato. Scout made her way out, hoping to see John.

"John?"

Before she made it within five feet of the top of the stairs, a hand clamped over her mouth and pulled her down to the floor, taking the gun out of her hand. "See, I told you I would get you," Jethro said. "Killing your own parents. I must admit you did a far cleaner job than I did with mine." He got close to her ear, so close that she could smell stale tobacco and alcohol on his breath. "Oh, you really are a diamond in the rough. But don't you worry, darlin', you and I are going to be really close. C'mon!" He dragged her out of the room, wrapping one arm around her good arm and hoisting her almost off the floor.

At the top of the stairs, they turned to head down only to see John at the bottom.

Jethro fired his magnum revolver at him and then pulled back behind the wall.

"Let her go, Jethro. She's just a kid."

She struggled in his grasp. "Stop it, kid!"

"Come on," John said.

"After I just got her? Old man, you are out of your mind."

"All your men are dead."

There was a pause. Scout looked down at her broken arm.

"Well, aren't you the little train that could," Jethro snorted.

When John had created the makeshift splint for her arm, he'd used padding from a sleeping bag. He'd tied that off with cord and then inserted two metal rods to offer further support. She touched the end of one and noticed how sharp it was.

Jethro shouted, "How about you leave now and the kid here gets to breathe another day?"

Silence stretched between them.

"Why did Frank want her?" John asked.

"What?"

"Frank Olsen."

He laughed. Now that was a guy with problems. "Oh, the chief. You know him?"

Scout wriggled in Jethro's grasp, causing him to put her down and readjust his grip. He slid his arm around her stomach and pulled her up like baggage under one arm, allowing her feet to just touch the floor to take off some of her weight. As Jethro continued to talk, she tugged on the metal rod until it slid out of the bandage and padding.

"Let's just say he paid a lot of money for this one. His first time. Her first time. You don't get any better than that. An ex-chief of police. The irony isn't wasted. But you see, old man. That's why I will win, and you will…"

Before he could get the rest of the words out, Scout drove the rod of metal into Jethro's thigh as hard as she could. He howled, dropping her and falling back, grasping at the rod. Scout scrambled, falling to her knees then getting up again.

"You bitch!"

She didn't see him but she felt his grasp on her leg as she tried to escape.

What came next happened so fast that when it was over she wasn't sure if it was her or him that was dead. Two rounds echoed, an ear-piercing sound so deafening that it left a ringing in her ears. Scout looked back at Jethro who had this stunned expression. Blood blossomed through his shirt. Jethro's body sank to one side, his eyes glassy and empty of life. Scout turned her head and saw John standing at the top of the stairs, firearm still pointing at him.

"John."

Within seconds John scooped her up and she hugged him tightly, although her other arm was in complete agony. "Let's get you out of here, kiddo."

24

Florida

Behind a curtain of rain, the sight of the Jackson residence was a welcome relief after battling the atrocious weather. The one-story home crouched at the corner of Emily and Tulane Drive — a suburb of Fort Myers. The property with stucco roofing was nestled behind a line of palm trees that were thrashing in the storm's grip.

Water sluiced from puddle to puddle as another flare of lightning tore the night apart. Its momentary brightness etched the shape of the home and the bleak setting. All the windows had shutters on, there were no vehicles outside and the street was lightless and devoid of people.

Laura set the bicycle down on the lawn and raced up to the door.

Please be there, please, she thought as she hammered with closed fists on the shutter covering the front door. "Charlie? Seth?"

No answer. She glanced across the street to the neighbors' homes, a line of one-story abodes that marched off toward the end of the road. On any other day, the commotion would have attracted curious onlookers peering out of windows, maybe even a call to 911 but not today. The ruckus was drowned out by howling winds. They were so strong now that Laura had to drive her feet into the ground to avoid being toppled. It had caused no end of trouble on the ride. Multiple times she'd come off the bicycle, landed in ditches, almost died as a wind-tossed sign missed her front tire by a few inches.

Seeing that no one was home, she had no other choice than to find a way in.

She believed the only hope of finding him was to be found inside that house. Laura skirted around the house and made a beeline toward a steel shed out the back. She slid the door open and dug around inside, shining her light into the darkened corners and tossing various gardening tools out, hoping to find a toolbox. She spotted it. Laura forged a path back to the house, pressing her face against the invisible adversary. Soaked to the bone, freezing cold and full of emotion, Laura tried to pry off one of the shutters on a window with a small tool but it didn't work. She wished he'd used something like polycarbonate or steel shutters. They were strong and easy to install and were only held in place by wing nuts. No, Seth's dad had opted for layered plywood that was held in place by small bolts drilled into the walls and then the plywood sat behind that. Not having much success with the one tool, she returned to the shed and found a power tool.

Hurrying to beat the storm that seemed to be getting worse by the minute, Laura took out some of the bolts, yanked the plywood away and smashed one of the lower windows so she could reach her arm in and unlatch the larger window.

As soon as it was open, Laura crawled in, dropping down into a dining area. She shook rain from her body like a dog sending droplets all over the floor. A wave of relief washed over her. Finally, out of the storm. Shining her flashlight around, she navigated through the kitchen, washing the light over the counters, looking for anything that would tell her where they'd gone.

It didn't take long.

Laura entered a room that was full of high-tech gear. Two of the walls were covered with whiteboards with scrawled text all over them, and a schedule for the month. There were different events Dawson had planned to attend, a tornado in Kansas, a tropical storm in Hawaii. Standing in the dark, Laura zigzagged her flashlight down the whiteboard until she saw the words Hurricane Fiona. There was various data, numbers, speed and a few different locations that he seemed to have in mind, but there was only one that was circled in red.

Sanibel Lighthouse.

"Bingo."

How had he managed to pull that off? There was no way the city would allow him to stay there. He had to have had someone on the inside or paid someone in high places to give him a key and turn a blind eye. It wouldn't have been the first time he'd gotten himself in trouble in pursuit of landing that highly coveted spot in a media broadcast. It was always the ones willing to push the envelope that seemed to attract eyeballs.

As Laura exited, she grabbed a towel from the bathroom to dry herself off. The Sanibel location was only confirmed by a reminder note on the fridge to have Charlie ask his mother for permission to go to the lighthouse. She shook her head and muttered, "Yeah, he asked. I didn't give him permission."

She growled under her breath.

Right then a huge gust of wind sent all the paperwork everywhere in the house. Glass shattered. Laura raced back into the dining room to find the drapes blowing in the wind like mad, and glass scattered across the floor. If she didn't get that shutter back on that window, wind and rain would continue to enter and there was even a chance of the roof being torn asunder.

Laura hurried through to the attached garage, accessing it through a side door. As soon as she stepped inside, she noticed a vehicle that was covered. She slid by it and opened the garage, a feat that seemed even harder now that the wind was causing an untold amount of pressure. Laura ventured out, keeping her head down and staying close to the house as she skirted around the back and reattached the plywood.

As soon as it was on, she went back in and pulled the garage door down.

Sanibel Lighthouse was a good hour away by bicycle, she figured, twenty minutes if she had a vehicle. She'd passed a few working cars but they were older models or classics. Out of curiosity but with her hopes not too high, she pulled off the cover to see a jet-black 1949 Chevy Truck 3100. No doubt it was a passion project. There wasn't a scratch on the damn thing. The leather interior was immaculate. It was old like those she'd seen on her journey over.

Could it work?

Glancing at the wall, she searched for a key but there wasn't one, only tools hanging up on racks above a wooden bench. There was order to the garage. This was a man who took pride in his property.

Take the car, she thought.

No, she shouldn't.

Then again, if this was what Richard believed it to be, material things would take a backseat to survival.

Laura stepped back inside the house to search for keys. She pulled out drawers, checked the cupboards, went in his bedroom and tried to think where he might leave the keys. Knowing him, with a valuable asset like that, he wouldn't leave them lying around. After ten minutes of searching, she figured she'd just have to head out using her bicycle and hope to God she wasn't lifted into the air like something out of *The Wizard of Oz.*

Going back into the garage to leave that way, she lifted the door and was thrust back inside by heavy wind. Outside it sounded like a jet engine. Heavy and unrecognizable debris sailed through the air, smashing into homes and scattering down the street. So much had changed in the span of the short time she'd been there. It looked like a car wash outside. Homes across the street were nothing but dark blocks.

There was no way in hell she was going to make it even a few minutes in that.

Laura squinted into the blackness as she manually forced the garage door closed, a task that was even harder the second time.

"I'm sorry, Charlie, I'm so sorry," she said, dropping to her knees in exhaustion. Laura remained there for an unknown amount of time before getting up and climbing into the Chevy, shutting the door and curling into a ball in the back under some covers. She figured for now it was the safest place, inside the home, inside the vehicle. She felt she was far enough away from the coastland that the storm surge wouldn't reach the home. It usually only went a few miles at the most and Emily Drive was at least five miles away.

As she bundled up to shelter in place, Laura only hoped her son was safe.

"God, don't take him," she said. "Not him," she muttered under her breath while outside the full fury of mother nature finally bore down on the landscape.

25

South Dakota

John never imagined he would have blood on his hands by the end of the day. Twenty-four hours. A lot could happen in the span of one day. After dropping off Scout and Eddy at Monument Health Lead-Deadwood Hospital to be treated, John walked the short ten-minute trip north and entered the police department alone. Whatever trouble the police had been dealing with in town that evening had been put on hold as everyone was driven back into shelter by the heavy thunderstorm.

At the late hour of eleven, he trudged into the lobby, water squelching in his boots, with one hell of a story. Heads turned as water dripped off him and he approached the front desk. Mabel's shocked eyes scanned him like a barcode from his bloody hands to his face which had an equal amount of blood splatter.

"Is Sarah in?"

She nodded, eyes wide, almost losing her footing as she backed up. "I'll go get her."

Behind Mabel several seasoned officers setting solar lights into corners of the room stared at him as if expecting him to tell them what had happened. Instead, he took a seat on one of the benches, stared into his hands and looked down at his muddy boots. He felt no guilt in killing those men as it very well could have been him lying dead back there. He only wished it hadn't come to that. It shouldn't have come to that. He didn't find joy in taking a man's life. There was nothing macho in it. Though at times it was a necessary evil.

Waiting, John turned his wedding band, glad that Katherine wasn't there to witness that, or worse suffer. Between the two of them, they had made short work of a handful of bikers. What worried him was that he knew that was just a sliver of the club. Once word got out that Jethro was dead, there would be hell to pay.

A door off to his right opened and several people strode out. "John?"

John turned his head to see Sarah and her father Frank.

He rose from his seat, glancing at Frank through new eyes. "You'll find the president of the Vipers Motorcycle Club, a handful of his men and Tammy and Ray at my property. They are dead. I killed them. All of them." He left Eddy's name out of the killing. Although he had cut down his fair share, he didn't want Eddy to get caught up in any legal hoopla, even though he didn't expect that since the EMP. And the kid, well, she'd suffered enough as it was. He had no plans to throw her under the bus.

Upon making that confession, John brought them up to speed on what had happened. Everything. That it was self-defense. That he was defending his home and his guest. That the Vipers were gunning for the kid, and well, he had no other choice. While he didn't expect a pat on the back, he knew he had a good case to avoid jail time as under the Stand Your Ground law in South Dakota, any person was justified in the use of force or violence against another person if they believed that doing so was necessary to prevent or stop the person from trespassing on their property. South Dakota had one of the strongest home self-defense laws in the country. If a person felt their life was in danger, there was no requirement to retreat.

Sarah shifted from one foot to the next.

She sighed, placing one hand on her service weapon and looking upward. "God, this is all I need." She let out a deep breath. "The Vipers, the Nomads, the Hell's Angels. Now you. Can this day get any worse!"

"I'm sorry, Sarah, to dump this on you," John muttered. "If it could have been avoided, believe me, I would have preferred it that way."

"Ah, it is what it is. This is not the first killing this evening and I'm sure it won't be the last." She filled him in. "A number of bikers got into a spat with each other. We're fortunate we had enough officers from the state and the sheriff's department on hand to stop it. Since the blackout, people are losing their shit. It's got everyone on edge. I don't even want to imagine what will happen tomorrow or the next day." She blew out her cheeks and said, "All right. Well..." She trailed off, overwhelmed. She glanced at her father.

Frank stepped forward and placed a hand on John's arm.

"You did what you had to." Frank then glanced at his daughter. "Go. We'll get this cleaned up, and then... uh... I'll help you deal with the logistics of this tomorrow. It's late. We should all get some sleep and..."

John shook off his arm and Frank noted it.

"Where is the girl, John?" Sarah asked.

"I promised you I would bring her in. I have. She's at the hospital right now being treated for an injury."

"She was shot?"

"No. It's a long story. But she's here and she'll confirm what happened as will Eddy."

"Eddy was there?"

"He was but he wasn't involved."

"So, you killed all of them by yourself?"

"That's right."

Sarah didn't believe it. He didn't expect her to. She knew him well enough to understand that he wouldn't want to get those he cared for into trouble.

"Look, there are others, Sarah."

"What? Dead?"

"No. Scout has siblings. Did you send an officer up to the house like you said you would?"

"No, with the blackout, we didn't have a means to get there. Then we had the incident in town with the MCs."

John held up a set of keys. "Not all vehicles are fried. Older models work. Those kids are going to expect their parents to return. I was planning on going to get them."

"And I was planning on putting you in a holding cell until we could get this cleared up with the court but... under the circumstances... well..." She stared at her father. Although she was confident in her abilities as chief, as she'd learned from the best, even for her this was overwhelming. A small town, a country without power brought with it multiple challenges, questions and threats. He could only imagine what she was thinking.

"Leave it with me," Frank said. "Go on."

Sarah let out an exasperated sigh, and her gaze darted between the two of them before she walked away. Frank turned back to John. "Can I get you a coffee?"

"Didn't you hear what I said?"

"Yes, we'll deal with the children but it's you I'm worried about. You seem a little off."

"You could say that. But then I guess that comes from learning things, Frank."

Frank's brow furrowed and he shook his head. "You've lost me."

John looked off toward the officers that were watching them through the plexiglass. He got close to Frank and whispered in his ear, "I know your involvement." He stepped back to gauge his reaction. Frank swallowed hard.

"Involvement?"

"C'mon, Frank. Don't play coy with me. The girl told me. Jethro confirmed it."

Frank's demeanor shifted, he glanced over his shoulder as if to check if anyone had heard or was listening. When he turned back to John, gone was the friendly expression he'd seen over the years, in its place was a cold-hearted face.

"I don't know what they told you but it's wrong."

"Is it, Frank? So then explain what you were doing at the Millers' residence, and why Jethro said you were about to or had paid him to spend time with Scout."

Frank took hold of his arm and forced him outside, out of earshot. "How long have we been friends, John?"

"A long time."

"And so you would take the word of a two-bit criminal and a girl who is clearly traumatized?"

John looked off down the road. Every year at this time the street would have been full of motorcycles roaring up and down the street going from bar to bar. Laughter. A carefree attitude, but not now. It was cold, wet and dark. A bleak reminder of what was to come. "John."

John turned back to him. "Why, Frank? Just tell me why? And does Gloria know?"

Frank took a few steps away and looked out as the rain came down in sheets. "Of course she doesn't know. But you've got this wrong. I wasn't going to touch that girl. I..."

"You were what? Huh?" John said, making his way over to him.

Frank turned on a dime, pointing at his chest. "Do you

think I'm the only one in this town that has made money from the Natives?"

"Unbelievable. So, it was all about money, is that what you want me to believe?"

"I don't care what you believe." He looked over his shoulder.

John felt disgusted by him. "You know, I thought I knew you. I thought you were my friend."

"I am your friend."

"No. You were," John said. "So out of a courtesy to Sarah and the pressure she is under right now with this town, the EMP and these deaths, I'm going to give you until tomorrow to come clean to her."

"Are you out of your mind?"

"If you don't tell her. I will. And Gloria."

Frank gave him an incredulous expression. "John. Do you know what you're asking me to do?"

John said nothing but just stared back.

"I... I..." Frank stumbled over his words. "You are in no place to tell me what to do. I helped you back there. If it wasn't for me, you'd be in a cell right now."

"Fine, I'll go in and tell her myself." John turned toward the doors but Frank grabbed his bicep.

"Stop. Just stop. Look. All you would be doing is making things worse. Sarah doesn't need this right now. Tammy and Ray are dead. Jethro is dead. Do you really think after what you just dumped on her that she is going to believe you? Her own father involved with the Vipers? C'mon, not even you can be that naïve. She'll never believe you or that kid."

"No. Maybe not. But four other siblings...?"

Frank gritted his teeth. "If our friendship means anything to you. I'm asking you." He paused. "No, actually I'm telling you. Drop it. Or..." he trailed off.

"Or what, Frank? You going to make things hard for me?" He snorted. "Or for the girl?" John pointed down the street toward the hospital. "There's a sixteen-year-old girl traumatized but with more balls than you will ever have. So, do what you must, say what lies you need to but if you don't tell Sarah the truth by morning, I will."

There was a long pause.

"Okay, John. Okay. We'll do it your way."

"So, you'll tell her?"

"I will."

Right then Sarah came out. "John, do you have a moment?"

Without taking his eyes off Frank, he nodded. "Sure."

"Everything okay, Dad?" Sarah asked after noting his sour expression.

Frank summoned a smile. "Yeah. Yeah." Then he waved her on in. "Go. I'll be inside in a minute. I just need some air."

John went back into the station. "You were right," Sarah said.

"About what?"

"Older vehicles. All of ours are new so none are working but one of the officers has an old Bronco that is running. He's going to let the department use it. I was going to take a trip up to the Miller house. Collect her siblings. With the blackout and all I'm not sure what we can do with social services but we'll figure it out. You want to come with me? We can talk on the way."

"Sure."

"I just have some things to do. We'll head out in about fifteen minutes."

He nodded and waited as she walked off.

∼

SARAH KEPT the conversation light on the way up to the Miller residence nestled a mile away from his home. John wasn't lying when he said he would give Frank time to tell his daughter. It was the least he could do for Sarah, not for him. Frank was dead to him. Whether he was telling the truth about only getting involved with Jethro and the Millers for money, or whether that was just a cover for his own depravity, it no longer mattered. By morning either Frank would tell Sarah or he would.

Sarah seemed interested in knowing more about the event.

"So, this EMP. You're familiar with it?"

"I'm not an expert if that's what you're asking."

"But you think it was an attack on America."

"What else could it be?"

"Well, it's just before the power went down, the media was talking about all these hurricanes and tropical storms happening all at the same time across the world. And then the power goes out, and 95 percent or more of vehicles are no longer working, communication is down. It just sounds fishy to me."

He listened but didn't reply, his mind was on Scout and Eddy. He was wondering how they were doing. The hospital was working with whatever they had on hand which appeared to be very little when he dropped them off.

The Bronco wound its way up through the dark mountains, the windshield wipers flipping back and forth at high speed, struggling to clear the rain.

"I've known you since I was a kid, John. Hell, you're like a second father to me. But this, tonight, it's out of my hands once the court gets hold of it."

"If the court gets hold of it. Remember, this blackout changes everything."

She glanced at him. "Blackout or not. There is due process involved. I will have to investigate and submit my findings."

John snorted, looking out the window at the wall of darkness. "Sarah. If this is what I believe it is, the lights won't be coming back on, communication will stay down, delivery trucks won't show up, and you know what that means?" John cast her a sideways glance. "You're going to deal with situations that will make tonight look like child's play. People will flee the cities and head to smaller towns, those with little will seek out those with more, and anyone who gets in their way is going to have a big problem. And right now, we have a huge problem. This motorcycle rally couldn't have come at a worse time. Five hundred thousand bikers gathered together, hungry, thirsty, pissed off. Now I know a large percentage of them are good people who will hike out of the Black Hills back home to wherever they came from, but not all of them will. If even 1 percent decide to stick around and cause trouble, you are looking at bare minimum five thousand riled-up individuals. And before you say you'll send for backup. Backup won't be coming. You're on your own. We're on our own. So, my advice… if you have people locked up from tonight, release them otherwise you could have a bigger problem on your hands."

He saw her grip the steering wheel tightly. "Well, we will deal with that when we get to it."

"I advise you to deal with it now. Not later."

"I appreciate the advice, John, but…" Before the words came out, they both saw a bright orange glow arcing over the forest. "Is that coming from…?"

"The Millers' residence," John added, nodding.

Sarah floored it and the Bronco weaved through the heavily forested area until they came to the neck of the road that led up to the Millers' property. The entire house was engulfed in flames. The Bronco bounced up the dirt driveway, coming around into a clearing. John squinted as he got out.

"Stay back, John."

He tried to find a way into the house but it was an inferno. Fire had already chewed its way through the walls and was consuming every room. Nearby John noticed three empty gasoline canisters. It was done on purpose. His thoughts flashed back to his conversation with Frank.

"C'mon, not even you can be that naïve. She'll never believe you or that kid."

"No. Maybe not. But four other siblings…?"

Had Frank torched the home with those children in it to cover his ass? Did he have plans to turn on John? In that moment he didn't know what to believe, all he could think about was Scout, and what she would say in the morning when she learned her siblings were no more.

Sarah glanced at John; she didn't need to say anything for they both knew that this was just the beginning of a whole host of trouble. Dominoes had fallen and now it was only a matter of time until the rest would collapse.

26

Florida

The night was brutal. What between worrying about Charlie and wondering if the roof would lift off, Laura barely got any sleep. As the storm passed over Florida, it had shaken the home with such fury that she was certain she was going to die.

But, when daylight flooded through tiny gaps at the side of the garage, she looked outside the Chevy and saw that everything was still in one piece. Although the winds hadn't died down, it was a far cry from the late hours of the evening.

Laura removed the blanket covering her, almost immediately she checked her phone. Habit, really. Still no service. She pawed at her eyes as she crawled out. Her boots sank into ankle-high dirty water that had washed in.

It was hot and humid inside and her mouth was dry.

She wandered into the kitchen and opened the fridge. It didn't light up. She pulled out a bottle of water and ran it around the back of her neck. It was still partially cold. She unscrewed the top and downed it all in one gulp before using the washroom.

Relieved to still be alive, Laura opened the garage to assess the damage. She expected to see storm surge at least a few feet high but due to the location of the area, it wasn't affected as badly. It was ankle deep, no more. She knew it would be deeper the closer she got to the coast. How long it would remain that way was unknown, as it depended largely on how much surge came in and the landscape it was traveling across. For the most part, Florida's terrain was flat and prone to flooding.

Standing outside, she noticed a few neighbors further down the street, assessing damage to their homes. Some folks who had used the wrong style shutters had huge holes in their windows. Others would have to contend with downed palm trees and broken-off signage, garbage cans and all manner of objects that had come to rest. One person had an entire tree through their home, another, their roof was gone and the worst was a home that was flattened.

Laura went back into the garage and got behind the wheel of the Chevy. She thought about her son, her father, Michael and her daughter. She knew there was a strong possibility that Charlie hadn't survived but she hadn't given up hope yet. As she flipped down one of the visors so she could look in the mirror behind it, a set of keys dropped into her lap. She frowned, staring at them for a second before lifting them.

Surely not, she thought, taking them and sorting through the keys until she found one that went into the ignition. She turned it over and it rumbled to life.

Laura looked on in amazement. "Out of all the places you could have put them and you put them there?" She chuckled and looked up thanking God. There was no telling what she would find outside, or how bad the streets were or if she could even reach Charlie, but she had to at least find out. Laura collected a few more bottles of water, some granola bars for her and Charlie just in case he hadn't eaten, and then rolled out.

Several neighbors looked on in amazement at the beautiful classic truck as she hung a left out of the road and headed down McGregor Boulevard. The tires rolled through deep water as she made her way south toward the Sanibel Causeway.

When Irma had hit, Sanibel Island was cut off from the mainland. The causeway was reopened within one day but that was only because work crews were out clearing the devastation and the waters had receded.

Maybe that's why her hopes were up that morning. She soon realized she was being too optimistic.

The devastation was intense. It looked as if a bomb had dropped on Florida. The storm had left plenty of destruction in its wake. No doubt many had died, and hundreds more would be at an ER seeking help for their injuries. The closer she got to the coast, the more it looked as if she wouldn't be able to get across. Flood waters were deeper after only a mile of driving.

Many boats had washed up in people's yards.

Signposts looked like crumpled straws.

Weak storm shutters had been torn off homes and strewn all over the street.

A large truck had plowed into a home.

Shingles, roofs, windows — they were all gone.

Hundreds of trees and power lines were down and blocking the roads. And with an EMP knocking out transportation, there would be no work crews to clean it up.

Laura went as far as she could before the water was too deep to go any farther. She didn't want to get stuck. With a heavy heart, she circled around and headed back for the house.

She'd have to wait it out until the water had died down before she made her way across to the island. In the meantime, she would go back and try and see if there was anyone who needed help. If she couldn't reach Charlie, she could help others. She could drive them to the hospital or simply clean up the street. It was the only way she wouldn't lose her mind.

Laura backed the Chevy into the garage and then got out.

You've waited this long, what's a few more hours, she thought.

Worst-case scenario, she was looking at a day or two until the water receded. Making her way back into the house, she tried to ignore the pain in her heart. Although it was daytime, it was still dark inside. She would find some candles, light a few, have something to eat and then head out and see what she could do.

Laura opened the fridge, shining her flashlight at what food was inside. She took out some eggs, thinking she would cook them up using the Coleman stove she'd seen in the garage. Laura turned and set them down on the granite counter, and went to collect the stove. When she returned from the garage, her mind occupied by Charlie, she noticed the eggs were gone. For a split second, she thought she was losing her mind, that maybe the tiredness of the night had worn her down — then, an icy chill went down her spine.

"Just in time for breakfast," James said.

Laura whipped around to see James near the entrance door to the garage. In his hand was a revolver. With the back of his foot, he kicked the door closed. "Take a seat over there," he said, gesturing with the barrel of the gun. When she didn't move fast enough, he bellowed, "SIT DOWN!"

Her hands started trembling.

"All right, all right," she said, keeping one hand out in front of her to try and keep him calm. Laura noticed his hand was bandaged up, as was his one knee that he dragged as he followed her into the house. He had this big grin. James set the gun down for a second, reached into his pocket and pulled out a piece of paper and tossed it at her. "You really should be more careful next time of what addresses you write down." He chuckled. "I bet you didn't think you'd see me again. Leaving me out on that bridge to die. Hell, I thought I was a goner." He leaned against the granite counter. "But, you'd be surprised at what kind people will do when they see someone in trouble. Shit. I thought I was imagining it when I saw a search and rescue group doing the rounds. Just ordinary folks trying to help people." The smile left his face. "Unlike you, they didn't leave me. But hey, I've got to say this, you've got more gusto than my ex had. She went down without a fight. Utterly pathetic and weak. But you, Laura. Oh, you've got spunk and moxie. I like that. It's very courageous," he said in a way that was condescending.

"Why are you doing this?" she asked.

"No, we've already had that conversation. You know why I'm here now." He looked around. "Charlie's not here. So, whose place is this?"

"A friend of his," she shot back.

"Huh." James continued looking but keeping a close eye on her now with the gun back in hand. "I see you came back with that Chevy. Where did you go?"

"To find him but the waters are still too high. It could take another day or two before it recedes."

"So, you know where he is?"

She didn't answer.

"Laura. C'mon now."

Reluctantly she replied, "Yeah."

"Where?"

Laura stared back, confused. "Why. Why do you want—?"

"WHERE?" he bellowed, cutting her off.

She lied. "Estero Island."

His demeanor shifted from a stern expression to a grin like he was Jekyll and Hyde. "Don't lie to me."

"I'm not."

"Laura, I already know he's at Sanibel Lighthouse. I saw it on the wall and the note on the fridge."

Laura shifted uncomfortably in her chair. "Look, just leave him out of this."

"Oh, no, he's very much involved. You brought this on yourself. Now since we're going to be here a while until the water recedes, how about you go ahead and whip me up some breakfast?"

"What?"

He scowled at her. "Do I need to repeat myself?"

She shook her head no. She got up and took the Coleman stove and set it down on the counter and kept an eye on him. He was observing in a way as if he had other ideas. The Coleman stove hissed as she lit it and a flame burst to life. "What do you want?"

"Eggs. What else can you make?"

She crossed to the fridge. "Bacon. Tomatoes. Beans."

"Sounds delicious. Get to it."

James made his way around the kitchen counter, dragging his bad leg though now being more cautious than ever. He took a seat at the table on the far side and set the gun down in front of him while he took out a pack of cigarettes and tapped one out. She was too far away to go for it but her brain was going a mile a minute, thinking of how to escape. "You know those search and rescue folks were like angels. Oh, they were all too willing to give me meds and patch me up. They wanted to drop me off at the ER but I convinced them to bring me here. Figured I would find you. Actually, I was almost ready to leave when you rolled in. I couldn't believe my luck," he said, blowing out smoke. "You did one hell of job on my wrist, Laura. But I'm a forgiving man. I know you didn't mean it. Did you?"

Laura filled the pan with oil and then an idea came to her. She poured in some extra oil until the bottom was coated in several inches. Cracked a few eggs and tossed a good amount of bacon into the pan and then set it on the stove to heat up.

"I'm talking to you."

"What?"

"I was saying that I don't think you really meant to hurt me, did you?"

This guy either had a severe brain problem from that knock to his head when she first met him or he was an idiot.

"You killed my neighbor. You tried to kill me," she said.

"Now see, that's where you have it all wrong. I could have killed you when you were in the water. Shot you and left you to drown. Don't you get it, Laura? You and I have something special. A connection that few others get in this life. That's why I'm willing to let what you did on that bridge slide. But I just need to hear you say it."

"Say what?"

"That you're sorry."

She turned away.

"Laura."

Not looking at him, she gritted her teeth. He tapped his gun against the table. "Laura!"

As much as it pained her to say it, she knew if she didn't say it, her life would be over before she had a chance to try and escape.

The oil began bubbling.

"SAY IT!" James demanded.

She pursed her lips then said, "I'm sorry."

"You're sorry for what?" he asked as if he wanted her to beg. She wasn't going to beg at the feet of this psychopath. The oil continued to bubble and then boil. Laura crossed to the fridge, took out a bottle of water and unscrewed the top.

"Hey. Hey!" James said, jerking his head to the stove where flames were beginning to rise along with black smoke. "Don't burn my fucking breakfast."

She had purposely left it that way, and purposely took her time to dig out the water from the fridge. Laura wanted him to think that she had overlooked it. But she'd overlooked nothing. In her time as a nurse in the ER she'd encountered plenty of accidents that had arisen from grease fires. And one of the worst came from when idiots introduced water to a burning frying pan.

Laura raced across the room and scooped up the fiery pan in one hand, while holding the water in the other. She removed it from the heat for just a moment so it would die down just a little. Just enough that he wouldn't think that she was trying to take control of the situation. She was but not the way he thought. "Damn it," she said.

"I hope it's not burnt," James added.

She set the pan back on and flames flicked to life again, smoke rising ever so slightly.

"What?" she asked.

"I said I hope it's not burnt."

"Oh, I thought you were talking about the bridge. You're right. I'm sorry," she said. What came next all happened in one quick motion. "I'm sorry I didn't finish you off." In a flash, Laura turned and squeezed water from the bottle into the pan while angling it at him. A sudden burst of fire exploded upward; a magnificent yellow tongue spitting boiling oil all over him. His reaction to deflect the flame caused him to fall back off his seat. Laura tossed the pan at him, it hit him in the head and clattered on the tiled floor. She went for the gun but he hadn't lost his grip on it. He lifted it and her eyes widened as she dove to her right.

A round erupted.

Laura dashed to the side door that led into the garage.

She wriggled the handle.

Locked.

Shit.

He'd taken the key.

James fired again, this time the round went through the wall a foot away from her. She turned back and saw him, screaming and wiping at his eyes which were covered in hot oil. Laura darted into the next room as he fired erratically around the room, unable to see her. Her body slid across the hardwood floor, her shoulder making contact with the wall. With all the windows and doors sealed shut by heavy plywood, the only way out was the garage and without that key, she wasn't getting out.

"Laura!" James shouted full of rage.

Frantically she searched for something she could use as a weapon.

But before she could spot anything, James came around the corner, firing another round. Laura darted into the dining area. All the while James continued to cry out her name and curse loudly. "I'm gonna kill you."

Another round, then another.

She moved fast, making her way through the living room into the dining room and back into the kitchen. The floor was now on fire, flames creeping up one of the walls. Smoke billowed, making her cough. She extracted a large ten-inch kitchen knife from the rack and slid off her shoes so he couldn't hear her and then pressed her back to the wall, listening.

"You bitch. When I get my hands on you..."

He edged around the corner, far more cautious than he was when he was on the bridge. This time James came bursting out gun first and then fired. Fortunately, she'd already moved, shifted into a new spot beside a huge armoire full of wine glasses. One look at him and it was clear he couldn't see clearly. He kept pawing at his eyes, and screaming in agony. They were red, raw, and the skin was peeling on his cheeks.

As James entered the room and made his way to where she was, instead of striking out, she did the next best thing, she forced her hand behind the armoire and pushed it.

The gun went off twice as the whole unit came crashing down on him, glasses smashing. As Laura went to run, he shot again and this time a bullet hit her in the thigh. She crumpled to the floor, crying out in agony.

Their eyes locked. He aimed the gun at her and squeezed the trigger.

She squeezed her eyes shut, ready to join her husband and then...

Click.

Nothing.

She heard another click, and then another.

Her eyes opened, a moment of hope.

"Fuck!" James shouted. Stuck below the armoire, he tried to crawl out as she clambered to her feet, thinking of only one thing — ending his reign of terror. With the knife in hand, she stumbled over to him as he clawed at the floor, groaning in agony and trying to free himself. He looked up at her as she loomed over him, tightening her grip on the knife.

James managed to summon a wry smile. "You don't have it in you. I was wrong. You're not strong. You're weak just like she was. WEAK!"

"Oh... that's where you're wrong." Laura drove the sharp knife down into the back of his neck so hard that the tip came out the other side and stuck into the hardwood floor.

A gargle caught in his throat as he choked on blood for but a few seconds before he breathed his last.

Laura staggered back, grasping her leg, the pain rolling over her.

Bleeding hard, she managed to fish into his pocket for the key to the garage. She stumbled down the small steps onto the concrete, and collected a first-aid kit from under the bench. Items spilled out everywhere, scattering on the ground. As she frantically searched for what she needed, Laura could see darkness creeping in at the corner of her eyes.

No. No. Not yet.

Undoing her belt, she slipped it out of her jeans and locked it around the upper portion of her thigh just above the bullet wound and yanked tightly, locking it in place as the world around her turned dark.

EPILOGUE

Florida
Two days later

Her world came rushing back, a kaleidoscope of liquid color and incomprehensible chatter. Caught between a foggy haze and a dreamlike state, Laura drifted in and out of consciousness for an unknown amount of time.

"When do you think she'll wake up? It's already been two days."

"Give it time. The doctor said she lost a lot of blood."

Laura felt her hand being squeezed. "I should have just done what she told me. If it wasn't for me, she wouldn't have been in this mess."

"Charlie, when I was your age, I made lots of mistakes

and you will make many more. Try not to be so hard on yourself."

Two days, Laura thought. Wake up, she told herself as her thoughts blurred together and sleep tried to pull her back.

But she was unable to.

Held prisoner by the dream world, all she saw was their faces, the people she loved, her mother, her husband and daughter. They looked radiant. Beautiful. Happy.

Libby. She was so beautiful. Laura wanted to reach out and touch them but she could never seem to get close enough. It was like there was this huge divide between her and them. Michael kept saying to her, it's not your time, while her daughter would wave and say she loved her and her mother told her that they were okay.

Laura tried hard to force her eyes open but they felt like they were glued together. She imagined if they did come loose, the skin would tear after so many days.

Then it happened.

She squinted as a bright light shone in her eyes. At first, she thought it was some kind of lamp. It wasn't, it was a band of sunlight bathing her face. Everything was cloudy. *Am I dead?* She wondered. *Is this it?* The moment that everyone talked about. No more tears, no more pain, no more suffering. She blinked hard.

This time she could tell that she was staring at a white ceiling.

Laura groaned as she moved. Pain coursed through her. Not severe but dull and achy from having laid in one position for so long.

"You're awake," said a familiar voice. She turned to see Charlie. He had on a red hoodie; his long jet-back hair was tucked behind his ears. He wore it the same way his father had. A smile formed while tears ran down his face. "I thought I was going to lose you," he said.

Laura looked past him. Dawson Jackson was standing beside him, clean shaven, mousy brown hair, short at the sides, long at the back, sticking out of a beanie. He was wearing jeans and a black North Face jacket. Near the foot of the bed in another chair was a brunette girl with highlights and deep green eyes. "Hannah, right?" Laura said.

The girl glanced at Charlie, then smiled and nodded.

"How did I get here?" Laura asked.

"I can answer that," Dawson said. "One of my neighbors saw fire coming from my house. The garage was open, they thought I was inside. They found you bleeding out on the floor and dragged you out. They would have checked the rest of the house but the flames had consumed everything including my..." He struggled to say it. "Well, that doesn't matter."

It dawned on her what he was alluding to. The classic Chevy.

"Anyway, we got back a day later once the water receded over the causeway and our neighbor told us they brought you to Lee Memorial Hospital."

Charlie clutched his mother's hand, bringing his face to it. She felt his warm tears roll over the back of it. "I'm so sorry, Mom. For everything."

Laura smiled, bringing her hand up to his face. Whatever anger she held in the days before this was gone. Laura was just pleased to be alive, and to see her son alive.

"It's okay," she said in a raspy tone. It felt like she had swallowed sand. Her throat was dry and lips cracked.

"What happened, Mom?"

Over the next ten minutes she brought them up to speed on everything. Their eyes and jaws were wide by the time she was done telling them about James. Before they had a chance to respond, Laura felt a sudden stabbing pain in her leg.

"Hannah, can you get the nurse?" Charlie said.

She nodded and exited.

Dawson chimed in. "You lost a considerable amount of blood. Had the neighbor not reacted as fast as he did, you would have died. Without a doubt. You must have some angels watching over you," he said. Laura thought about her mother, husband and daughter.

She coughed hard.

"Here, have some water," Charlie said, bringing a glass to her lips.

"And the power?" she asked, hoping for some good news.

"Still out," Dawson replied.

"Where's Seth?"

Dawson jerked a thumb over his shoulder. "In another room down the hallway. Ironically, he has an injury to his leg, much like yourself. The doctors said he will be released this evening."

"Dawson. I'm sorry about your house and car and... I..."

"Don't worry. With all that's happened in the country, I think it's the last thing on my mind. I was on the road more than I was home. Look, I was planning on heading up to my cabin in Maine anyway. Homes can be replaced. People can't."

"Still..."

"By the sounds of it, Laura, burning the house wasn't your intention. Surviving was and you appear to have done that well." Dawson took a deep breath as the nurse came into the room. "Well, I should go check on my son. You want to come with me, Hannah?" he said, gesturing to give Charlie some alone time with Laura.

She nodded. "Nice to meet you, Laura."

"You too, hon."

Once they were out of the room, the nurse gave Laura some more meds and then left them alone. "I like her. She's cute."

Charlie went red in the cheeks. "Yeah, she's something else."

They stared at each other. "Look," they both said almost immediately.

Laura was first. "I want to give you more space. I know I've been on your case lately, it's just... well..."

"You don't need to say it, Mom. I understand." He paused. "You were right. You know, when I was out on Sanibel Island and the hurricane was shaking that lighthouse. I thought I was going to die. I really did. I thought a lot about dad and Libby but in that moment, it was you I wanted to speak to, just one last time." More tears rolled down his cheeks. "I didn't think I would get to. I'm sorry, Mom. I just got lost. I didn't know how to cope."

She welled up. "You and me both."

He leaned in and she gave him a kiss on the forehead. "However, if you ever do that again." She got this glint in her eye and began to laugh before it turned into a groan. Charlie wiped away his tears and pointed to the window.

"The storm is gone. Florida is a mess. I'm pretty certain our house is under water. So, what now?"

Laura took another sip of her drink and spoke in a soft and slow voice. "Well. Once I'm better and can walk, we'll head for Uncle Tommy's and then on to South Dakota."

"That's a long way."

"Yeah, it is, but I need to know they're okay. And like what Dawson said. With all that's happening in this country right now, there's a chance things will get worse before they get better. At least in Deadwood we'll be with your grandfather."

Charlie frowned. "But you said you would never go there again."

"We say a lot of things we regret later. Now go on, go see your friend Seth. I need a moment alone." Charlie leaned over and kissed his mother on the forehead before heading out. Once the door was closed, Laura said a silent prayer of thanks for saving both him and her. She glanced out the window at the devastation that had befallen Florida. The hurricane was over but the storm of the EMP was just beginning.

THANK YOU FOR READING
When The World Turns Dark
Book Two, When Humanity Ends is now out
Please take a second to leave a review, it's really appreciated. Thanks kindly, Jack.

A PLEA

Thank you for reading When the World Turns Dark: : A Post Apocalypse EMP Thriller (After it turns dark book one). If you enjoyed the experience this book gave you, I would really appreciate it if you would consider leaving a review. It's a great way to support the book. Without reviews, an author's books are virtually invisible on the retail sites. It also lets me know what you liked. It also motivates me to write more books. You can leave a review by visiting the book's page. I would greatly appreciate it. It only takes a couple of seconds.

Thank you — **Jack Hunt**

VIP READERS TEAM

Thank you for buying When The World Turns Dark: A Post Apocalypse EMP Thriller (After It Turns Dark Book One), published by Direct Response Publishing.

Go to the link below to receive special offers, bonus content, and news about new Jack Hunt's books. Sign up for the newsletter. http://www.jackhuntbooks.com/signup

ABOUT THE AUTHOR

Jack Hunt is the International Bestselling Author of over sixty novels. Jack lives on the East coast of North America. If you haven't joined *Jack Hunt's Private Facebook Group* just do a search on facebook to find it. This gives readers a way to chat with Jack, see cover reveals, enter contests and receive giveaways, and stay updated on upcoming releases. There is also his main facebook page below if you want to browse. facebook.com/jackhuntauthor

www.jackhuntbooks.com
jhuntauthor@gmail.com

Printed in Great Britain
by Amazon